The Prism Effect

PSYCHIC SOLUTIONS MYSTERY #6

PATRICIA RICE

Please Join My Reader List

One

"Sasquatch." Idonea Malcolm lifted the mewling ragdoll kitty in her palm and tied an *I need a good home* ribbon on it. Useless, she knew, but the kitten would have fun pulling it off.

Iddy was officially a veterinarian, but unofficially, her clinic overflowed with unwanted pets. The county needed a shelter. She desperately needed more space. If only the gods really did provide. . .

"Yeti," Loretta, her cousin's about-to-be adopted ward, countered, picking up Sasquatch's furry litter mate to tie another ribbon. "No one will adopt kittens named Sasquatch and Yeti, and then I can take them home."

"Evie would kill me, and then you couldn't stay here while she's honeymooning, and Jax will murder us both if she calls off the wedding." The judge had said Loretta's adoption couldn't go through until Evie and Jax were married, so the kid grimaced at the warning.

"Besides, *Yeti* isn't any worse than *Iddy*." As a vet, she was called Dr. Malcolm by strangers, but the entire town of Afterthought knew her as Iddy, Slate Cooper's weird bastard daughter.

"What was your mother thinking?" With her shoulder-length brown hair enlivened by purple streaks to match the frames of her glasses, the precocious eleven-year-old tapped into her notebook computer. "Idonea, meaning *suitable* in Latin, Norse, *to love again*. . ."

Iddy could have said her mother was thinking with her lower parts, but Loretta was a little young to understand. Slate Cooper was every woman's wet

"

dream. As a father, he sucked. He'd hied himself off to Hollywood at the first opportunity, seeking fame and fortune. He'd achieved infamy, anyway. All Iddy had ever received from him was her height and presumably Native American coloring. Her father's claim to Cherokee heritage could easily be as much a lie as everything else that came out of his mouth.

Apparently, he hadn't been lying when he'd told her mother a film production company would be coming to town, though. He probably had been lying when he said he'd sent them here. Her mother had curled her graying hair and bought a whole new wardrobe just in case he arrived with them.

In this past week, the film company had blown into town like an April storm, practically redesigning Afterthought's historic Main Street. No one had mentioned Slate's name. Iddy was staying out of it.

Shrieking a warning, La Chusa flew in the back window Iddy left open for her. The raven glided around the examining room, skillfully avoiding hanging fluorescents and walls of cages, while setting the other birds to squawking. Polly Parrot erupted in her usual stream of invectives. The macaw had outlived her owner, a Navy man whose daughter had small children and couldn't take its foul —beak.

"La Chusa, perch," Iddy commanded, slipping off her confining lab coat while trying to focus on the bird's warnings. Ravens could learn words and think to some extent, but La Chusa projected mental images best. "Quiet. Let me see."

Wide-eyed, Loretta cuddled the kittens and waited.

What little Iddy could translate from the picture she received had her reaching for the tranquilizer gun and shouting at her almost-niece. "Call Sheriff Troy. If this is the film crew's idea of producing footage, I'm stopping it. Tell him a bull is heading in the direction of town, chased by a herd of wanna-be cowboys."

Loretta was already on her phone, while simultaneously typing a group text alerting the family on her notebook computer. Iddy didn't have time for a family freak-out. She grabbed tranq darts and ran out through the empty reception room. It was too early for clients, thank the goddesses.

Crossing the gravel parking lot, Iddy opened her mind to seek the bull's panic and caught images of more than one terrified animal—*shoot, sugar*. The morons really did think they were cowboys. Where did they find the horse?

Wishing for the umpteenth time that she had enough space for cattle, she threw open her gate. Her parking lot and tiny paddock were the last piece of open space between the farms to the west and the town to the east. Afterthought wasn't large. Once past her place and the feed store, the highway ran by old bungalows and became Main Street. Downtown wasn't crowded at this hour, but there were still cars and pedestrians.

She backed up and parked her heavy Tahoe at a slant across half the highway. Climbing out, she opened a bag of grain in the paddock and checked that there was water in the trough. She could hear the roar of engines racing toward her, and she worked faster. What the *Hades* did they think they were doing?

The poor beast's panic was so great that her mental probes didn't connect. Sensory stimulation needed. She inhaled the scent of fresh grain and water, conveying welcome aromas with her calming reassurances.

The rampaging bull charged over the hill, a rider on horseback on his flank, crowding it to the side of the road. A massive Ram pickup and two motorcycles roared and maneuvered around each other in an effort to what? Start a clown derby?

Seeing a rifle sticking out of the truck's back window, Iddy allowed rage to roll over her. She didn't do fury often, but to shoot a poor animal for doing what comes naturally. . .

Stepping out on the highway, she raised her tranquilizer gun and aimed it at the vehicles.

To her relief, the cowboy on a terrified roan spotted her open gate and angled the bull in that direction. With fury shutting out any admiration for the movie star action, she held her dart gun on ready. She concentrated on thoughts of grain and water to lure the bull.

Her oversized SUV funneled the bull toward the paddock and blocked the pickup and bikes from interfering. The posse of clowns stopped in the far lane to shout and wave their weapons.

"Better call off your men or I'll shoot them," Iddy told the rider, relaxing her mental lures as the bull followed the scent of food. She continued aiming her gun, daring the morons to come closer.

"Be my guest," she thought he shouted over the roar of powerful engines. The rider slammed the gate after the bull limped into the paddock.

Or maybe she just hoped they were on the same wavelength. Once in a while, it was nice to imagine sensible men existed. She'd seen little evidence of it.

Exhausted, the animal trotted over to the grain as if that had been its goal all along.

The battle had taken mere minutes. Sirens were just now screaming from town. Iddy eased her gun to her side, ready to lift it the second anyone went after that poor bull.

Even though he was wearing a linen suit and gator boots that screamed city slicker—or movie star—the cowboy on the roan swung down with expertise.

He was broad, almost barrel-chested. And tall. She was five-ten, and he towered half a foot over her, with an unshaven jaw and a black expression to match his overlong black locks. Holy smokes. This glowering, square-jawed beef-cake resembled her father thirty years ago—a very good reason not to lower her guard. She held her gun steady at her side under his simmering anger.

He looked her up and down, making her much too aware of the skimpy T-shirt and jeggings she usually wore under her lab coat. She was skinny. She knew that. But she wrestled cattle and hundred-pound sacks of grain for a living. She was no weakling.

She glared back. "What the hell did you think you were doing? Holding a rodeo?"

A deputy's car halted on the road shoulder on the far side of her Tahoe. Recognizing the man climbing out, she tossed him her keys. "Got it under control, Cal. You might want to interrogate the clown squad over there."

The giant in linen gestured at his crew to move on. They were already hastily making U-turns.

Not bothering with the posse, Cal used her keys to pull the Tahoe off the road, then strolled over with his notebook out. "Disturbing the peace at this hour?"

"Escaped cattle," the cowboy said curtly. "The production crew must have left a gate open." He gestured up the road.

Production crew, right. Iddy rolled her eyes. "All that, and they weren't even filming?"

Now that authority had arrived, Loretta popped out of the office, waving her ever-present computer notebook. "You're with Mackie Productions!" she crowed. "Has Betty George arrived yet?"

The grim giant acknowledged her bespectacled niece with a nod. "Miss George arrived last weekend. And yes, I'm with Mackie."

He said it with such distaste that Iddy watched him a little closer. His expression didn't reveal anything as he handed a business card to the deputy. "Caden Garcia. I'm the line producer, just trying to keep everyone legal."

"How many animals are there and who is in charge?" Iddy demanded.

Caden Garcia of Mackie Productions raised a dark eyebrow.

Before she could spit in his arrogant brown eye, Cal spoke up. "Dr. Malcolm is the county animal control officer. If you'll be using livestock in your production, you need to check in with her."

"Malcolm?" The linen-suited cowboy changed his attitude. "Dr. Idonea Malcolm? I was told I should consult with you."

It was her turn to raise a haughty eyebrow.

He nodded acknowledgement. "I apologize if we started out on the wrong foot. I have family familiar with this area, and your name was mentioned as an animal trainer."

His family mentioned her? Not her father? She could believe that.

"What family?" Loretta asked eagerly. "My father has California family. You're from California, aren't you?"

Recently orphaned Loretta really loved calling Evie and Jax her mother and father. Holding the dart gun with one hand, Iddy squeezed the kid's skinny shoulders with the other.

A little warily, the stranger replied, "I'm told I have a distant cousin, Damon Ives Jackson. I was hoping to call on him."

The deputy sighed and shoved his notebook in his pocket. Loretta jumped up and down, shouting, "I knew it!"

Iddy didn't share her excitement. Jax's California relations usually called on him when any weird problem popped up along this coast—*because of Evie*. She wasn't about to become one of her cousin's psychic solutions.

"You arrived just in time for the wedding," Iddy warned. "I'd suggest you call Jax before you mention whatever your problem is, or he's likely never to speak to your side of his family again."

Two

"IT'S A REAL LIVE *BULL*, NOT A GHOST," GRACIE SAID THROUGH A MOUTHFUL OF PINS. "Animals are Iddy's job, not yours. Hold still, Evangeline, or I'll stick this pin in you!"

Standing on a stool, Evie twitched restlessly at her sister's admonition, causing the sea-foam green taffeta to rustle. She loved the rustle and swing—standing still, not so much.

Fine, she wouldn't talk about restless bulls. Loretta's call had indicated more was going on, but she could wait. A little bit. Loretta was an Indigo child, with insights even Evie couldn't achieve with aura reading. The kid just needed a little more experience.

"I still think the striped gown would have been cooler." Evie tugged at the sweetheart neckline and studied the sag over her unfettered boobs. Old-fashioned gowns needed confining underwear she didn't own.

"*Cool*, as in downright drafty. You need a wedding gown, Evie. Great-Aunt Val must have worn that plunging rainbow number to an orgy." Gracie shoved a final pin in the front hem. "Wear heels. This is the best I can do without ruining the silhouette."

Evie's dressy wardrobe always came from their Aunt Val's vintage closet. Val had been married often enough to have wedding gowns stashed away, but she'd apparently either ripped them to shreds or in the case of this one—dyed it.

Evie loved the convenience of instant clothes, but unfortunately, she was short and Val was not. Mini dresses fell to her knees. Floor-length—well, wedding dresses should have trains anyway.

"You are a wonderful sister, and I thank you. What color goes with green, so I don't make any fashion faux pas?" Evie wriggled out of the gown, letting it drop to the floor.

"You don't need any other colors! We'll make a bouquet of pink roses, add some baby's breath, and voila. Perfect for a garden wedding." Gracie gathered up the taffeta in a sheet. "A corset would be good, and no, it can't be red."

Evie ran her hand through her naturally orange hair. "Pink," she demanded, knowing it would make her sister crazy.

"*White*. For once, you will not look like a flaming sunset. The wedding photos will be fabulous. Your descendants will never know you were actually a bag lady."

Descendants—she'd have to have children for that. Did adopted ones count? Actual babies. . . scary. Weddings, commitment—all scary. But she'd learned to conquer fiery ghosts. She could learn responsibility. Maybe. Someday.

"Now may I make sure our unsocialized cousin doesn't have my soon-to-be daughter examining bull testicles?" Unfazed by Gracie's description of her fashion choices, Evie yanked on her purple T-shirt stating *Normal is an Illusion*.

Evie was still practicing saying *daughter* instead of *ward*. She was thrilled to the marrow that Loretta wanted her as a mother. She wasn't so thrilled that the Atlanta judge wouldn't sign the papers until the wedding had taken place, which made sense. No one had ever considered her more than dog walker material before.

"I've already checked," said Jax, her real-life hero, striding in from the front hall, phone in hand, his office jacket over his shoulder, dark hair temporarily raked back. "Loretta is fine and trying to weasel her way onto the film set to see Betty George, who is apparently some famous wildlife expert."

"What wildlife do we have here?" Gracie scoffed, packing up her sewing box. "Raccoons? Possums? Or maybe they mean Guns and Hoses."

Grinning at her normally quiet sister's opinion of the local tavern, Evie wound herself around her fiancé and tried to peer at the phone in his hand.

Knowing her tricks, Jax shoved it in his pocket, lifted her, and kissed that idea right out of her head.

Then he plunked her on a counter seat to check the contents of the refrigerator. "Can't you persuade Pris to move back in? No one ever goes to the grocery anymore."

"No one here but thee and me to do the cooking these days. Want to start a garden? We're out of Val's canned goods." A year ago, before Jax and Loretta entered her life, Evie had survived on peanut butter and apples despite a pantry full of canned green beans and tomatoes. In this past year, the house had filled with family for one reason or another and the larders were now bare. "We have eggs and bread. I can make an egg toast sandwich."

"I can grab lunch at the diner. I was looking for drink." Jax closed the door of the ancient harvest gold fridge. "Apparently, my California family has sent another cousin our way. This business of tracking generations of our family tree is wearing thin."

Evie laughed. "I sent a wedding invite to your cousin Conan and told him to bring any of his family who'd like to come along. I want to meet the brother who flies planes. Isn't he the one married to the genealogist?"

She knew Jax was thrilled to discover he and his sister weren't alone in the world. Since he'd been orphaned as a child, he'd simply never had the experience of dealing with large family as she had. He'd learn.

Jax filled a glass with water. "Conan's other brother is in the film industry. I assume he's the one responsible for sending Cade here."

Evie slid off the stool to fill a kettle so she'd have ice tea for lunch. "Cade?"

"Caden Ives Garcia, goes by Cade. I just got the run-down from Conan. Garcia's uncle owns an insurance company that works with Hollywood's studios and stars, and Cade has taken up some kind of production job as a result."

"Your family is usually more technical than insurance sales." Evie set the kettle on the table and waved Gracie good-bye. Her sister preferred discreet pursuits like grading exam papers, writing, and sewing. She lacked Evie's curiosity and hadn't asked the burning questions raised by Jax's comments.

Once Gracie left, Evie swung on her stool and demanded, "Now that you've successfully diverted the topic from wild animals, why is Garcia here?"

Before Jax could carefully word a reply—Evie knew her lawyer man was being evasive—her mother blew in like a summer storm. Wearing a caftan of spring flowers on a sky-blue background, her graying hair streaming from its bun, she waved a tarot card. "The stranger brings swords! Stay away, Evangeline. We don't have enough time before the wedding."

Oh, yeah, there it was Evie beamed, swung her swivel seat around to the butcher block counter, and helped herself to a banana from the fruit bowl. "Do tell."

Jax glowered at her mother. Mavis had called him a dark cloud before she'd ever met him. He could certainly be that. Dark, studly, built solid as a tank despite his desk-jockey profession, Jax was the best black cloud to ever blow her way. Even after a year of her vagaries and eccentricities, he still wanted to marry her—and it certainly wasn't for her empty bank account and weird family.

She wiggled her unfettered boobs to distract him from her mother. It worked, and she beamed.

"I ran the cards after Loretta's text message." Mavis poured the boiling water into the prepared teapot. "I'm sure the Fool is the film company. The bull is Strength. He knows something. Swords surround them—probably the production crew. Keep Loretta away!" She grabbed the last donut from the box and swept out the back. The dogs in the yard barked in greeting. Psycat, the Siamese, peered out from his hiding place on top of the refrigerator now that it was safe.

"My mother is a storm cloud. She'll rain from now until our wedding day if there really is a problem." Evie pulled her phone out of the pocket of her shorts and wiggled it at him. "How do you want to do this?"

"Not at all. Let's run away and get married in the Bahamas. Loretta will be fine with your family. I'll have LaWanda notify my clients I won't be in until next month. . ." He snatched the phone from her when it rang but settled on the other counter seat in resignation after reading Caller ID.

Roark—she'd set his ringtone to play *Secret Agent Man*. Evie's business partner could smell a lucrative job from a thousand miles away. Hackers were a little more reliable than tarot readers.

She propped her chin on her hand, fluttered her lashes, and held out her hand for her phone.

~

DISGRUNTLED, CADE FLUNG HIS SUIT COAT OVER THE RENTED FARM'S PEELING wooden fence and watched the lanky vet commune with animals.

Commune—as in *talk*—to *animals*.

What the hell had his family got him into this time? He knew he should have changed his name and moved to Outer Slobbovia the instant he'd paid off the family farm's mortgage. He'd done his time. Someone else could take up the reins of responsibility.

If he had half a brain, he'd be on his way to Thailand now, as planned. He'd earned this opportunity to work with a company that wasn't all about the bottom line.

But his uncle had helped his family dig out of the wreck his parents had left behind and offered Cade an opportunity to get an education so he could support his siblings. He owed him. So, he'd agreed to this one last job.

At the time, it hadn't seemed too onerous. Visit the southeast coast, a place he'd never been, admire the Spanish moss, mint juleps, and antebellum mansions, and move on. His math skills certainly hadn't been stretched by the production company's limited budget.

But then he stupidly hadn't quit the instant he learned Sandra was part of the job. With Thailand beckoning, he'd assumed he could endure a few weeks of her attitude. But apparently Sandra couldn't endure him, and she'd walked off without even a formal resignation, leaving the production with a farm full of animals and no animal wrangler.

In desperation, he'd accepted the advice of his Oswin cousins. They'd given him the vet's name and told him about their east coast relation. He should have known better than to listen. The Oswins had married into a psycho family. Dylan's rock star wife wrote children's books because she feared her voice was *dangerous*. To throw away a fine instrument and lucrative career for weird superstition. . . Inexplicable.

Apparently, he'd sent his brains to Thailand and left a lump of stupidity on the job.

So here he was, watching a presumably intelligent woman with a medical degree *talk* to a goat. Dr. Malcolm didn't look insane. She was dramatically stunning, in fact. But she was taking notes just as if the bovid's bleats made sense. And that weird raven flying about and landing on her shoulder. . .

But he was desperate. Since his arrival and Sandra's departure, the rooster had crowed all night, the chickens attacked anyone in the vicinity, the goats and pigs escaped at every chance, and the bull still needed tranquilizing. He had to wonder if Sandra had put hallucinogens in the feed.

The film's star climbed up on the fence beside him. "What the freaking hell is she doing?"

Betty George was a dainty blond who didn't look a day over thirty, thanks to the best surgeons Hollywood could provide. Cade had read her file. She was past fifty and still insurable, but with her heart condition, her days of trekking the outback were numbered—especially if she insisted on smoking those cigarettes she carried everywhere. Given that she'd apparently had the safety removed from her lighter so the flame remained on the way old-time lighters did, he gathered the addiction was long-term.

"Animal control," he answered laconically.

Wayne Wright wandered over to join the audience. Cade had read his file, along with that of all the others in Mackie's tight production crew. Cade suspected Mackie held onto his crew because he was the only one who would hire them. And vice versa. Mackie had a reputation as a first-class asshole.

Wright wasn't Wayne's real name. He'd changed it after he'd been released from prison for assault and drugs. These days, he was Mackie's right-hand man, which probably meant he was still doing wrong. His official title was production assistant.

"What's she doing?" Wright repeated Betty's question.

"Holding the attention of every male in the vicinity," Betty answered dryly. She offered Wright a cigarette and lit it with her gold-plated lighter. Maybe she carried tobacco for goodwill purposes. Who knew?

But yeah, the leggy vet held Cade's attention. He almost had to admire her for coming after him with a tranquilizer gun. He'd like to borrow that when the rooster started its routine at midnight. But then, he'd have to talk to her, and he wasn't going there. He was gone the moment this insane job ended.

As the raven-wielding vet finished inspecting the facilities, a limo rolled in bearing the principals who had chosen to commute from a Charleston hotel. It was Saturday. Filming didn't start until Monday. Cade didn't question why they were here. As line producer, he simply counted pennies and made Mackie toe all the lines he was infamous for crossing, as he'd promised his uncle.

There really should be security posted at the entrance, but Mackie had vetoed the expense. He apparently assumed rural folk were too polite or too ignorant to hunt movie sets for autographs and photos.

An up-and-comer in the industry, Brice Kennedy, the director, stepped out first. Cade wondered how Mackie had persuaded real talent to take on this second-rate, low-budget documentary. But despite his legal and financial difficulties, Mackie still held a lot of strings. Kennedy's might be one of them. Ignoring the paddock, the director aimed straight for the old farmhouse.

Roy O'Bryan climbed out from the passenger front seat. Betty's male counterpart, the actor wasn't more than five-feet-six, but he wore wedges in his boots and swaggered like an old-time cowboy, which he was not. He was a graduate of a respected acting school and had played the part of cowboy in dozens of films over the years. He was just a bit long in the tooth for action parts now.

Sean Mackie, the film's producer, rolled his corpulent body out of the back seat without glancing in Cade's direction. Mackie knew why Cade was here and didn't like it, but Cade's presence was a condition of the financiers invested in the film.

Stamping out his cigarette, Wayne Wright scurried over to meet the trio.

Not a people person at the best of times, Cade swung over the fence, avoiding the newcomers. He took the arm of the enigmatic Dr. Malcolm and escorted her toward a different gate. "Keeping in mind that my job is to assure the insurance company and investors that all is well, what conclusions have you drawn about the set conditions? Sandra spent most of this past week overseeing repairs and construction to ensure the safety of the animals."

"Sandra?" Removing her arm from his grasp, the vet strode toward her Tahoe, her long blue-black ponytail swaying with her hips.

Cade appreciated the view of rounded posterior in tight jeans, but he was only here to keep Mackie in line, not hang around the locals, especially the psycho ones. "Sandra is the trainer Mackie hired to keep the animal rights people off his back."

Despite being a pain in the posterior, Sandra was normally a damned good animal wrangler. Cade shoved his hands in his back pockets and aimed for impartial and impassive—when he wanted to grind his molars at being left in the lurch at her abrupt departure.

The lady vet leaned against her SUV and regarded him with interest—probably not feminine interest but more as if he were a curiosity—not exactly the reaction Cade was accustomed to. But he wasn't here to charm.

"I'm gathering you and Mackie are not on the same page?"

"No comment. If you give the set a clean bill of health, you will be paid for your time, and that's that." He realized he was testing her. Sandra had informed him that he was obnoxious like that, along with his multitudinous other faults.

"I doubt you'll be interested in paying me when I tell you the animals are on edge, wary, and in the case of the bull, angry. Something or someone is disturbing them. The structures are sound. I'd like to meet your trainer. She and the crew have done a good job. The livestock appear well fed and cared for. And still, they are seriously unhappy and acting out."

As if to confirm her opinion, the goat bleated and attempted to climb the gate of its pen. A trio of chickens emerged from the barn, squawking as if a coyote was on their heels. And the bull bellowed furiously.

Cade glanced over his shoulder. Mackie and his posse were on the porch. It was almost as if the animals protested his arrival. Now *he* was succumbing to superstition.

Dr. Malcolm watched him with curiosity. "And *that's* why you're here?"

He gazed with dislike at the fashionable crew entering the old farmhouse they were using as office and lodging, understanding she referred to them and not the racket. Silver-haired Mackie in Armani in a barnyard—almost made sense. The man was more uncivilized animal than intelligent human.

"I'm here to keep production legal and under budget." He corrected any assumption that he cared one way or another about Mackie and company

Her phone beeped. She checked her messages and shrugged dismissively. "In my professional opinion, you need to call in my cousin Evangeline. That's why your Oswin cousin really sent you to Jax. But if all you want is reassurance that the animals are well cared for, I can give you that."

She opened her vehicle door.

Cade knew he should leave it there, write his report, and go back to the city and spreadsheets.

Unfortunately, his instincts agreed with hers. Despite his intellectual assumption that Sandra had walked out in spite, his gut said she wouldn't have willingly abandoned her horse or her lucrative career in a snit. She would have at least dumped manure on him and given him an ultimatum.

He caught the Tahoe's door. "Why am I calling in your cousin Evangeline?"

The vet had huge marine-blue eyes that reflected wells of concern. "Your animals are haunted. Evie sees ghosts."

Yanking the door from his hand, she climbed in and sped off, leaving him to ponder changing his plane ticket to Thailand to tomorrow.

Three

HAD JAX STILL BEEN WORKING IN HIS FANCY SAVANNAH LAW OFFICE, HE'D BE ON THE golf course right now. One of the disadvantages of a small-town career was that he was always on call. Of course, back then, he hadn't had much family to interfere either.

Jax regarded his *cousin* filling the antique Morris chair and suspected Garcia was uncomfortable with the case he'd brought in. He could sympathize. A year ago, that had been him, seeking the rational in Evie's irrational world.

"Think of it as energy," Jax suggested. "Iddy is telling you that the animals are disturbed by some energy we can't sense but she and Evie do."

Cade Garcia frowned and crossed his alligator boot over his knee. "I've seen spooked cattle, but this. . . cannot be written up in a report. A chemical dump, maybe?"

"Call it what you will. Talk to our Oswin cousins. Are you familiar with their wives? They'll tell you that the women are not crazy, just differently *percepted*, if I may coin a word. Evie's *team*, however, are trained investigators. You won't have to report more than that you hired them to find the animal handler. I take it she did not have a habit of disappearing?"

Jax could see some resemblance to himself and the rest of the family he'd met this past year when Garcia set his square jaw, narrowed his eyes, and nodded. Ives weren't pretty men, just carved like granite on a strong bone structure.

"Intelligent women have a habit of walking off on Mackie," Garcia admitted. "That's why I'm concerned. He's being sued by half a dozen women for sexual harassment and assault. If he hit on Sandra, she'll sue. I'm supposed to be preventing that from happening."

"Reuben and Roark will investigate Sandra's financials, see if she can be traced so you can talk with her. Idonea is an animal trainer who can help with the animal problem. If she brings in Evie. . . You might get answers you won't like, but that's up to you to report." Jax hoped and prayed they found this Sandra, settled the animals, and could sign off the case quickly. Iddy's prediction of poltergeists meant bad luck for the wedding happening in a little over a week as planned. "The crew may simply find snakes in the barn. Has the wildlife expert examined the premises?"

"Betty?" Cade snorted. "She reads her script well, looks good on screen, and isn't afraid of spiders. That's the extent of her expertise."

"Haven't they filmed her with big cats and elephants?" Jax rose when his new client did.

"Trained, not wild. The insurance would have been prohibitive if she walked up to a wild lion. Her BS degree is just that—she paid for one online. I expect that to be kept confidential." He strode out the door without looking back.

Loretta would be disappointed to learn her idol was just an actor, after all.

Jax texted Evie to expect a call. Then he sent messages to Roark and Reuben, Evie's Sensible Solutions team, telling them everything Cade had told him and setting them to hunt Sandra Harris, animal wrangler. The file Cade had left on his desk showed Harris as thirty-five, former owner of a now bankrupt California horse farm, with an unfinished degree in animal science. Divorced, no children, parents in Charlotte.

If she'd only just walked, her family may not have heard from her yet. Jax scanned in the file Cade had left on the crew and emailed it to R&R before returning to his own case load. He wasn't pulling down the kind of income he used to make at his old law firm. He needed his clients to afford the trip to the Keys he'd planned for their honeymoon.

He just had the itchy feeling he should whisk Evie off right now.

IDDY LOCKED UP HER OFFICE THAT EVENING AND GROANED AT SIGHT OF THE SENSIBLE Solutions van waiting in the parking lot. Evie leaned out the passenger side window and waved. Roark, the big Cajun hacker, sat at the wheel. Which probably meant Reuben, professor of engineering, was in back, spinning computer wheels.

"I haven't eaten all day," Iddy protested, crossing the lot. "Can't this wait?"

Evie handed her a brown sack. "Pris and Dante have the restaurant kitchen up and running. We come bearing food."

Their cousin Pris had been a busy caterer before she hooked up with her Italian count. She'd spent these last six months bouncing back and forth across an ocean, setting up a restaurant here while Dante worked his archeology career there.

Iddy took the sack, smelled garlic and fresh bread, and figured it was better than the frozen meal she'd meant to nuke.

"Fine then, I'll sit in my car while you sniff for ghosts. I don't know what you expect of me." She'd brought this on herself, so she had no one else to blame. Those animals were crying out for help she couldn't provide.

"At least sit on the fence and warn us if the bull means to attack." Evie rolled up the window and Roark gunned the engine.

For one of Pris's meals, she could do that.

The farm the film crew rented wasn't far away, just past the Shepherds' pot farm that had been raided a few months back. Driving the Tahoe, she'd barely nibbled her eggplant sandwich when they pulled up the drive. She sipped from her water bottle and watched the big cowboy swagger down from the farmhouse porch. How did Garcia persuade all that thick black hair to behave so stylishly without grease? He was in jeans tonight. His T-shirt, however, appeared to be silk and clung to bronzed arms in a way plain cotton would never do.

He approached *her* SUV instead of Evie's. *Dang.* She supposed introductions might be in order. With a sigh, she finished chewing, slugged from her water bottle, and climbed out.

The bull was calling menacingly from behind the barn. A herd of geese and goslings waddled, protesting loudly, toward the woods. Two pigs in the paddock had joined forces to batter at a fence railing while another dug at the post. Now that was truly weird.

Aware that she was still wearing the jeans from this morning, splattered with blood, fur, and vomit, Iddy didn't approach their host but gestured at Roark's van. "I'm not fit for human company. I'm only here to keep an eye on the bull."

Garcia eyed her skeptically and maintained his distance. Evie bounced out of the truck to join them. Iddy made the introductions. Her cousin didn't dress for success any better than she did. The purple T-shirt and pink shorts with her orange hair said it all.

"Good to meet you, Miss Carstairs." Garcia shook Evie's hand and glanced over to her partners, who were working with equipment in the back of the van. They didn't appear to notice the pigs determined to undermine the fence at their feet.

Evie beamed. "That's Reuben and Roark. They're here to check if electronic energy is disturbing your cattle. They're probably also hacking your internet. Jax says you're missing an animal trainer, and that's their direction."

Ever the strong, silent type, the cowboy waited expectantly.

Well, it wasn't as if he would ask how Evie hunted ghosts. Iddy gestured at the paddock and barn where the livestock was definitely not settling down for the night. "The animals are disturbed. You should probably start there and not with the trainer."

Ignoring her advice, Evie studied Cade with her spacey, third-eye gaze before nodding. "He harbors a lot of secrets, some angry, but he isn't overtly lying. Yet. Just be wary." She trotted off toward the paddock.

Iddy sighed and reached inside her vehicle for her sandwich. "Don't let me keep you. I'm still working on supper. I don't think you'll disturb the ghosts if you watch."

Caden Garcia's bronzed, high forehead wrinkled in perplexity—she thought. Maybe it was a frown. He didn't seem to be steaming. Yet.

"Who has secrets?" he finally asked, apparently unable to add two and two and get Evie. Good to know he wasn't completely brain dead.

Iddy shrugged, finished chewing, and watched her younger cousin climb the fence. "I'm assuming she means you. Evie reads auras. She does it with more comprehension than most people who claim to see rainbows or whatever. I've never tested her accuracy, but she's managed to stay alive all these years by knowing things others don't."

"Staying alive is a problem for her?" Now, he was glowering.

"It is when she's prone to saying the preposterous and acting on it. People who don't like their secrets revealed are inclined to want her dead. My niece looked up your Mr. Mackie when she decided you didn't like him. You won't want to introduce him to Evie. If he's guilty of all he's accused of, she's likely to gut him, slowly and painfully." Finishing her sandwich, Iddy leaned against her SUV and watched Evie scratch a goat head and dodge a rooster racing at her.

"Your niece, the child who wanted to meet Betty?" Apparently unmoved by her explanation, he leaned against the SUV with her instead of doing the intelligent thing and closing in on Evie. Maybe he didn't notice the stench of manure currently emanating from her boots.

The late April sun was descending behind the trees, throwing spectral shadows over the landscape. Iddy hoped R&R were keeping an eye on Evie. They were closer than she was, and she wasn't in a mood for wrestling pigs. She had the tranq gun in the seat, but it wasn't loaded.

"Loretta sees things in people that others can't, not even Evie. None of us understand what she's seeing, and she's learning more every day. Catching your dislike of Mackie is apparently child's play. If you have secrets, you should probably avoid Loretta." Iddy nodded at the paddock. "Evie's made contact with the Afterworld."

Her colorful cousin appeared to be talking with thin air.

Jaw shadowed by scruff, the cowboy watched grimly—until the farmyard noticeably grew quiet. The pigs stopped rooting, and the fowl returned to pecking for food.

That raised his heavy dark eyebrows. "The mare has calmed down and is tossing her head as if she's listening, but your cousin isn't even close. I thought *you* were the animal trainer."

"I've had a long, exhausting day, and I'm not doing a thing. I don't understand what Evie does, but she tells me she can see and hear spirit energy. So maybe animals can too." Even though she was familiar with her family's odd abilities, Iddy was a trained scientist and preferred to put her understanding into precise terms. She figured the Doubting Thomas beside her would appreciate language he understood. Mention *animal poltergeist* and he'd probably freak and fire them all.

A couple of men stepped onto the farmhouse porch. Iddy kept an eye on them.

"That's Wright, Mackie's assistant, and Steve Nancy, the camera operator." He nodded his head in the direction of the porch. "If you read animal minds, have a go at them. Mackie's crew isn't of the most wholesome."

Huh, he really didn't have a high opinion of the staff. Interesting, but not her circus. "People are not animals. Animals are much simpler to understand. If you don't trust those two, steer them back inside. Evie will report back to you later."

Iddy drifted toward the paddock, putting herself between the porch and Evie.

R&R got the message and settled against the fence, arms crossed, looking as intimidating as only former Marines can do. Since moving in with Jax's sister this past year, Roark had tamed his black curls and removed a lot of his metal. Reuben had replaced the bone in his topknot with a stylus but couldn't conceal the self-inflicted tribal scars on his cheeks. Since shacking up with the mayor, he'd learned to wear shirts with collars and khakis, but his deliberately intimidating posture screamed African warrior.

Garcia strolled beside her, blocking her view of the porch, he was that broad.

As they watched, a whirlwind of dust and pebbles abruptly flew through the paddock, causing Evie to step back. The bull bellowed as if whipped, and the horse kicked its stall. Iddy sought the minds of the closer creatures while Garcia climbed the fence, presumably in preparation for diving to the rescue.

As before, Iddy detected animal uncertainty and distress.

She glanced at the men on the porch. A couple more men holding beer bottles had joined them. A frisson of fear shivered her spine at the crescendo of animal protests.

Frowning in the fading light, Evie trotted toward the fence and safety, to Iddy's relief.

The door to the horse stall abruptly flew open under an unseen hand. The roan burst free.

A saddle flew out after it. *Uh oh.* She'd seen flying picture frames when Gracie was around, but this. . .

Caden Garcia broke into a run, but Evie caught his arm and stopped him. The horse circled the paddock, tossed its head, then trotted back to the feed sack.

"I'll make notes and send them later," Evie told him. "Keep those men away from the animals or the company might be liable for more than they understand."

He tilted an invisible hat in acknowledgment, hefted the mysteriously mobile saddle, and proceeded toward the barn and now calm horse. Iddy checked over her shoulder to see the men laughing and pointing their beer bottles at the scene. She understood some of Garcia's animosity toward the slackers.

Evie climbed the fence. "Thanks for coming, Id. You're right. I'm not sure how to handle this, but I'll ponder."

She was right—the animals were haunted?

R&R tossed Evie into the van and waited for Iddy to return to her SUV. In tandem, they all left the big cowboy dealing with a farm full of angry animals and useless idlers.

Four

Evie sighed as her team, including Iddy, followed her into the kitchen of the Victorian home her great-aunt had left in her haphazard care. Jax was waiting, along with Dante and Pris. Someone had evidently gone grocery shopping, because Pris was rolling out dough, and Dante was noshing on nachos. The kids, thank all the heavens, were nowhere in sight. Dante's five-year-old twins were adorable, but discussion was difficult in their presence. Loretta must have them in hand.

Trying to formulate a report that would not be well received, Evie gave her rescued Schnauzer puppy attention and a treat, then sent her out into the yard so Psycat could come down from the refrigerator. The Siamese didn't approve of a dog in the house.

Apparently reading Evie's mind, Pris produced glasses of ice and poured suspiciously green liquid into them, happily distracting all that male intensity with the libation. Evie took out her iced tea pitcher. Alcohol, ADHD, and ghosts were a bad combination.

She helped herself to a tortilla chip, waiting until everyone had settled before announcing, "I don't think the animal handler left the farm."

Amazingly, R&R nodded agreement. "No action on her credit cards or bank account since Wednesday, when she deposited a paycheck. We haven't found any vehicles in her name. The film company rented a limo and a few other vehicles, so she could have left that way. We've called the sheriff for a welfare check.'

Apparently not filled in on the story, Dante appeared confused. Jax looked resigned. Evie wanted to hug him, but the kitchen was pretty crowded.

"Did you make contact with the spirit?" Iddy asked, helping herself to the iced tea too. "The animals seemed to calm down for a while."

"Furious, incoherent energy," Evie confirmed, sorting through her impressions. "A recent spirit. There are others, but this one dominates. She's lashing out, which disturbs the animals. She just turned her attention on me for a spell."

"She won't harm the animals?" Iddy asked in alarm.

Evie thought about it. "No, I don't think so. She's not angry at them. She may be worried about the horse. Did she own the beasts? Is there a dog? I sensed concern for a large. . . has to be a dog. The goats aren't that long-haired."

Jax got out his phone and began texting. Evie assumed he was asking their client about a dog. He was good with details. And she was relieved he wasn't shouting about the wedding. Yet.

"But you don't know what happened to her?" Pris asked, rolling up her flattened dough.

None of the men asked questions, but they listened. Evie counted that as a plus. After a lifetime of being mocked, she appreciated their respect, even if they lacked understanding.

"Usually, a ghost doesn't remember their death, especially if it was a sudden one. They really are just energy when new. It takes time for their spirits or souls or whatever to coalesce. I don't claim to understand." Evie plugged in her phone. The battery was almost drained.

Having learned the routine, R&R did the same. Jax had thoughtfully provided cables all over the house. Her team had tried to determine if she was draining the batteries, or if the ghosts were, but it wasn't an exact science. Talking through the Veil had always been physically draining. She'd never attempted long conversations until this past year—when she'd acquired her first cell phone.

"Cade says Sandra brought her dog and horse with her. Dog is a collie, and it left with her. We should let the sheriff handle this," Jax said with finality, setting down his phone. "She could have just gone to visit her parents. But if there's any chance at all of a new grave out there, let Troy find it."

"Without evidence, he can't get a warrant to search." Reuben sprawled in the breakfast nook across from Dante. He was an engineer, not a lawyer, but they'd all learned a lot from recent investigations.

Jax glared at his friend. "We should call the trainer's parents, ask if they've heard from her. Check her phone records. Evie doesn't need to be involved more."

Loving the man too much to point out the fallacy of his theory, Evie swung on her counter stool and sipped her tea. Jax knew as well as she did that women went missing all the time. By the time law enforcement tracked them, they usually turned up as bones along the highway. She wished she might find Sandra alive, but she knew there was a recently dead woman out there. Whoever it was deserved justice sooner than later.

"Is the big cowboy paying us to investigate?" Roark asked.

Jax threw back a large gulp of his drink before nodding. "It's complicated, but he's working for both Mackie and his uncle's insurance company to keep Mackie in line and on time. He has an authorized budget by both companies. Garcia is a wild card. Be careful how you present your information."

Because R&R illegally hacked resources, Evie knew. "We can always say Pris read minds," she said with laughter. "He can get his own subpoenas once he knows where to look."

"We're assuming this poor woman is dead then?" Iddy asked worriedly. "And that someone on the farm knows it?"

That silenced the room, and Evie grimaced. "Way to crash the fourth wall, Id. It's easier in the abstract."

"Not safer though." Roark held up his plugged-in phone. "Social media. Sandra Harris and Caden—aka Cade— Garcia were an item two years ago."

Iddy slammed down her tumbler. "It's been a long day. I'm heading home."

The men were all digging into their phones and merely waved acknowledgment. Evie exchanged a glance with Pris as the door closed behind their cousin.

"What's your take on him?" Pris murmured, slicing up her roll of dough.

"Not a killer any more than Jax and friends—although they're ex-military and have quite possibly killed. So, there's that. Hiding secrets, thus not totally honest. That he didn't tell us the missing woman is an ex proves that." Evie sipped her tea and studied Jax and Dante, both distantly related through some centuries-old ancestor, as was Cade Garcia, apparently. "We'll have to invite him over for dinner so you can meet him."

"If he has Iddy worked up already then, yeah, let's do it. If his family owns an insurance company, he comes from money. Maybe they'll want to invest in a café."

Evie snorted. "Gracie's beau is calling it the Mad Café. Do you have a theme yet?"

Pris whacked her dough harder. "I'm thinking we'll have a poison appetizer du jour."

Her cousin had been accused of poisoning the former tenant of the café building and still harbored resentment. "Is Lawless Jane still in jail?" The blogger had started the nasty rumors about Pris being a murderer.

"In jail or a mental ward." Pris set her rounds of dough in a pan. "Her blog was shut down the last time I looked. But we have press crawling all over with the film company in town. I'm terrified they'll pick up on that old story and ruin us before we open."

"That's why we have Gracie's Nick, our very own personal marketing professional. You've seen what he's done to the Antique Barn. She's found herself a keeper." Evie was still amazed that her quiet, cautious sister had taken up with the relentlessly cheerful marketing pro.

"Wedding bells in the offing?" Pris inquired.

"You tell me. You're the mind reader. What about you and Dante? He's being incredibly understanding."

"He's learning to prioritize family over work. It's not easy. He loves being in the field, keeping an eye on his students and the dig, especially now that they've discovered an Etruscan tomb on the farm. But he's good at obtaining funds for the work, and he can do that from home. And coming here opens up new resources. Gotta adapt. I'm learning Italian." She covered the pan and slid it into the refrigerator.

Evie understood nothing of grants and tombs, but Pris's aura was calm for the first time in her life, and Dante's had broadened. Looked promising to her.

Finished with their drinks and discussion, R&R slid out of the booth. "We'll report back when we have anything," Roark called, opening the back door.

"Cake," Reuben added. "You need to choose a wedding cake. And a color theme, pronto. Larraine wants to coordinate her scarf and robes."

Larraine, Reuben's partner and mayor of Afterthought, was officiating at the ceremony. She'd obtained an online ordination and was working on a notary license, to be doubly certain the wedding was legal.

"Rainbow colors," Evie called after him. "If I'm wearing boring green, everyone else has to provide the color!"

The men departed, laughing. Mildly disgruntled at being left out of the investigation, Evie regarded her fiancé with a frown. "Why aren't you the one planning cakes and color schemes? You know I don't care."

Jax pried himself off the wall and leaned over to kiss her. "Because you can do three things at once, and I can't. And I'd rather they're wedding things and not investigating graves in a nest of potential killers. OK?"

"Well, when you say it like that. . ." Except she wasn't about to abandon the distressed and tortured spirit haunting a farmyard.

It was still early on the west coast. Cade called his uncle's number. Enrique picked up with the first ring.

"What has the muckface done now?" his uncle demanded.

"I don't understand why you keep insuring him," Cade snarled wearily. It was an old argument.

"None of your business," his uncle said. "Just keep him clean. It's only a three-week project. He's kept clean for the first week."

"Not necessarily. Why did he hire Sandra?" Cade rubbed a goat head as he made his rounds of the barn. "There's a perfectly good trainer here in town and probably dozens of handlers in driving distance."

"Her mom's sick. She applied for the job so she could go home. Mackie moved her animals for her. Convenience. I don't want to know more. They're grown-ups, and you were done with her years ago. Now tell me what he's done to have her walk away."

Cade contemplated saying *killed her*, but that was just his dislike of the producer. So far, no one had ever accused the pervert of murder. "Her horse is here. She isn't. The crew claim she left in a truck and hasn't been heard from since. I've hired local investigators, but you'd better let me find a way out of this contract. Once the sheriff is called in, the press will be bad and production will crawl."

"You didn't have to call the law," his uncle shouted.

"Yeah, I did, *Tío*. That's why I'm here, isn't it? Because Mackie holds nothing over *my* head. Take a nice vacation. Catch up with family. Better yet, give me authority to cancel the contract."

Because saddles didn't fly on their own. . . Who was the special effects person on this job? He didn't think the budget allowed one.

"Closing the production would bankrupt both of us. Only Mackie's investors would come out clean. My employees, Mackie's employees. . . they'd all lose their jobs. Hold his nose to the grindstone, Cade. I'm counting on you." He hung up.

His uncle's *employees* were Cade's extended family. The insurance company and his father's farm had supported them for years. Then, his mother died and his father fell into a funk and eventually committed suicide, leaving adolescent Cade and his brother struggling with young sisters and unfamiliar management while they were still in high school.

The hard knock school of learning had left the farm heavily in debt. They were just now out of the woods. Cade was experiencing his first glimmer of freedom.

If a behemoth client fell, it would leave a lot of casualties, including his escape plan.

Mackie's bad press had made investors wary of his films. Without insurance that the production would finish on time, the producer hadn't been able to obtain funding. Cade didn't know what Mackie held over his uncle for Enrique to reluctantly agree to insure even a documentary. Hiring Cade as line producer to keep production legal and on schedule had been a requirement. His job was to see that there were no animal rights protests, no women charging assault, nothing that would break the budget. He'd flown in when notified of Sandra's disappearance, a budget breaker if there ever was one.

In a better, smarter world, he'd be here to shut Mackie down if he'd violated the contract, but he wasn't running either company.

He canvassed the grounds one more time, checking stalls, locks, and gates. He'd grown up with animals, recognized their uneasiness, but unless there was a wolf wandering the premises, he could find no reason.

The weird scene with the vet calming the animals fretted at him. Sandra used to have a soothing effect on the animals she trained but not a whole barnyard at once. And the flying saddle. . .

He'd inspected the stall. No one had been inside. No secret exits. The saddle was lightweight, but it would have taken a tornado to fling it without a human hand. He needed to take another look at employee files. Had Mackie hired someone new?

Unless they were planning sabotage, a new tech would not be flinging saddles.

He threw the bolt on the barn door, locking it for the night. He wished he'd stayed in Charleston, but he'd opted for moving into the farmhouse until he'd found out more about Sandra's disappearance. If he had to remain much longer, he'd rent an RV and park it out back, like Betty. She claimed she needed it so she could have her assistant with her,

The barn door bolt he'd just closed rattled. Cade swung around and watched in disbelief as the heavy bar fell out and the door swung open.

The goats bleated and shot out as if their tails were on fire.

Sandra had done that to him once when she was angry.

Dammit, she had to be hiding around here.

Five

THE MAD CAFÉ. SUNDAY MORNING, EVIE PEERED AT THE MIDNIGHT BLUE SIGN painted in gold lettering and decorated in moons and stars and a crystal ball. "I thought you were joking. Why Mad Café?" she asked the man sitting on the tile floor adding the finishing touches to the sign.

"Gracie's suggestion. Pris liked it. I can work with it. I'm thinking a Mad Hatter theme, but Pris shipped in all these nifty Italian pieces from Dante's villa." Nick Gladwell stood and dusted off his paint-spattered jeans. "I'd call it the Mad Italian but Pris isn't actually Italian."

Pris was definitely the mad partner. Evie's mindreading cousin had reason to be. "Dante is Italian, and it's his belongings and money she's appropriating. That makes him pretty mad, as in totally nutsoid." Evie studied the artwork and artifacts her sister was arranging on the walls. Nick and Gracie came in a pair these days. "You need a Mad Hatter hat and a rabbit."

Gracie climbed down from her stool and pointed at the order counter. "Pris is thinking about a mural with Alice and the Hatter sitting on Etruscan ruins. I have no idea what's going on in her head."

Evie chuckled. "Pris thinks in metaphors. She's probably the Hatter serving tea. Etruscan represents Dante's more solid foundation. Who knows what Alice represents?"

"Exploration," Gracie suggested. "Adventure. I've read an analysis of *Wonderland*. I'd be surprised if Pris has, though. She just likes weird."

"Pot calling kettle," Nick warned, pointing his paint brush at her. "I've read your book draft. Anyone not knowing your family will call it weird."

Gracie blushed and turned back to situating art on the wall. "I write what I know!"

If she was writing up their cases, she'd never sell them. Evie didn't worry. "I'm supposed to be here to look at designs for my wedding cake. Where's Pris?" She wandered deeper into the high-ceilinged café, remembering the glossy boutique that used to occupy this space and far preferring Pris's simple black and white design with wild pops of color.

"Something about the delivery of equipment. She's probably casting spells on some poor devil. She left books on the counter." Studying the artwork she'd just hung, Gracie straightened the frame without climbing up again. She was learning to use her telekinesis a little at a time. Ever cautious was her sister.

"You could go with a fairy theme for the wedding," Gracie suggested. "The kids would love that."

Nick snickered.

Evie rolled her eyes. "Rainbows and unicorns. *Larraine* will love that."

Gracie nodded enthusiastically before noting their expressions and blushing again. "Sorry. I'm a grade schoolteacher."

"With a six-year-old," Nick added solemnly.

"Rainbows are better than witches and black cats, which would be Pris's theme. I like color." Evie opened a book of cakes, but she'd rather taste than admire. "Let's have one of everything."

In time to hear that, Pris emerged from the kitchen bearing boxes labeled *flatware*. "Let's you do the baking," she said pointedly. "I have to bring my catering gear out of storage, but if I remember correctly, I have one set of wedding tier pans and half a dozen sheet cake pans. Which do you want?"

Evie crinkled her nose. "I want enough cake for everyone and extra for extras. I just want a big party with yummy food."

"You're afraid to call it a wedding." Gracie opened a cake book and flipped the pages. "Just because everyone in our family comes from a failed marriage, including me, doesn't mean you and Jax are doomed."

"Maybe." Evie studied a cake decorated in cats that Gracie showed her. "Jax said his birth parents were happy. And his California cousins seem to be happy. So maybe his family breaks the jinx. And I don't want furry animals on any cake I eat."

Pris turned a book around for her to see. "Sherbet layer cake. Choose an icing color. If all goes as planned, I'll have ovens installed by then, if not freezers. I'll have to bake them all in one day, but it's doable."

Evie admired the multi-colored sheet cake. "Wow, how do you do that? It's perfect!"

"Green icing," Gracie demanded. "Let's try to keep some theme here."

"Green eggs and ham too?" Nick suggested, laughing.

"More than one cake, different icing on each. Can you use real strawberries and not artificial coloring for the pink?" Evie's phone rang as Pris nodded agreement.

"Limes for the green?" Gracie asked dubiously.

Recognizing Iddy's number, Evie put the phone on speaker. "What's up? You're not supposed to be working on Sunday."

"Animal control has no day off. Renters at the Shepherd farm say the pit bulls have cornered a collie. They've locked it in the shed for safety. The photos on Sandra's social media show her with a collie. I want to take the animal over to the film farm after I examine it. I thought maybe you should go along."

"You thought right. Have you called Cade yet?" Forgetting about cakes and weddings, Evie aimed for the door.

"After I examine the dog. I'll go now. Meet me at the office."

Iddy's office wasn't far outside of town. Figuring if she started working off wedding cake now, she could indulge later, Evie hopped on her bicycle. Until this past year, it had been her only mode of transportation. She'd been getting lazy since acquiring a car.

Iddy's SUV was just pulling into the lot by the time Evie arrived. The Shepherd farmhouse was less than a mile away, so Iddy didn't have far to drive. But it was miles from the film set, if this was Sandra's pet.

"She's terrified but in pretty good shape," Iddy called as she opened the animal pen in the back of the Tahoe. "I want to calm her down before I try any mental connection."

"Let's not take too long. If the dog really is Sandra's, it may be the reason she's lingering." Evie didn't think so, but she could hope.

She also hoped that wasn't the missing trainer whose aura haunted the barn, but coincidences of that size simply didn't happen.

Inside the hospital examining room, Evie set out food and water while her cousin pried burrs and ticks out of the collie's once-gorgeous mane.

"I should bathe her, but she's pretty shaken." Iddy continued the soothing combing while the dog scarfed from the bowls. "Poor baby. Wonder how long she's been loose?"

"Until we have a ghost—or body—to consult. . ." Evie grimaced. "Dogs can't count, can they?"

"No, not unless trained, and then only for specific tasks, not days. She's tired and wants to sleep. Call Garcia. I think it might be easier if I wait until we're at the farm to probe for images."

The cowboy showed up on a motorcycle before Evie's investigative team arrived. Cade took one look at the dog and nodded wearily. "Classy. Sandra called her Classy."

He stooped down and held his hand out for the collie to sniff. The dog yipped recognition. Evie waited for Cade to express grief, but she only saw confusion.

"Sandra always took care of her animals. She had to have left the dog with someone." He stood up again and punched text into his phone.

Evie wanted to add him to her suspect list, but his aura reflected concern and fury—for what? His job? He was all business robot. If she kicked his shin, would he react or just dent?

Her phone beeped with incoming text. "Roark has the van. He said he'll meet us out there."

At Iddy's questioning look, Evie shrugged. "I promised Jax to let them know where I am. If Sandra's ghost speaks. . . We probably need backup."

"I called in the welfare check last night," Cade disclosed, holding the door open so they could lead the collie out. "Sheriff is out there now. There's no filming on Sunday, though, so most of them are in Charleston."

"If it's Troy questioning, and not one of his deputies, we're good. Let's roll." Evie climbed in the Tahoe's passenger seat while Iddy shut the dog into the pen in back. Cade raced off on his motorcycle ahead of them.

Except for the sheriff's car in the drive, the farm appeared deserted as they drove up. Roark's van pulled in shortly after they'd parked. Warily, Evie stood by while Iddy opened the back. The collie sniffed the air and sank down, head on paws, reluctant to jump out. Cade had to kneel and scratch its head before she could be persuaded.

"I'm picking up confusion," Iddy murmured, focusing on the dog. "An image of a blond woman, curls, curves, rhinestones?"

Cade grimaced and shook his head in apparent disbelief. "You're describing Sandra. Have you seen her recently? She can't act, but she dresses like a film star. It draws the attention she likes."

Evie didn't need to open her extra senses to see the dance of attraction and distrust between her cousin and the cowboy. Iddy wouldn't have a lot of patience with a doubting Thomas.

Ignoring them, she studied the deserted barnyard. "The spirit energy is concentrated in the barn. Let's take Classy over there. Hold the leash tight. Animals don't react well to ghosts, and if I'm sensing Sandra. . ." She wouldn't predict what would happen.

Keeping Iddy's description of Sandra in mind, Evie climbed over the fence. The animals began their clucking, bleating routine, and the horse crashed against its stall. Roark texted that he would stay with the van and keep an eye on the house.

People were more dangerous than animals. Evie got that.

Cade ordered them to stay out of the barn until he signaled it was safe to enter. When he opened the door, geese and chickens dashed out, flapping and squawking. The pigs and goats apparently hadn't escaped their pens yet. He gave an OK sign, and Iddy and Evie entered together with the dog.

On a sultry April day, the barn felt air-conditioned.

A rush of love and relief hit her. Against the dim backdrop of dusty rafters and wooden stalls, Evie located an aura coalescing near the dog—grounded earth colors, not angry ones. Yet.

The collie sniffed and yipped eagerly, as if detecting its owner.

Iddy whispered, "She's sensing a familiar presence and puzzled that she can't see her."

"Sandra's here. She's happy to see the dog. I hate disturbing the moment of peace. Her aura is stronger today." Evie checked her phone battery and slapped her backup on it. "But I can't wait too long."

Cade returned from checking stalls. Previously warned about Evie's battery problem, he indicated a panel of USB plugs in a wall outlet. "Crews need tech. You're covered."

The instant Evie stepped over to the panel and away from Cade, the earthy aura straightened into almost human height and flared red. A second later, a pitchfork flew off the wall in Cade's direction.

SWEARING, CADE DODGED THE FLYING FORK, SNATCHING IT FROM THE AIR BEFORE IT could harm the fowl running around like. . . chickens with their heads off.

In disgust, he examined the tool, looking for how flight had been accomplished.

"Nice job." Betty stood in the doorway, accompanied by a bulky older man in uniform. "Mackie should hire you for special effects. A haunted barn would be a hell of a lot more entertaining than the plight of the American farmer."

The copper-haired ghostbuster hastily shooed them all outside. Despite her diminutive stature, she received no argument. Everyone filed into the paddock and away from any more flying implements, although the leggy vet lingered to be certain no fowl had been harmed.

"Tell me the guy in the van invents electric pitchforks," Cade murmured, lagging behind with the vet and the dog. He didn't like any damned thing about this set-up his uncle had dumped him into, but the vet made good scenery.

"If Roark had witnessed that scene, he'd be tying and gagging Evie and flinging her in the van. Nope, if that's your girlfriend's ghost pitching fits, she's not happy with you." Iddy followed the others out, ponytail swinging, collie on her heels.

His *girlfriend*? Cade studied the empty barn before closing the doors. He dated. He wasn't celibate. But long-term girlfriends were no longer on his agenda. Sandra had cured him of any notion of settling down. . .

Sandra. She knew about Sandra. *Shit.*

Yeah, he could believe Sandra would pitch a fork at him. They hadn't parted friends. Was she hiding and rigging this set up? What would be the point? To shut down Mackie's production? Revenge?

The chattering group climbed the fence. He should probably introduce them to the concept of a gate, but under the circumstances, he was comfortable with leaving it bolted. Having shown off her athleticism, Betty returned to the comfort of the air-conditioned house, no doubt to tell tales of flying pitchforks or learn who had set up the trick.

The earring-wearing Cajun leaned against his utility van, keeping a wary eye on Evie. He didn't approach the sheriff. Jax had said Roark was a computer engineer. Had the pitchfork been some weird 3-D projection? Except it had been damned real when he caught it.

"Know your way around pitchforks, do yah?" the sheriff asked as Cade approached.

Cade was here on business and had dressed accordingly in blazer and slacks. In the sheriff's eyes, he probably looked like a dude. He didn't care. "I grew up on a farm. I know how to pitch a bale. I'm not, however, in the movie business. I don't know my way around special effects."

Evie hooted but steered the conversation away from flying forks. "The presence in that barn knows Sandra Harris's pet and recognizes Cade. Unless someone else who knows them well is missing, I'm sticking my neck out here to say that the presence is Sandra. A ghost generally lingers where it was killed. Doesn't mean her body is there, but we should search."

Cade's gut took the full impact of that possibility and twisted into a deadly knot. *Sandra, dead. . .*

He refused to believe in spooks. Working with his uncle's firm, he'd been around the movie business and knew the magic gloss Hollywood spun to hide reality. Dozens of women would love to see *Mackie* dead. They could be plotting against him by having Sandra disappear and sabotaging the film. If it weren't for his uncle and his family, Cade would leave them to it.

"I have no evidence for a search warrant, Evangeline," the sheriff chided. "From all reports, Sandra Harris climbed into a pickup of her own free will on Wednesday evening. Her room is empty, so she presumably took her purse and her baggage. Her parents say they spoke with her on the phone Wednesday, and she was cheerful and liked her job. She promised to visit when the filming was done. You can be wrong occasionally."

The sheriff didn't appear disgruntled at a potential nut job demanding a

Sunday morning wild goose chase. Cade took a chance on questioning him. "When I asked, no one could tell me the make and model of the pickup she left in. Did you have better luck?"

"They say it was dark, and they only saw taillights. The bull started trying to break down the fence, and no one dared venture out."

"The bull smelled blood," the lanky vet explained. "He's still trying to escape the scent. The other creatures are unsettled after witnessing violence, but it's impossible to tell if it was a coyote grabbing a chicken or worse. If Sandra disappeared Wednesday night, that's too long a period for them to recall actual events. Their current behavior is mostly a reaction to an unsettling experience or presence they sense *now*."

Cade liked the vet's looks, but he wasn't buying animal mind reading. All he'd wanted was someone to look after the beasts and keep production in line. Once he got off this job, he was heading to Thailand and never speaking to any of his family again. A lawyer like Jax really believed this crap?

Garbed today in an almost painful clash of red and pink, his cousin's fiancée wandered off, presumably in pursuit of invisible beings. She might be as psycho as the Oswin wives.

Cade rubbed the back of his neck and tried not to sound as if he were interrogating the law. "Is it possible to trace Sandra's cell phone?"

The Cajun answered for him. "Already have. Evie never reads our reports. Give me your email, and I'll send it over. The victim's phone lost service around midnight Wednesday. The last ping was near the interstate ramp. Can't tell whether it was going north or south."

Sheriff shrugged. "There ya go. Her folks can call in a missing person report if they like, but she's an adult. We have no reason to believe she's in trouble. Your concern now is the butt load of animal rights people around here. They'll be down your back if you don't have anyone looking after them animals."

The contract required an experienced animal handler—no Sandra, no film. Insurance would have to cover investor losses. That's the reason he was here—to prevent that happening.

This was starting to look like a setup. He needed to find a replacement for Sandra, pronto. His gaze automatically swung to the ideal candidate.

"Don't look at me," Dr. Malcolm warned, holding up her hands. "I'm working 24/7 as it is, and sometimes 36/8 if you want to believe in extra dimensions."

He might not believe in ghosts, but he respected the concept of horse whisperers. She'd calmed those animals yesterday. She knew what she was doing.

"We can pay you Sandra's salary and hire someone to help you." The budget would take a hit, but he named an amount that caught her attention. "The contract only requires a professional to oversee care. It's not as if anyone will be riding the bull or putting the goats through hoops. This is a documentary about farmers, not a circus. You only need to be certain they're all healthy and treated well."

"Vet school graduating this month," Evie called, proving she listened.

The animal doctor had expressive, long-lashed eyes that lightened to almost turquoise in longing—before she set her wide mouth and shook her head. "Hiring a student for two weeks, then letting them go, is cruel."

True. "Let me make some calls," he stalled. "We're talking shutting down a multi-million-dollar project for the sake of a few thousand in salary."

"And the town loses all that nice business," Evie pointed out, returning to the paddock. "The film company is paving broken sidewalks and adding potted trees. If Pris can open her kitchen tomorrow, she could start with a bang. Hank at the hardware store is salivating, and the print shop is already working overtime."

Cade hadn't considered the film production's effect on surrounding business. He was just covering his ass. One more damned responsibility to add to his yoke.

"Good luck finding anyone interested in a rural animal hospital," the vet said dryly. "I'm paid on goodwill and canned goods half the time. I've been looking for help for a year."

"If you're planning on staying for a while, Cade, we have plenty of room at our place," Evie suggested. "You're family. Then you can offer an assistant your room here on the farm—free rent really helps when you're starting out. Just make sure he's male."

The sheriff tapped his cap in departure, ignoring that jibe at Mackie's reputation. "I'll leave y'all to it. Let me know what you learn."

Cade mentally uttered a few of his uncle's Spanish imprecations at realizing he was stuck here, then politely accepted Evie's invitation. He wanted to be close to the production, not in Charleston, and he'd prefer not to stay in this nest of vipers.

With resignation, as the sheriff drove off, Cade studied his unlikely group of detectives. Unlike the sheriff, he had to go with his gut and believe something had happened to Sandra, or she'd deliberately set out to ruin the film. "All right then, we seem to be on our own. Mackie's crew isn't likely to talk to me. Anyone want to hire on as extras?"

"Will that get us into the house?" Roark eyed the porch where Betty and a few of the crew had settled with cigarettes and iced drinks, probably alcoholic even at this hour on Sunday.

"If you need inside the house, you need to be part of the tech staff," Cade warned.

"Dat works. You got a sound tech who'd like to take a vacation?"

Seven

Too shattered by Cade's job offer to think clearly, Iddy performed her daily routine on automatic. The soothing repetition of scratching furry ears, filling water containers, even scooping poop, cleared her head.

Cade Garcia had offered her a princely California-style salary that in this cheaper rural area would allow her to expand the paddock and the shelter. She could take in larger animals, maybe even start a pet hotel. More work, but also better paying clients so she might hire minimum wage help to do what she was doing now.

She really needed a full-time assistant so she might one day take a vacation, see something besides cotton fields. She might at least go to the beach, go shopping. . . Well, money for fancy clothes was wasted on her.

Expecting a vet school graduate to settle in Afterthought was insanity There simply wasn't enough money to pay for the education.

She only stayed because her family's eccentricities were accepted here. People in Afterthought didn't care if she walked around with a raven on her shoulder and dogs on her heels. She'd even had clients ask her to read their pet's mind when it quit eating its favorite food. The locals understood as no one else would —as Cade obviously didn't.

Here, she'd been able to take over an established business with minimal investment and live at home while she paid school debt. Her father certainly hadn't helped, and her mother barely scraped a living.

It had worked well. She'd saved enough to buy the used Tahoe she someday hoped to use for hauling a horse van. And she had enough credit to buy this RV to sit on the back lot, allowing her to move out of her mother's apartment. Convenient for monitoring her surgical patients overnight. Inconvenient when people pounded on her door while she was showering. . .

She wrapped herself in a towel and shouted, "Hold on!" Tugging on a clean pair of shorts and a denim work shirt, she wrapped the towel around her hair. Expecting a tearful client with an injured pet, she almost slammed the door as soon as she opened it.

Cade Garcia didn't appear apologetic for disturbing her. Looking like he'd just walked from a James Bond movie instead of an insurance office, he shoved his hands in his back pockets as if he wore jeans instead of tailored trousers and looked her over with masculine interest. "I brought resumes for potential assistants."

Had he said anything else, she would have slammed the door. Having spent the day dreaming of what she could do with money and an assistant, she couldn't say *no* now. She ought to, but she couldn't.

Ungraciously, she waved him in. "You're quick."

"Not when it counts," the usually grim giant said, offering an earth-shattering grin that left no doubt as to his meaning.

She'd been celibate for so long that she had no notion of how to react. So, she didn't. She simply pointed at her tiny red bench couch. "I'll be back in a minute."

He almost had to duck beneath her low ceiling.

Then she abandoned him there, dwarfing her miniature RV furniture, while she escaped to comb out her hair before it was hopeless.

When she returned, he'd helped himself to a glass on her drain board and poured water. She was a horrible hostess. He was a rude guest.

Ignoring protesting hormones, she held out her hand. "Resumes?"

"Email. Will the one on your website work?" He pulled out his phone.

She signed in exasperation. "You didn't have to come over to send me an email! That's the whole blasted point of the internet!"

"Not when I need an immediate response. Production starts tomorrow. As much as I'd like to cancel Mackie's contract and Mackie personally, my uncle stands to lose a fortune and his reputation. It's a cutthroat business."

She grimaced and reached for her laptop. "Fine. Have a seat. I can offer iced tea or juice, if you prefer."

"Water's fine. I'm not much into syrup." He took a seat on the low-back bench, sprawling his long legs halfway across her sitting area.

"I have unsweetened tea, but that's a cultivated taste too." She opened her email, found one with attachments, and slid in behind her tiny table to read it.

This was a camper, not a full-sized mobile home. She wasn't sitting close to testosterone personified. "How did you find three candidates so fast?"

"Hollywood glamor and money. I told Mackie if he wanted this film, he needed to personally offer a sizable contribution to the vet school, in return for the names of students who weren't starting jobs immediately."

"And you put Mackie Film Productions in the header, and you're inundated. I want to hate you." Instead, she examined the student emails he'd received. "You have a dozen replies in this file! How did you narrow it to three?"

"The only men who replied. I'm not putting another woman in jeopardy. Sandra left without notice for a reason."

"That grates in so many ways. . ." Seeing no point in arguing when he'd handed her the golden jackpot, Iddy skimmed quickly, then sorted out several to study more.

"The male candidates already have other jobs lined up, starting in June," he said. "This would just be a fun interlude for them, rubbing elbows with film stars and getting paid. I like the one who grew up on a horse farm."

"He'll ignore the chickens and goats," she said absently, having already rejected him as a privileged son stepping into a planned vacancy working with racehorses.

Her agenda was different. She wanted an assistant who would *stay*.

She had second thoughts when she rejected all the men. He was right. They were all able-bodied and prepared to move on when the job was done. It was that last part she resisted.

"Compromise." She shot him the file holding all her hopes and dreams. "A woman who might want to keep working here. I'll move in with Evie for the interim and let this candidate stay in the RV so she doesn't have to live at the farm."

"She's deaf!" he shouted, reading the cover letter. "If the bull goes on a rampage, she wouldn't even hear it. It's a liability issue."

"That excuse will get your pants sued off if you use it to reject her. Open your narrow mind and look—she grew up on a cattle farm. Do you think she doesn't know how to handle cattle? She's worked with a small-town vet in summers. She's a straight-A student with excellent references. If she hadn't been forthright in declaring her disability, we wouldn't be having this discussion. She'd have her pick of the best animal practices in the country. It's blatant discrimination that she's not already hired."

He glowered and growled but studied the file. "At least she won't hear the sexist crap Mackie's crew spews."

"Bonus. Of course, she says she reads lips, but turning her back fixes that. She might reject *us*, though. She isn't doing this for film credit. She says right there that she hopes this is an opportunity to show what she can do. All that hard work, and *she can't find a job.* That is so grossly unfair." Trying not to show how much she wanted this kid, Iddy stroked the three-legged kitten that finally got brave enough to crawl from under the bed.

Cade studied her. "You're hoping she'll stay?"

She couldn't carry off indifference when her hopes were leaping for the sun. "I'm going outside to do a prayer dance the moment you leave. I'll never see anyone this qualified darken my door again. I can't begin to pay her what she's worth. But I can give her experience until she finds the right position."

He looked dubious. "She can't hear a dog bark trouble or a cat in pain. I'm not a complete rube. I can't—"

"Just look at her resume! She's been doing it for years. It's not ours to question how. Let's bring her here. I'll go with her to see what your job requires. I'll have my receptionist reschedule routine appointments. Having us both available ought to fulfill the contract."

He shoved the phone in his pocket but continued to study her. "I'm thinking there's a conspiracy to shut Mackie down. What happens if there are more flying pitchforks, and this kid gets injured?"

"The same thing as if it happened to one of your privileged males, except he'd shout louder and file a lawsuit. And I understand you don't want to accept what Evie is telling you, but keep your eyes and your mind open. If anyone is after Mackie, it's his crew. Ghosts are simply collateral damage."

He rubbed his head and rumpled his thick black locks. "Your dad said this place was weird. I see what he means."

Iddy froze. "You know my father?"

He blinked in surprise. "Of course. Didn't he tell you? Mackie hires him all the time. Mackie likes to prove he's culturally sensitive or whatever."

"My father wouldn't know culturally sensitive if he sat on it, so I suppose it's fitting that he works for a sexist pig. Hire this girl and then you can go back to the city or wherever and not worry about weirdness." She stood and opened the door.

He stood, too, his head brushing the ceiling, but he didn't leave. "I apologize if I hit a nerve, but Slate seems proud of you. I thought that's why he steered Mackie here."

A man who apologized, there was a new one, but she was too irate to care. "He sent you to a *weird* town where the women talk to animals and the After-world? Ponder that. Let me know if this Asia person accepts our offer."

He departed, somewhat reluctantly. If he'd hoped she'd throw herself into his arms in gratitude, he'd blown it by mentioning her father.

Scooping up the kitten in consolation, Iddy called Evie to ask about temporary quarters—just in case miracles happened.

"Excellent timing," Evie cried. "Dante and Pris have finally moved the last of their things into the apartment over the café! They left the beds at least. Come on over. We're having a going-away pizza party. You don't happen to cook, do you?"

Only then did Iddy remember that Evie had also offered her huge Victorian to Cade.

EVIE HAD FINISHED CHOPPING THE GARLIC AND PEPPERS BY THE TIME PRIS RETURNED from her most recent run to the toilet. She gestured casually with the paring knife. "Pick up a license at the courthouse, and Larraine can marry you at the same time as us. Get more for our money."

"The wedding is not costing you any money, except groceries." Not acknowledging Evie's assumption one way or another, her cousin rolled out the pizza dough.

"Maybe we should persuade Nick and Gracie to the altar at the same time," Evie mused, tasting the pizza sauce. "Beltane. Think about it. Our kids could all be the same age."

"I'm trying to imagine you with an infant. You'd see a ghost, wander off, and leave it in a grocery cart. Does Jax want kids?"

"He claims he doesn't care. We have Loretta. I don't think it matters what we want though. If the spirit of one of our ancestors decides to return and the time is right— Bingo. All protections are useless." Evie liked the idea of leaving children up to their ancestors. They were probably smarter than she was.

Pris wrinkled her nose and filled the pizza pan. "So, we should have stayed in Italy? This is the fault of this house and the ghosts of our ancestors?"

"Dante doesn't want more kids? I mean, if you're both staying home to take care of the twins, it makes sense to have another. And Dante has Malcolm ancestry, too, remember. The villa or the homes of any of his relations you've visited—"

"Charming, so old crones who once stirred cauldrons can just reincarnate any time they grow bored with haunting us? Or maybe they decide video games are worth another walk through life. Or, knowing our family, maybe they figure this time around they can rule the world?"

Evie decided her cousin's aura was calming down now that she was admitting that she was knocked up. Her job here was done.

"I'm not certain that spirits are that well defined when reborn. Look at us. We're mostly a product of DNA and environment. It's just some—*qualities*, like curiosity and open mindedness and. . ." She gestured with the knife again. "Those are the things the spirits of our ancestors provide to make us who we are and to accept our anomalies."

"That, and our mothers eagerly encouraging the weirdness of their precious infants." Pris grated cheese with furious vigor. "I don't think telling Dante that the spirit of an ancestor has moved in will help much. We've been taking precautions."

Evie shrugged. "You don't have to marry. The advantage of the twenty-first century is that you can take care of your own kid without a man. You have family. Marriage is just a tax break."

"A visa loophole," Pris suggested grimly. "A marriage of convenience as they say in Gracie's romances."

Ah, there was the heart of the matter. Dante was the strong, silent type with no facility for admitting emotion. "You know he adores you. Why else would he put up with your grumpiness?"

"Because I understand his kids, and he needs me."

Evie laughed as the doorbell rang. "He could hire a nanny instead of putting up with you. Tell him. See how he reacts. That's Iddy. Did you see how she and Cade looked at each other? No, you weren't there. The house spirits will have lots of opportunity this Beltane."

Just the talk of babies had all Evie's hormones banging pots and pans and the spirits humming with excitement.

She almost warned Iddy not to come in when she met her at the door.

But for the first time in years, her older cousin's aura was on fire with excitement. Who was Evie to stand in the way of fate?

Eight

Monday morning, at Cade's request, Jax called in Reuben and Roark to meet at his office. He didn't like working behind Evie's back, and he stated that right up front. "I'm getting married in less than a week. Keeping Evie out of this meeting doesn't bode well for a long-term relationship."

Cade Garcia paced Jax's office, not taking the offered seat. "I don't wish to hurt her feelings, but I'm not buying into ghostly exhibitions. My uncle's insurance company and Mackie Productions stand to lose their reputations and millions if this film shuts down. Mackie has enough enemies who would enjoy seeing that happen. Ghosts aren't part of the equation."

When Cade didn't take the massive Morris chair, Reuben, acting as the mayor's liaison, did. The top-knotted professor had the ability to crack military code and hack corporate computers, but he was currently practicing lawfulness. "Larraine is hoping the film will put Afterthought on the map. I'm pretty sure that doesn't mean with more notoriety."

Murdered mayors and lethal judges had been the local headlines last year. Jax agreed that an intelligent documentary could only improve the town's image.

"Ain't much Ariel and I can do investigating da financials dat you don't already know." Roark leaned his broad shoulders against the wall and crossed his arms. "Mackie is operating on a shoestring. No major funds to siphon, although he's sucking a few hundred at a time from the ATM."

Cade grunted at that. "I told him he had to stop that. Production isn't paying for anyone's drugs. Or other bad habits."

Roark shrugged and continued. "Da missing woman hasn't done more than bank her paycheck. No credit charges, nuttin'. She didn't have a vehicle here. She apparently sold everything she owned in California. She paid off debt then. No inexplicable deposits on her accounts. 'Fraid she's more ghost than saboteur."

"Sandra has no reason to hate Mackie as far as I'm aware." Cade rubbed his hand through his hair, apparently the only signal that he was upset. "She's worked with his company before and took the job knowing he's being sued by former female employees. Mackie is an old-style casting couch producer, and Sandra is too low level to meet with him. Brice hired her. Since Mackie has a lot at stake with this production, he's condescended to visit the set, but it's not his usual routine."

"So, you suspect conspiracy to harm Mackie now that he's unprotected by his normal environment? Could Sandra have been kidnapped to make him look bad?" Reuben tapped his stylus on the chair arm.

"That. . ." Cade hesitated. "Or her cooperation can be bought. She worked on a production with another of our clients. The owner of the horses being used paid her a hefty sum to claim his animals were mistreated on the set so he could sue the producer. Insurance would have had to pay, so she probably thought it was no big deal. I proved his own trainer had caused the injuries. She hasn't worked much since. Hollywood is a small town."

Roark whistled. "All right, yeah, she's got da hates for you and your company. We better start investigating everyone involved in the production, including Mackie. Anyone else in particular you think would want you or him taken down?"

"Not that I know. I was thinking any of the women he's assaulted over the years might want his head and lower parts. A lot of them didn't join in the lawsuit. They're too afraid of his power in the industry. Sandra might be after me, personally, but anyone else may be using her as a tool to get at Mackie." He didn't look happier for having said that.

"This isn't necessarily a case for Evie?" Jax said in relief. "She hasn't identified the ghost as Sandra?"

Roark answered when Cade hesitated. "She and Iddy say Sandra's horse and dog recognize their owner. They want us to plow up da farm."

That wasn't happening, Jax knew. *Damn.* Once Evie dug her fingers into a case. . .

"I can get ground-penetrating radar to search for cadavers." Reuben punched keys on his notepad. "Maybe bring in some dogs. That should keep the women happy."

"And keep Evie out of trouble," Jax said in relief. "It's taken me nearly a year to bring her this close to commitment. I have the plane and hotel booked. I don't want interference now."

"Look at the man sweating it," Reuben scoffed. "And what about the Cajun here and your sister? You pushing them to be legal?"

Jax didn't even want to think about his fragile, neurodivergent little sister sleeping with the half-civilized Cajun. "I'll settle for knowing she's happy. She knows her own mind."

"And what am I? A hunk of ham with no say in da matter?" Roark pushed off the wall. "Let's keep dis to business. Send me a list of anyone, anywhere involved in the production, plus the women suing Mackie. I'll compare it to da lists I have."

Jax hid his wince at the result of Reuben's overstepping. Roark avoided the personal, and his relationship with Ariel was intensely personal. And Ariel, naturally, was noncommunicative.

Cade headed for the door. "I have to meet Iddy and the student we're interviewing for Sandra's position. I'll gather any information I can find after that. Mackie won't approve the expense for the investigation so bill your time to Garcia Insurance. If my uncle wants to deal with tarantulas, he can foot the bill for the poisonous results."

∾

MONDAY MORNING, WITH HER HOPES SOARING, IDDY REARRANGED HER APPOINTMENT schedule to postpone anything not an emergency. Now, she waited eagerly for her possible new assistant to arrive. She prayed Asia Brown was as sensible and personable as she sounded—and that she wouldn't flee at the sight of the concrete block office and RV home.

Right on schedule, a battered olive-green Kia rolled into the gravel parking lot at the same time as Cade on one of the crew's motorcycles. Iddy watched from the plate glass front window as Cade parked the bike, then opened the Kia's door and helped the student juggle her briefcase and purse. Despite his reservations, he was leaping right into the fray.

She wished he didn't look so good doing it. Movie executive stylish looked too confining for his big frame, which might be why he wore cowboy boots instead of tight polished leather.

She studied the student as they approached. She had been stereotyping a differently-abled student as frail and fearing she wouldn't be strong enough to handle some of the patients. But Asia was pretty much average everything, height, weight, even coloring—lighter than Iddy's native brown. The student carried herself with assurance, which was what was important if she meant to win over Iddy's rural clients.

Iddy opened the door to welcome them in. She'd read up on talking with deaf people and made certain to face Asia and speak clearly. "Thank you for coming. I'm Idonea Malcolm." She even wore her name badge so Asia could read the unusual name—although Iddy supposed she'd looked up the website and knew it already.

"Thank you for asking me, Dr. Malcolm," the student replied in a slow, thick, but comprehensible voice. "I am excited to be here."

Iddy could feel all her bones and muscles relax into semi-liquidity. This was going to work. She cast Cade a grateful look which he didn't notice as he escorted his new hire toward her office.

Iddy and Asia immediately aimed for the cages instead.

They bonded over a discussion of pet rabbit disease. La Chusa flew in to check out the new person and flew off without complaint. Asia exclaimed in excitement over having a place of her own instead of a dorm room, then tucked the three-legged kitten into her blazer pocket.

Iddy rejoiced in learning that Asia had no more finals, so she didn't have to make trips back to school. She was move-in ready.

Brooding, Cade followed them about, apparently resigned to hiring a kid straight out of college. He really didn't look as if he belonged in business suits. Taking pity on him, Iddy suggested they drive the Tahoe out to the farm to visit the animals they'd be responsible for over the next two weeks.

"They've already taken the foul fowl into town this morning," he warned them. "The crew has a block of city streets shut down."

"We can't be in three places at once." Iddy spoke slowly, facing Asia so the argument didn't go over her head. "Is their camera footage online? Can we access it? I'd like to check on the farm first."

"I'll arrange it." He started texting while he talked. "I've called Sandra's parents and told them she's gone missing from the set and advised them to file a report. They didn't seem terribly worried until I told them her horse and dog were here and needed to be moved."

Iddy bit her tongue on her first reaction. She didn't want to scare off Asia with talk of ghosts. But if that was Sandra's spirit out there, and if they removed her animals. . . She suspected the result would not be pretty.

How much should they tell the new hire about the situation? Her family's weirdness was always an obstacle with strangers—like Cade. Iddy supposed she ought to be relieved that modern science had erased most superstition so they weren't burned as witches, but science had also erased belief in anything beyond book knowledge. That's why she'd hunted for local boyfriends who accepted weirdness, unlike hardheaded outsiders like Garcia.

He took the motorcycle back to the farm, and Iddy drove Asia. A silent partner would be relaxing, rather like working with pets who only spoke when needed. The student didn't even ask what movie stars she might meet but intelligently inquired over the number of animals involved in the film.

Pulling up to the chaos that was the farm—Iddy checked her guest for alarm. Asia's eyes widened as she watched the goats trample over a truck parked in the drive and Sandra's horse race in circles around the paddock. The bull, as usual, bellowed its protest.

If Sandra's spirit caused this havoc, she was danged good.

Unable to explain, Iddy simply climbed out of the truck and began with the horse. They weren't the smartest creatures, but they responded to mental reassurances and a carrot or two. She produced bribes from the box she carried in her back seat, and soon even the goats were eating out of her hand. Cade and Asia led them back inside the fence.

Wayne Wright, the middle-aged banty rooster Cade had introduced as Mackie's right-hand man, sidled over. Thinning dishwater hair hanging over his furrowed brow, tight jeans revealing his bowed legs, Wright looked like walking trouble.

"Thought you was supposed to have someone here to keep these animals in line." He carried a gun in a holster on his hip as if he'd just walked out of a spaghetti western.

"I hope you have a license for that weapon," Iddy countered. "If you're from California, South Carolina doesn't recognize your permit."

Wright scowled and turned to Cade. "That bull nearly took Parker's ass off this morning. Who's feeding it? I've got someone lined up if Sandra ain't gonna show."

He did? And he was just saying so now? Throwing out feed for the remaining fowl, Iddy listened as Cade leaned against the fence to respond.

"Who do you have lined up? The contract requires a professional."

"One of the crew says he has experience. We can save a little money and have him walk around the barn every evening and throw out feed in the morning. It's not as if the animals need training to do what they do." Wright cast Iddy and Asia a look of suspicion.

She didn't need Pris's mind reading ability to know Wright didn't want her on the premises. She wasn't Evie either, so she didn't smile and deflect. Instead, she pointed at the horse. "The mare has injured her right hock. Your crew qualified to fix that?"

She left the jerkwad glaring at her and opened the gate. Asia followed her in. Sandra's collie trotted over, and she scratched its head, wondering if the parents were on their way to pick up the animals.

"They don wan us here?" Asia asked quietly.

Crossing over to look at the horse's leg, Iddy turned toward Asia so she could see her speak. She kept it simple. "Money and women problems. Ignore him."

"Text later?"

She wanted a better explanation. That should be fun. Iddy nodded, then directed her toward the barn. The student wandered off to look around.

Cade came over to help her with the mare and to show her his phone. "Here's the private cloud account with the video of the filming downtown. There's a slow delay but you can monitor activity. I sent you the link."

Ascertaining the hock wasn't seriously damaged by the mare's earlier antics, Iddy took his phone to examine the action while Cade petted the dog. Judging from the video, Mackie wasn't a pretty man. Massive, almost corpulent, wearing a ludicrous silver wig and a perpetual Hitchcock pout, he was swearing at some poor cast member. "I thought the video would be what they're filming. What is this?"

"Apparently your cousin's *solutions* agency has cameras aimed at the production. They might be more useful than the documentary, which doesn't pick up behind-the-scenes action like this."

"Whew, I'll have to go downtown and watch this in real time. Is Mackie allowed near the animals?" Iddy handed the phone back.

"He's not an animal lover. The crew member Wright wants to assign to your job is basically a handler to transport and keep the animals penned until they're needed. But the contract specifically calls for a trained professional. If you or Asia can go downtown daily to see that they're being treated well, we can sign off as having done our parts."

"I know you don't believe, but I'm thinking the animals all need to be moved elsewhere," Iddy murmured, voicing her concern. "Classy is almost traumatized. The others are agitated and afraid, and something or someone is letting them loose from their pens. They'll hurt themselves under these conditions."

Just as she said this, Evie puttered up in her little red Subaru. Reuben climbed out with her and reached in back to produce a machine on wheels.

The animals screamed in unison.

Nine

WHILE IDDY'S NEW ASSISTANT LED THE AGITATED MARE BACK TO THE BARN, CADE greeted the mayor's liaison and ex-spy. With his scarred cheeks and man bun, Reuben had the appearance of an African warrior dressed in business casual. Like any good warrior, his focus was entirely on the distant ground he had to cover, if that was the radar equipment he was rolling.

To Cade's surprise, Evie opened the back of the wagon to let out a German shepherd. "Surprise!" she cried. "Meet Oscar, the cadaver searching dog."

Reuben angled his head in the dog's direction. "Friend in the police business. You hired us, so we have permission and don't need a search warrant like cops, right?"

Cade could see Wright on the porch, yakking frantically on his phone. This could get interesting. He still wasn't believing in ghosts, but if the animals were restless because they scented blood. . . that at least made sense.

He picked up the broad-brimmed hat he'd left on a fence post and slapped it on his head. "If Mackie calls off the search, I can shut down production, and they know it. My uncle won't like it, but if this is what it takes. . . Do you know how to operate this stuff?"

Long black hair swinging, the vet approached the dog, holding her hand out for sniffing, then scratching behind its ears and praising it in a low voice. Even Cade felt the effect. He'd be twitching his back leg and turning over to have his belly scratched any minute now. He needed to keep his distance from temptation. Thailand called. The world would be his oyster shortly.

Reuben shrugged. "Ex-military. Finding bodies part of the job. I'll start in back, near the woods. Seems most likely."

Distracted by Iddy, Cade had almost forgotten his question. Now, his gut ground as if he'd swallowed glass at the notion of Sandra out there in the mud, but he nodded. "It's rained quite a bit since Wednesday. Field's been plowed, so there's a lot of disturbed earth to cover." Including in and around the bull pen, where the mud had been trampled thoroughly by sharp hooves.

Holding the German shepherd's leash, Iddy followed her cousin into the paddock where the new assistant watched, baffled by the activity. If the vet wanted to deal with a deaf assistant, she'd better start learning sign language. He grunted as he realized Iddy had her phone out, texting with one thumb. Okay, so maybe they could communicate, and he was a bigot.

Before he could follow them into the barn, where Evie was apparently leading them, Wright and another of Mackie's crew intercepted him.

"What the hell is going on?" Wright demanded.

"Your new animal handler agrees that something is disturbing the animals, and they'll be injured if it isn't stopped." Cade enjoyed keeping the asshat puzzled. He tilted his hat brim so they couldn't read his face.

"A dog will make them behave? Or the dude with the lawn mower?" Wright pulled out a cigarette. His companion lit it.

Cade ran down a mental list of employees and decided this was Darren, one of the sound techs. Young, surfer blond, he was too tanned to be spending time bent over an equipment board. Muscular, he was not however. Tanning bed, actor wannabe Cade decided.

"Not mine to question the professionals." Cade shrugged. "Heard from Sandra yet?"

That shut Wright up. His phone rang, and he wandered off, undoubtedly to report to Mackie. Leaving the blond tech behind, Cade strode after the women.

He didn't want Sandra to be buried in a shallow grave in this backwater. Sandra might have her problems, but the last he'd seen of her, she'd been bright, alive, and sexy. They'd had fun while it lasted. He could see no reason to believe she'd come in harm's way, unless she'd been stupid enough to attempt blackmailing Mackie. Still, murder wasn't Mackie's *modus operandi*.

They said she'd left in a pickup. He far preferred to believe that she was leaving the pervert high and dry after an attempted assault. Mackie had weight, but Sandra had muscle. Vanishing and causing Mackie a boatload of grief would be her idea of revenge, while she looked for a lawyer.

"She's not wanting to tell us anything," Evie called as he approached. "Or if she is, I'm not interpreting. New spirits don't always communicate well, unless they were communicators to begin with, I suppose."

It took Cade a second to realize she thought she was reaching Sandra's *spirit*. He grimaced on recognizing that particular truth. "Sandra mostly talks to horses." Playing along with her fantasy, Cade studied the scene as Jax's fiancée followed a crooked course through the dim interior, chasing noon shadows. Or noon shadows, since it was lunchtime. Iddy and Asia had apparently taken the cadaver dog out back with Reuben.

Cade thought about his time with Sandra. What had they talked about? Anything? Just their work, mostly. They'd eat, fall in bed, and go back to work. He was a numbers wonk. She wasn't. Another good reason to stay away from the vet. "You'd probably have better luck if you ask her about the horse's hock."

That was as far as he'd go with her superstition. Giving up on talking shadows, he went out the back to watch the others. He returned to his mental list of employees, but there were few women on the crew, and they were all accounted for except Sandra. Why was he thinking if anyone was buried out here, it would be a woman? Why would he imagine *anyone* was buried here at all? Because a vet said animals smelled blood?

Still, not wanting to be caught off guard, he did a mental rundown of men. The company had hired locals for various jobs, but they only came to the farm for meetings. The crew sleeping at the farm were all accounted for. There would have been no reason for extras to be around last week since filming didn't start until today.

Reuben was out in the plowed field, near the trees. Asia and Iddy walked the dog around the bull's paddock. The bull snorted and paced. Iddy snapped her fingers and pointed at the water trough. The massive animal shook its big head and trotted over to drink water.

Okay, he didn't just see that. Even Sandra couldn't command a bull with a finger snap, and she was good.

Squealing pigs rushed from the barn, straight for the mud and the women. Cade had personally checked that pen just minutes ago. It took a lot to make pigs run. Cursing, he ran to cut off the enormous swine, swinging his hat to divert them from trampling dog and women.

On the other side of the bull pen, Iddy handed the leash to Asia, stomped her feet, and clapped her hands. Before Cade could intervene, the pigs dashed past, stopped short as if hitting a wall, and began rooting through the trampled grass.

Gathering she had the animals in hand, however she did it, Cade slammed his hat back on and returned to the barn to see who could have let the pigs out. Classy was lying near the stall with Sandra's horse. Evie stood on a wooden bench nearby, a pitchfork in hand, although she was holding it the wrong way to stop a pig.

At sight of him, she jumped down. "Your girlfriend isn't happy with me. Or you. A spirit who can manipulate the physical this early in the game is dangerous. I had one once that could short out the electricity for half the town. This one prefers animals."

Would this diminutive weirdo release massive swine from the safety of their pen to prove a point? He was already paying her. What did she stand to gain?

"And pitchforks." He eyed the one she held. "Did it go flying again?"

"Nah, I was holding on to it. If there's anything else sharp in here, you probably ought to move it elsewhere. If she can open doors, there's no tying down tools or animals." She handed the fork over.

She wanted him to believe a *ghost* had let out the pigs? Even though he'd seen the stall open on its own earlier, that was still hard to swallow. But he couldn't insult Jax's fiancée by accusing her of scamming him, even if logic demanded it.

Evie swung around, searching the shadows, then shook her copper curls. "She's gone." She continued out the back, into the sunshine.

Cade couldn't take much more of this. He threw feed in a trough and drove the pigs back inside, slamming them into their stall when they obeyed. He would not believe it was because the vet had given them mental directions.

Outside the barn, the German shepherd yipped and dug frantically at a trampled mud pit that might once have been a hog wallow.

At the dog's frantic behavior, Evie watched her client freeze like a giant statue of Hercules. Today, Cade Garcia wore a cowboy hat in the hot sun, so his expression wasn't obvious. From his aura, she gauged he was in serious denial and unhappy with their operation. He really wanted his ex to have run off with. . . who? Had anyone even asked who Sandra might have run off with? Her friends were all back in Hollywood. No one else was reported missing from the company.

While Iddy held back the dog, and Reuben pushed his machine toward the mud pit, Evie phoned Jax. "Send the sheriff, Big Boy. The dog is digging in the old hog wallow right outside the bullpen. There's a reason the bull isn't happy."

Jax cursed. She made smooching noises and hung up. Thank goodness Loretta was in school or she'd be here now. The kid's curiosity would take her far, if she survived childhood.

Apparently observing from the house, Wayne Wright and the blond boy wandered out to watch Reuben run his machine over the trampled pit. Iddy pulled the dog back and fed it treats from her bottomless pocket of goodies. Evie walked over to introduce herself to Asia, while Cade called his boss or whoever.

"Maybe you should go downtown and observe the filming," Evie quietly suggested to Iddy. "This is likely to become awkward, and you don't want to be caught in the middle."

Her cousin threw a glance to Reuben running his radar. "The cadaver dog only knows the scents he's been trained to locate. It could be pig bones for all we know."

"Troy won't be happy either way. And your insurance man is looking as if he'd grind bones between his teeth if he could. That's one impressive hunk of masculinity. Why on earth is he in the insurance business?"

"Cade is not my insurance man, and why don't you ask him? He knows a few things about animals, so he hasn't always been a suit. But yes, we should check on the film set to see how they're handling the fowl. Watch out for the Mackie person if he shows up. I just saw a clip of him in action, and he's not a nice guy." Iddy pulled the leash on the dog and trotted back to the barn.

With a backward glance of interest, her new assistant reluctantly followed. Vet students probably had gruesome imaginations, but Evie didn't want Iddy to lose her much needed help if this turned into a murder investigation.

Once Iddy and Asia were gone, Evie sat on the back step and watched as Cade and Reuben found shovels and stripped off their fancy coats and shirts. Such lovely half-naked masculinity. . . But she preferred Jax. "You'd better wait until the sheriff arrives," she warned. "You could be destroying evidence."

"Or chicken bones," Cade called back. "Do you know what they feed hogs?"

"Don't want to know. And we'll hope you're right, but I don't want in any more trouble with Troy than I usually am, all right? You two look real pretty doing the strong man thing, but the pit isn't going anywhere."

She smiled brightly at the mean-looking shrimp crossing his arms and glaring at the scene. "Maybe you should call your film crew, make a documentary of real farm life."

Wright shot her a scowl and didn't bother replying. His aura screamed misogynist, but she'd wanted to prove it to herself.

The blond, bronzed boy looked uncertain. "Should I look for a shovel too?"

"Probably not if you were out here when Sandra disappeared. How many people were here?" Evie snapped off a grass stem and chewed on the end. She knew she looked small and harmless and people thought her half crazy. Her pink shirt saying *Don't quit your daydream* probably added to the image.

"Most everyone stays in Charleston when they're not on the set," surfer boy said, looking worried at the distant sound of sirens. "There's just me, Wayne, Sandra, Nimrod, and Nancy staying here. And Betty and Ray Ann out in the trailer." He nodded at the humongous motor coach parked between the house and field.

"Nimrod and Nancy?" Evie didn't try to hide her amusement.

"Set design and camera. They're both Steves, so we call them by their last names."

"His name isn't Nimrod," Wright grudgingly contributed. "That's just what Mackie calls him. Don't rightly know his name anymore."

An established crew, got it. They'd lie for each other, if necessary.

It was harder to see auras in broad daylight, but Evie kept watch to see if any spirits showed up. "So, all of you saw Sandra leave that night? And she didn't say why?"

"She called us pigs for not washing our dishes. I just figured she got tired of cleaning up after us. Betty and Ray Ann were out in the trailer and didn't hear the blow up. I was in my room when she left and didn't hear her leave." Surfer boy didn't seem real concerned.

There was a lot of that going around. Poor Sandra, if her ex was the only one who cared enough to look for her. And Cade was only forced to do so to prevent shutting down production.

The sirens stopped out front. Troy had to be really irritated if he ran the sirens. That's why she'd had Jax call in on the non-emergency number, in hopes that if there was nothing out there, the sheriff wouldn't yell too much.

Cade strode into the barn, presumably to meet the law and lead them back here. Reuben leaned on his shovel, waiting. Now that she'd sent Iddy and Asia away, she was the only female present. Jax wouldn't be happy.

Instead of Sheriff Troy, his deputy Cal accompanied Cade, and on his heels was Philomena Arquette, detective wannabe and Evie's nemesis. Lovely. Well, now she wasn't the only female around.

Remaining in the shade of the back porch, ignored by everyone, Evie watched for any aura at all. In the bright light, she could just barely see the colors of Mena's competitive arrogance. Cal never had much color. Reuben was Reuben, all science and no visible emotion. Cade. . . even in daylight, he radiated a clear, grounded red, and healthy, intelligent orange in all the right places. He was also shadowed with concern as he talked to the law.

She checked the barn door again, and there she was. . . the spirit colors she called Sandra. They were too dim to discern well, but the anger was vivid.

Evie didn't think warning the men would help. She really didn't want to become an object of Mena's attention or the investigation might go sideways.

There wasn't much she could do if Sandra pitched forks again. Maybe she'd just let out the goats this time.

Cal had brought his own shovel. After some discussion, the three men divided up the pit and began digging. Mena took notes and talked to someone on the phone. She was skinny for a cop and wouldn't have been any better at digging than Evie. She also had more brains than easy-going Cal, but Mena wouldn't believe Evie if she warned they were disturbing a ghost.

"You'd better keep an eye on the animals," Evie warned the two men on the porch doing no more than watching others work. "I can hear that horse kicking his stall." She couldn't, but it would be soon, if she read the signs right. The collie was already standing watch in the doorway.

"Ain't our job," Wright said, predictably.

"It will be your job lost if Cade shuts down production." If it weren't for his uncle, he was probably one step from doing so, Evie figured.

A murmured consultation sent bronzed boy off to inspect stalls. She doubted he even knew how to lock one.

Reuben shouted and crouched down to dig with his hands.

The aura in the doorway exploded in fury and vanished. Doors slammed. Animals squawked, neighed, bellowed, and bleated.

And the stampede began.

Ten

At Evie's urgent call, Iddy hastily dropped Asia at the office to deal with an injured dog emergency, then sped out to the farm. The fowl on the downtown set had been fine. The people, not so much, but they weren't her concern.

A body in a pig wallow and a stampede. . . That was not fine.

Her heart sank as she drove up the farm drive. It looked like the entire police force had arrived but none were out here in animal chaos. A shirtless Cade was on the mare, attempting to prevent the bull and the sheep from hitting the road. Evie ran around shooing geese, who pecked viciously in their attempt to escape. The bronzed boy had a broom, chasing goats from everything that looked tasty.

Iddy grabbed a tote bag of treats and started with the bull. The bull was acting out of fear with no clear-cut reason other than scent or startlement. Iddy worked on the fear, calming it, approaching slowly, calling up images of green pastures and dappled water.

"Put feed in the trough," she called to anyone who would listen.

Cade hesitated, understandably not wanting to leave her alone with a mad bull. But when the animal made no threatening move, he rode over to the barn. He was back in an instant with a bag of feed that Evie couldn't have managed.

Once the bull settled, the sheep and goats took a little more persuasion. She found their leaders and focused her effort there.

"The pigs?" she called to Cade once they'd wrestled the main packs into the paddock.

"Found food in back. They're good." He drove a wandering goat back where it belonged.

By the time they'd rounded up the strays, a convoy of expensive vehicles was pulling up—filming must be done for the day. A Hummer of equipment continued around the house to the back, but the limos parked in front. Iddy wanted nothing to do with the film people, but Evie seemed intent on studying each person as they emerged.

Leaving her cousin to her investigations, Iddy joined Cade in leading the agitated mare into the barn. The big man looked seriously disgruntled. The collie tagged forlornly at his heels.

"Did you have to identify the remains?" she asked in sympathy, guessing the body must be Sandra.

"Yeah." Without further comment, he entered the stall with the mare and grabbed a curry brush.

The man knew his way around a horse. He'd been riding bareback. Admittedly, Iddy was curious. He hadn't gained those muscles sitting at a desk. She soothed Sandra's dog and determinedly refused to watch rippling bare flesh. "I'm sorry. That had to be hard."

"Bastard wrapped her in the old Navajo blanket she carried with her everywhere." He kept his voice even so as not to scare the horse.

"That would indicate someone strong enough to carry her." She heard loud voices raised in the yard. She probably ought to leave. But if Sandra's spirit lingered as Evie said. . . It didn't feel right to abandon cousin or spirit.

Apparently considering her suggestion that someone had to carry Sandra's body, he mused aloud, "We've been told only four men were here when she left —if they can be believed. Sandra was a big girl. The camera operator, Steve Nancy, and Darren, the sound tech, might have carried her on their own. Not certain Nimrod or Wright could even lift her. Sheriff only just arrived. Coroner isn't here yet to say how she died."

"Coroner comes from another county. Do you need to be here when Mackie starts throwing his considerable weight around, or you want to slip away with me and have lunch?" She didn't know why she offered that, except she figured he was bottling up so much steam that he was likely to take off someone's head at the slightest excuse.

Evie trotted in, blocking the daylight for half a second before finding them. "I'm going up in the loft to sit with Sandra and spy on proceedings. Sheriff Troy is threatening to have Mackie flung in jail for obstruction. Auras are gyrating so badly even my ADD can't keep up. Bring me back a sandwich?"

Cade flung down the brush, patted the mare, and threw it some oats. "Your cops can be trusted to protect the body?"

"That's Mean Mena out there. She'd chew the arm off anyone trying to interfere. Go. I'll tell Troy where to find you." Evie grabbed the ladder to the loft and swung up with expertise.

"Evie really can take care of herself," Iddy promised. "And Mena loves guns. Anyone stupid enough to go near whatever she's guarding is a danger to everyone in the vicinity. Pris was planning a soft opening for her café today. Let's lend her some support."

Cade grabbed a shirt off a hook and shrugged it on. Grimacing, he called up at Evie, "If you see Sandra, tell her I'll find the bastard."

He was believing in ghosts now?

"She used up all her energy opening the pens. I'll tell her if she shows up again," Evie called down.

"I feel like an idiot talking to the dead." He buttoned his shirt as he tagged after Iddy. "I'm still wondering if your family didn't plant the body."

"Now you know why my dad is in Hollywood and not here. Men don't like being unable to see or hear what we do." Iddy wasn't sympathetic. Evie had found a man who understood. They existed. They just appeared to be truly rare.

"Your mother talks to ghosts?" He held the driver's door open for her.

Iddy gave him credit for not taking charge of her vehicle. She waited until he climbed into the passenger seat. "Mom makes magic charms and amulets that work. I don't know which one set my father off. I was an infant when he left."

"I don't like being scammed," he said, apropos of nothing.

"Understandable. Our family has been called crooks and frauds for centuries. Some of us moved away and pretended we're normal—Loretta's parents and grandparents, for example. They did well out there in the real world, but they're still dead. I could go elsewhere, keep my mouth shut, and do what I have to do, but why should I? My mother needs me. The town needs me. I'm comfortable being the local eccentric vet."

"You're paid for your knowledge, just like any vet. No scamming involved, unless you're selling magic pills. Your cousin Evie though. . ." Obviously struggling with finding his ex's body and the weirdness that had uncovered her, he shifted uncomfortably and glared out the windshield.

She almost sympathized. Evie was hard to take even for those who knew her.

Rolling down Main Street, they saw evidence of the film production everywhere. Iddy had to drive around the block to avoid taped off streets. She parked in the city lot. "Yeah, Evie gets that a lot. Cultivates it, truth be told. She plays a cheerful idiot who walks dogs for a living. No one really wants to know that she can see into their soul."

"She can do *what*?"

"Never mind. Let's get lunch. We should probably take some back for everyone, including Asia." She climbed down from the Tahoe and started down the street.

Cade caught up in a few strides. Hot, sweaty, and rumpled looked good on him. "I'm barely working my way around ghosts, don't hit me with any more, all right?"

"Sure." She shoved open the door of the building that had once housed an expensive boutique. Pris was rapidly turning it into the Mad Café she called it. It was a work in progress, with only a few mix-and-match tables and chairs and art on the walls, but the black and white background, colorful Mad Hatter theme, swaying crystals, and blaring music was all Pris.

Wearing the gray stripes in her hair dyed bright green today, apparently to match her apron or spring greenery, Pris was unloading a tray of cookies in the glass display case. She glanced up the instant they entered. "Whoa, take the bad vibes outside. I don't need that kind of jinx on opening day!"

Cade growled. Iddy patted his arm. He had, after all, just learned of a friend's murder.

"Meet Caden Garcia and give us a break. We are having a freaking bad day, and we want to buy lots and lots of box lunches for a bunch of very unhappy people." Undeterred by her grumpy cousin, Iddy proceeded to the counter to read the menu.

Pris studied them for a moment, then nodded and produced a fresh loaf of bread and a knife. "I'm sorry. I hadn't realized they found the missing person. Is it all right if I make a selection of cheese, mushroom, and ham sandwiches to go? The take-out containers for the soup and salad haven't been delivered yet."

Apparently ignoring Pris's knowledge of Sandra without having been told, Cade glanced around at the eccentric interior. "May we taste the soup and salad while we're waiting? Do you cater?"

"Do I cater, he asks." Pris finished whacking the bread before calling back to the kitchen, "Mom, you want to fix a couple of bowls of vegetable soup and some of that potato salad for Iddy and friend?"

"She used to cater," Iddy whispered. "Until she was accused of poisoning a client. She *can* do it. Whether she will or not is another matter."

"Poisoning Mackie and crew might be a good idea," he muttered back. "I'll recommend her without tasting then."

She smacked his muscled bicep and helped her aunt carry the trays of soup and salad to a table. Aunt Ellen looked just like her own mother and Evie's—frizzy gray hair, chubby, and dressed in dowdy maxi skirts most of the time. Until recently, Pris's mother had worn glasses so thick they hurt her nose, but she'd had eye surgery recently and was apparently stepping out in the world again.

"Where are the twins and Dante?" Iddy asked, since Pris's ready-made family was usually under foot.

"Upstairs, practicing the alphabet using dinosaur bones," Aunt Ellen said with a shrug before meandering off.

Right. Iddy sampled the vegetable soup, confident that Pris had made it with vegetable broth and not chicken. "If you need meat, ask for the ham sandwich. Pris cooks her own meat so it doesn't contain any of the processing chemicals store-bought has."

"You're vegetarian?" Now that she hadn't fallen over in a poisoned stupor, Cade tasted his salad. "That makes sense, I suppose."

She assumed that was a reference to her occupation, not her animal mind-reading. She wasn't letting him off the hook.

"Even lobsters have a mind I can sense, so yes, eating animal flesh isn't for me. And Evie will tell me that plants have sensory receptors that talk to each other, but I can't hear them, so I don't care. Shall I continue distracting you with meaningless dialogue or do you want to avail yourself of town gossip and learn more about the film people?" Iddy savored the delicious seasoning of Pris's potato salad.

One of these days, if Asia could be persuaded to stay, maybe she'd have time to take lessons in cooking so she didn't eat nuked food every night.

Cade sipped the water Aunt Ellen brought over. Apparently choosing not to comment on lobster minds, he considered what he'd like to learn about the crew his uncle was insuring. "I want to know what hold Mackie has over my uncle, and why they came all this way to film chickens in the street."

"Excellent questions." She signaled her aunt, who wandered over to see if they needed anything else. "Do you have any idea who lured the film crew to town?"

Ellen combed a graying curl from her forehead. "You should probably ask your mother, dear, or even your Aunt Mavis. The mayor was looking for ways to improve our reputation, but I wasn't in on the discussion. Aunt Val might have been. Her husband is in the film business." She turned to help a customer coming in.

"And there you have it." Iddy waved her fork. "The mayor and the coven got together and things happened. I assume some financial deal went down along with the sales job. I can't speak for your uncle's connection."

He didn't look enlightened. "Coven? Aunt Val? You're saying your family is in the film business?"

"I'm saying they have connections *everywhere*. My father didn't end up in Hollywood by accident. I suspect my Great-Aunt Val was an influence. She's scary, but she married well three times and has money. Her current husband is a retired director. She likes historical reenactments, not Hollywood, but these aren't amateur productions. Some of them are background for several well-known movies."

"And Mavis?" He remained impassive, not revealing his opinion of her family's contacts.

"Evie's mother. Mavis reads crystal balls and tarot. Her interpretations leave a lot to be desired, but the family listens and acts accordingly. And yes, please do take all this with a grain of salt. Even science isn't perfect. We all learn as we go. But just as scientists learn which molecule has what reaction when put under pressure or whatever, we have to experiment with what we learn from our gifts." Iddy had never attempted to learn more from animals than where they hurt. But if Sandra had been killed in front of them. . .

"Gossip isn't facts. Mackie came here for a reason. He is a producer, concerned with making money on his investment. But he spent money to bring the production out here for some purpose that isn't immediately evident. Normally, he wouldn't have had much to do with hiring someone as low level as Sandra, but I'm not ruling out anything. I'm not sure any of this matters or if this was a crime of passion." He finished his lunch and sat back.

"Cookie?" Pris held up wrapped goodies. "I've added chips, apples, and condiments to the boxes. I don't think you need plasticware for sandwiches. Cookies will cost two dollars extra per box."

Iddy left Cade to negotiate and pay with his company card. She wasn't a detective. She'd be far happier back at the office with Asia, treating puppy paws and feeding the kittens. But she had the gut feeling that the animals had witnessed Sandra's death, and that poor woman deserved justice.

Pris bagged up the boxes. Iddy took four bags while Cade took the rest. She examined the taped off streets as they wandered back to the car. The production crew had cordoned off part of the city parking lot for animal pens and cages, but there was nothing and no one here now.

"Isn't it expensive to be on location and not be filming?" she asked as they loaded everything into the SUV.

"They'll be filming in scenes. They may have changed them up so they're shooting at the farm this afternoon. Your family knows the mayor, right? Do you think they can ask her how or why Mackie contacted her?" He scrolled through messages on his phone.

"Call Jax. He'll talk to Reuben. That way you get the straight, pragmatic answer. I'll talk to Evie and have her question Mavis and maybe Aunt Val. You won't like their answers, but it might help me." Iddy wasn't entirely certain she wanted to be involved, especially if any roads led back to her father. But for the sake of her fellow animal trainer, she'd do what she could.

The coroner's van was parked in the large gravel circle in front of the farmhouse when they returned. Roark's Sensible Solutions van was parked next to the limos, so Evie and team were still around. Iddy backed off the road, near the paddock. Praying food would calm roiled waters, she climbed out and filled her arms with Pris's carry-out bags. Even at this distance, she could hear loud voices.

As they approached the farmhouse, Loretta's idol, the blond actress who played a wildlife expert, stepped out on the porch. With her, still in makeup, was a swaggering, aging actor Iddy recognized from old cowboy films. He wasn't much taller than Betty George. She couldn't recall his name. Following them out was a lean, bespectacled, balding man with what Iddy assumed was a script in hand. At sight of them, he trotted down the stairs.

"Cade, excellent, I need to talk with you." He gestured at the actors. "Put the food on the table, will you?"

The actors didn't do as told. Cade continued heading for the house, bags in hand, introducing her as he walked. "Our new animal trainer, Idonea Malcolm, meet Brice Kennedy, director. We can talk later, Brice." He jogged up the stairs.

A director who couldn't make people do what he told them? Interesting. Iddy nodded at the introductions and followed Cade. Brice scowled and did the same. It wasn't as if there was anyone else to yell at.

She caught a glimpse of Roark working on a lamp fixture in the parlor as they strode down the hall toward the kitchen. He was pointing a screwdriver at the blond boy flipping a wall switch. Knowing Evie's cast of spies, she figured he was bugging the place right under their noses.

From the sounds of it, everyone else was out back arguing. They deposited the bags on a trestle table in the kitchen.

Betty George checked the contents of a box and shrugged. "Better than pizza, I suppose. C'mon, Roy, let's play guardian angels and deliver manna from the heavens."

Roy O'Bryan, right. Iddy recalled the actor now. In real life, he had more wrinkles and gray hairs than she remembered from the old films, but she gave him credit for aging gracefully. Betty George. . . well, not so much.

"Cade, we can eat in here." The director grabbed a box and headed back to the front room. "I want to talk to you about the budget for. . ."

"A woman died out there, Brice." Cade shook off the director's hand. "I'm not talking budget until I know what happened."

Iddy didn't think of herself as a people person. She worked with animals, and people just came with them. But watching Caden Garcia in action was almost as good as watching a movie. He cut through crowds like a ship through water.

She followed him out to the back yard where forensics experts were working on the gravesite while men in uniform hovered. Evie and Reuben weren't in sight. The film crew circled the two actors setting bags of food on a picnic table. Obviously miffed, the director stomped out after them to grab a box.

Leaving Cade to feed the masses, Iddy drifted to the pen to be certain the bull wasn't too disturbed by the activity. The agitation of the animals had her nerves on edge.

La Chusa flew in, cawing. The raven could circle for miles but usually stayed close to home. Worried that something was wrong at the office, she held up her wrist for the bird to land. The bird sent her a flash of an image of a huge vehicle rolling—

Already twitchy, Iddy swung to see the enormous equipment vehicle rolling down the back hill, straight at the crew around the picnic table. Without giving a thought to how crazy she sounded, Iddy shouted, "Hummer! Run!"

Eleven

Alerted by an uproar outside the barn, Evie slipped from her hiding place to peer through the loft window. Outside, the film crew scattered, shrieking, across the yard. She didn't have time to be horrified at sight of the rolling Hummer before Cade flung the picnic table behind the vehicle's wheels, slowing it down enough for one of the crew to open the door and yank the brake.

That was some scary action. The idiot driver ought to be fired.

Checking to be certain no one seemed hurt and that her friends and family were safe, she dropped down behind the hay bales again. She ought to have Roark put his spy devices in here. The barn appeared to be a popular meeting place.

Equipment to catch ghosts on film might be entertaining. . .

Below the loft, Sean Mackie was berating his bandy-legged assistant over the presence of cops and demanding to know who had hired Sandra.

Hadn't Cade said Brice did the hiring?

Wright insisted that he'd had nothing to do with her. Evie thought she ought to check his aura for lies, but she didn't want to be seen.

Neither man turned a hair at the commotion outside. Not until the doors of the stalls began to slam open and animals—once again —escaped, did Mackie cease his harangue to kick at one of the chickens the crew had returned earlier.

"Sandra, you have to stop this," Evie hissed. "How can we do our jobs if you keep throwing toddler tantrums?" Irked to have her observation spot exposed, she slid toward the ladder before the producer started breaking chicken necks.

Pigs. They're all pigs.

The ghostly aura vanished with a last shove of a hay bale from the loft. It missed Mackie by a hair. Charming time for Sandra to start talking.

Mackie screamed as if he'd been shot.

No way was Evie climbing down now. The chickens sensibly fled.

"It's that damned Garcia," Wright protested, making it sound as if falling hay bales were Cade's fault. "He acts like he *owns* us. How much is he paying those freaks to poke around and make trouble? If it wasn't for him—"

"He isn't the one who fired the damned handler! What the frigging hell's been going on out here? I can't leave the lot of you alone for one night. . ."

Wright had *fired* Sandra?

A third voice interrupted before she could hear more. Evie peered over the hay bales but couldn't see the door. The collie lay beside the horse's stall, as usual, watching with every appearance of intelligence.

"Sheriff wants to talk to us. He's taking over the house. Can he do that?" an unseen male complained.

"Call our lawyer," Mackie shouted. "What are we paying him for? We need to stick to the damned schedule. Let's film the scene with the bull."

Evie didn't think that the smartest idea while Sandra stormed about. Glancing back out the window, she saw Iddy communing with the terrified chickens while everyone else surrounded the Hummer.

She texted her cousin. MACKIE WANTS TO FILM BULL. SANDRA STILL MAD.

Iddy scattered some feed, then checked her phone. She sent a grimace emoji and jogged over to talk to Cade, who was examining the Hummer with Roark.

Noting her battery was almost dead, again, Evie waited for the barn to clear before climbing down.

Mackie and Wright had very bad auras, and not just unhealthy bad, although that was there too. Mackie had violence in his sacral chakra—sexual. And Wright harbored strong resentment, but it appeared general, not focused. She'd stay well away from them, but she could see why they worked together.

R&R met her as she climbed down. Her team didn't look happy.

"Someone let out the parking brake and shifted gears on da Hummer," Roark said before she could speak. "Don' know who coulda done dat except da driver, and dat's Parker, the camera guy. But he swears it wasn't him, and we have no proof. Brake handle too smudged for prints."

Evie didn't think the ghost could have or would have manipulated equipment, but she reserved judgment. Sandra had not been visible all the time she'd been up here. Who else would do it—and why? She petted the quiet collie, wishing she could take it home with her, knowing the dog wasn't ready to leave.

"Jax is bugging us to remove you from here. We have mics and cameras in place. We don't need to be on the set." Reuben held his radar equipment, ready to leave.

"Did you put cameras in the barn? I'd like to prove we have poltergeist activity." Evie was ready to go. Dealing with spirits was draining. Fearing killers was worse.

Reuben pointed at a couple of cameras hidden in the rafters. "Did those earlier. Place is too large for effective signals but should catch flying saddles."

"Has Iddy left? I can't leave her if someone is tampering with equipment. It sounds dangerous." She stepped into the back doorway to find her cousin.

"She says she wants to watch them film the bull. Garcia can look after her." Reuben headed for the front.

"Not leaving her alone with an angry spirit," Evie called after him. "Tell Jax to pick up Loretta from school. I'll be fine."

She'd prefer a good long nap, but she'd pulled Iddy into this situation. She'd have to stick it out.

R&R didn't argue as Jax would have. They left her plugging in her phone. She climbed on a grain bin and half hid behind an old raincoat hanging on a hook. Texting Iddy her whereabouts, she closed her eyes to catnap.

Jax sent her a collection of angry icons. She sent him hearts and flowers. Gracie texted to say the dress hem was basted, and she needed Evie to try it on. Jax had probably told her sister to do that. Pris texted to ask how the crew liked lunch.

Realizing she hadn't been given a sandwich box, Evie gave up on napping, and left her phone charging to go in search of leftovers.

The coroner had left with Sandra's remains. The sheriff had apparently commandeered the house and crew, so maybe there wouldn't be any scene filming. She found Iddy at the bull's pen, keeping it calm while Cade and a crew member crawled around the massive Hummer.

Evie found an unopened lunch box dumped in the dirt with the picnic table upheaval. She unfolded the wrappers and checked to be certain the contents weren't covered by ants before climbing up next to her cousin. "Deliberate sabotage?"

"Or your ghost," Iddy said dryly, accepting the half cookie Evie offered. "I think they all need to go back to Hollywood."

"I think Cade agrees with you." Evie ate her half of the oatmeal pecan cookie first. "His normally grim aura is even more unhappy than usual. And Mackie and Wright are unhappy with him. If they hadn't been right where I could see them, I'd blame them for the car."

"They wouldn't sabotage their own production. As I understand it, Mackie needs to make this film pay if he wants to stay in business. Any more bad publicity, and he's in trouble. Are there news vans out front?"

Ugh. Evie hadn't given the media an ounce of thought. "Haven't heard anything. They probably got bored watching chicken runs all morning. And the sheriff isn't likely to let the crew out for a while. If they're not filming, you should go back to work R&R have the place bugged. We've done all we can do."

Iddy shrugged. "The animals are still edgy. Did you tell your ghost to lay off?"

"I did. She doesn't listen well. I'm guessing she's still mad about whatever it was that got her killed. Until that's resolved, she won't go away. And until she learns to communicate better, I can't do anything." Evie finished nibbling her sandwich and watched Cade prop concrete blocks behind the Hummer's wheels.

"Don't know if Cade will leave, but it's probably better for all concerned if he does. I'll try to send him your way. I need to check in at my office." Iddy slid down from the fence.

Evie ate her apple, decided nothing interesting would happen with the sheriff around, and went to fetch her phone.

The blond sound tech was using it.

Even though Evie and Jax's dinner table offered iced tea instead of the alcohol the day demanded, Cade relaxed in the family atmosphere. It had been a long time since he'd been home. He'd forgotten how distracting children could be from the day's stresses. He didn't exactly miss his siblings, but now that they were no longer a burden to bear. . . Well, they weren't as annoying.

"Your bubble is sorta like my dad's," the brown-haired child in purple glasses declared over her plate of spaghetti. "It's silver. I think that means you're an Ives, and your family is weird like mine."

Cade merely lifted his glass in acknowledgment. He was an Ives through his mother's side. *Weird* was undefinable.

Jax knuckled the kid's head as he sat down with a second helping of pasta. He'd opted for meatballs. "It's impolite to call guests weird on the first night."

"It's impolite to call guests weird at any time," Iddy corrected. She was eating from a second dish made with mushrooms. "Even if they are." She threw him a laughing look.

He liked her better in this more relaxed atmosphere. It had been a harrowing day. The vet had kept Cade's temper in check much as she'd calmed the animals.

He didn't think it was mental telepathy. She simply reminded him that not everyone was evil. He needed that.

They'd invited Asia to join them, but good student that she was, she declined in favor of settling into her new home and making notes on the clients. Pris had sent over a vegetarian plate with meatballs on the side, not knowing Asia's preferences.

"How was your first day at the cafe?" Cade asked, to be neighborly, as Pris checked on the twins eating at their small table in the corner.

Verifying everyone had food, Pris pulled out her chair. "Entertaining. Your film crew called in an order for four dozen cookies and no food. Are they having a pot party?"

"If the sheriff finally left, probably. But Mackie and Company will be back in the city by now, hitting the bar." Cade was an observer, not a detective. He supposed he should have gone with them.

If he'd arrived earlier, Sandra might still be alive. He hoped the position in Thailand came with no responsibility beyond spreadsheets. If not, was ditch digging still an employment opportunity?

Not if it meant digging up more bodies.

"We can go to the cellar and hook up Reuben's video feeds later." Jax ended ditch digging thoughts. "We don't need to be on the scene."

Everyone deliberately avoided talking murder over the dinner table. Cade appreciated that. The dinner was delicious, but he was having a tough time feeling hungry.

Dante, father of the twins, regaled the table with tales of what he'd seen in the videos his students had made inside their Etruscan excavation.

Cade hadn't sorted out all the family connections yet, but he thought the third child at the small table belonged to Nick and Gracie. They seemed a perfectly normal couple until Nick asked to have the Parmesan passed—and it floated precariously down the table to his plate. Cade refused to search for special effects when Gracie giggled.

And Evie's kid thought *he* was weird?

As a guest, he was excused from the massive clean-up effort after dinner. He and Iddy followed Jax outside to the cellar door. The April night looked stormy, with the wind whipping the trees, but it wasn't raining yet. Iddy stopped to rub the head of an eager Schnauzer and let it inside.

Reuben and Roark were already downstairs, running video to the multiple monitors and television on the wall. They apparently had headphones for each video stream and were taking notes. Impressed, Cade simply watched the screens until he identified locations.

Jax headed for the pool table.

"How do they stay employed when they have no murder to investigate?" Cade asked as Iddy stopped beside him, studying the screens too.

"With Evie the ghost hunter around, there are no shortages of suspicious deaths." She grabbed a beanbag chair and settled on it. "But they're also good at financial fraud and the like. They're developing a reputation and stay employed."

"Isn't this illegal as hell?" Cade watched the actor, O'Bryan, on the screen sneak outside for a toke. Was this monitor real time? Apparently. He could see the trees swaying. O'Bryan had a room in the city. What was he doing still there?

Betty was already on the porch, rocking in the swing, martini glass in hand, cigarette in the other. Without makeup and costumes, they were just two middle-aged people watching the world go by.

"You hired Evie and her team," Iddy reminded him. "It's like companies that install cameras to catch employees shoplifting. Probably illegal without your permission." She didn't seem concerned.

Evie joined them not much later, taking the beanbag chair beside Iddy's.

"Did you check to see who surfer guy was calling on my phone?" Evie inquired.

"You mean Darren?" Cade tried to keep the conversation from getting out of hand before it started. He'd noted Evie had that effect. "The sound tech was using your phone?"

"Phone records show he called Parker. That was the guy driving the Hummer, right?" Reuben flicked a video back to the arrival of the limos and equipment.

"Yeah." Cade frowned. "When was this call?"

"When everyone was supposed to be in the house with the sheriff." Evie popped back up to start the popcorn machine. "He told me he had to call his girl-friend, and his phone was dead. Does Parker qualify as a girlfriend?"

"Parker's the pony-tailed, surly film director who looks like a biker hood-lum?" Iddy asked. Evie bobbed her head in agreement.

"And why would Darren have to call from the barn if they're all over at the house, and he can just talk to them?" Jax whacked a cue ball.

Roark halted the video of the farmhouse parlor at the point where the sheriff had gathered the whole crew in there. "They're all in this shot except Darren and Wright. Wright was in the back room talking with the sheriff. Parker is pacing and glancing out the window. He checks his phone but doesn't answer it."

"They all bickered and roamed back and forth to the kitchen," Reuben pointed out. "I've gone over it a couple of times. Darren simply doesn't show up for about fifteen minutes. No one notices or cares. Sheriff's men don't know who he is or that he even exists."

"He was there the night Sandra died." Cade tried to picture the pretty surfer boy with Sandra, and even though Darren was younger, it made sense. "Parker wasn't."

"He coulda been," Roark pointed out. "He coulda been in da barn or da truck they say they heard."

"No motive." Evie handed out bowls of popcorn. "They're both just technicians with nothing to do with animals or production budgets or anything important. Anyone could have been at the farm the night Sandra died. Did the coroner give a time frame? Are we sure it was last Wednesday night?"

"Without an autopsy, he covered his ass by saying anywhere from noon Wednesday to noon Thursday," Cade told her. "The crew at the farmhouse claimed to have seen her until she stomped out on Wednesday night. No one saw her after that. That's all we have."

"Anyone or everyone could have lied," she pointed out. "Everyone had opportunity unless you can prove they were in Charleston. It all comes down to motive."

And that came down to Cade to determine. He crunched on a popcorn kernel and wished he'd break a tooth so he had an excuse to bow out. He wasn't ever working for his uncle again.

Evie waved her phone in the air. "Texted Aunt Val and Mom about Mackie. They claim Iddy's dad sent him this way when Larraine was looking for movie productions."

"Yeah, that's what Larraine said too," Reuben said, still studying his monitor. "She put out the word to your dad."

Cade glanced at the vet, who was covering her eyes and cursing under her breath. "You want me to call him or you?"

Twelve

Iddy sat on the tailgate of the Tahoe in the city parking lot the next morning, watching a hot air balloon float over the courthouse. "If I intended to sabotage a film, I'd start there," she told Evie.

"Ghosts are all I can manage. You and Cade can have conspiracy theories." Evie leaned against the Tahoe's fender to watch the action.

A single news van sat in the lot, filming the balloon lift off. Betty George waved from the wicker basket and held up a cage with a rooster. Iddy assumed the movie production cameras were over on Main Street, recording this inane episode for reasons beyond her comprehension.

"At least she's not flinging out turkeys." Evie scratched the head of a curious goat through the parking lot pen.

"I told them that rooster doesn't fly. If she lets that thing loose, I'm shutting them down." Iddy wanted to send them all home anyway.

"You probably should be the one calling your father to find out why he sent Mackie here. You know he won't tell Cade." Evie dodged Iddy's kick.

"If he wanted us to know, he could have called. Not that I'd believe him anyway." Iddy remembered a childhood of broken promises. She hadn't talked to him since she was a teenager pleading with him to attend graduation. She hadn't bothered sending him an invite for her college ceremony.

Last night's storm hadn't completely blown over. The bright red and yellow balloon looked like a circus tent floating into the clouds that gusted across a gray sky.

"What fool thought this would be a good day to fly a kite?" Cade asked, striding across the parking lot from the direction of Jax's office.

He'd finally given up on business suits and wore jeans with an open-collar, short-sleeve shirt. South Carolina humidity did that to a person. Iddy wondered what the surly businessman looked like in shorts, but the bare arms were inspiring enough.

"Your boss, one assumes." She winced as the balloon's gondola swayed and the rooster crowed its warning. "It's a good thing our courthouse doesn't have a steeple."

Even as she said it, the balloon emitted an ominous pop, the basket swayed erratically, the rooster squawked, and Betty screamed.

"Didn't they say she had a pilot's license?" Iddy asked in alarm, sliding off the SUV's roof.

"Like her college diploma, it's probably BS." As the balloon began to descend, Cade took off running toward the courthouse, Iddy right behind him. Evie, with shorter legs, got left trailing in their wake.

The balloon's tether slackened as the envelope quit filling with air. The wicker gondola swung closer toward collision with the courthouse roof.

"Follow me." Evie caught up when Iddy hesitated at the front stairs of the building, where a crowd strained to see upward. "I know the way."

Behind them, Brice Kennedy and the balloon crew screamed orders. Onlookers simply screamed as the basket rolled with the gusty wind. Iddy noticed a couple of men in uniform shove through the crowd to run up the stairs after them. She had no idea what any of them could do, but the courthouse was the tallest building around.

They scrambled up the main stairs to the second floor, then through a service door to the attic ladder, and out a trapdoor to the roof. Cade shoved through first, hauling Iddy out as if she were made of nothing, while he examined the sky. His hand was strong and not shaking like hers. Climbing out, Iddy caught at her wind-whipped hair and studied the scene.

The tether rope sagged against the parapet. Gradually collapsing in the brisk breeze, the balloon envelope descended toward the far side of the courthouse. If it passed the roof, it would plummet three stories into the street, on top of cars and pedestrians. Terrified, Betty clung to the ropes and screamed.

Cade grabbed the tether with his massive fists and hauled. The firemen on their heels added their weight in a tug of war with an enormous balloon and the wind. Iddy held her breath as the gondola halted its slide and dangled just above the parapet, the nylon envelope blowing in the wind yards above the edge.

"Ladder," Iddy shouted at the terrified actress, remembering Cade insisting on safety equipment earlier. "Is there a ladder in there? Throw it over the side."

Dropping the rooster cage in the bottom of the basket, Betty stooped down to find the rope safety ladder.

More people climbed out of the attic. Whispering words of prayer and invective, Iddy directed them to the tether. She didn't recognize any of the film crew arriving to assist, but the balloon operator joined her and Evie in catching the ladder Betty threw down.

Jax appeared with what seemed to be a grappling hook, although where he'd found that was questionable. Maybe from the rest of the balloon ground crew following him.

With men in uniform, lawyers in suits, and the general populace adding their weight to the tether, and the balloon crew and Jax hooking and grabbing cables, the basket edged back toward the roof.

"It's safe now," Evie called up. "You can climb down."

Iddy wanted to demand that the stupid woman carry down the rooster cage, but the actress didn't appear well enough to pull herself over. Just as it looked as if someone might have to go in after her, Betty George collapsed inside the basket.

More shouts. Medics arrived while the balloon crew hollered about propane tanks. The fire seemed to have gone out. No wonder the balloon was deflating.

With the basket finally stabilized on the roof, its cables holding off the blowing nylon, Jax scrambled inside. Iddy tried not to swallow hard as the whole contraption shook and shifted while he lifted the actress over the side into the arms of a pair of sturdy medics.

"Rooster?" Iddy called once the unconscious woman was on a stretcher. As long as he was in there. . .

Jax held the cage over the side. Before Iddy could reach it, the cage door flew open and the terrified bird flew out, hitting the roof and flapping, squawking, through the crowd. Iddy chased after it, but the rooster's mind was too fried to reach. She could appreciate the terror.

With others now hauling cables and securing the basket and nylon, Cade jogged over to wrestle the rooster before it attacked anyone. Thanking the heavens, Iddy grabbed the cage Jax supplied.

"Damn crew should be filming this." Cade shoved the fighting, scratching bird into the cage. "Rooster Pilots Balloon for Fainting Actress. Practically writes itself."

If she weren't already swooning over his sweat-soaked shirt, she'd do so over a man who could joke while wrestling roosters. The damned bird had sharp claws.

"There are people with cameras everywhere. I'd rather not be in any of the stories." Letting Cade carry the cage, Iddy aimed for the stairs, her pulse still racing as sanity prevailed over sheer terror.

Sabotage, just as she'd predicted. There was no other good reason for those propane burners to go out. On top of the Hummer yesterday. . . Someone was trying to shut down the film.

So the murderer could leave town?

HUGGING AND KISSING JAX'S NECK IN GRATITUDE THAT HE HADN'T BROKEN IT FOR A basket case, Evie reluctantly let him slip away with the other suits and uniforms. She couldn't hold him back any more than he could her, and discussions of lawsuits and insurance were his thing. Ghosts were hers. She slipped down to the courthouse's second floor back stairs.

It had been a while since she'd stopped in to visit former mayor Block's spirit. She'd tried to send him on, but his black soul had been tied to controlling this town for so long, he couldn't let go.

The excitement had emptied the courtrooms. She wandered around until she found his icy spot and tuned in.

Block's aura hadn't faded. In fact, he seemed more visible now, propped against the wall, watching the excited masses chattering in the rotunda.

"Movies?" he asked cynically when Evie greeted him. "Is that what your half-baked mayor thinks will put us on the map?"

"Better than a killer judge. Toby's doing good, in case you care." Evie didn't like that Block had always put his job and the town in front of his only son, but that was old news.

"He still around? That's a first."

They both knew Toby had always avoided Afterthought because of his father. Now that Block had moved on. . . Well, no point in discussing it now. The mayor had never listened when he was alive.

"Toby is working with Judge Satterwhite and a local committee. They're hoping to turn the land over by the school into a family friendly shopping and entertainment experience. Are you sure you wouldn't like to let all this go and see what awaits beyond?"

Block snorted. "Entertainment! I hear things. Your movie people are in trouble up to their fat necks. Get rid of them."

He vanished. With a sigh, Evie slapped a battery pack on her depleted phone, but Block didn't return.

As far as she was aware, Block couldn't leave this place where he'd died. The only fat neck on the film crew was Mackie's. If the ghost had seen him, it had to be here. Why?

She called Jax. She could tell from the background noise when he answered that he was still with the medics or balloon crew or both. It was noisy. She kept it simple. "Why would Mackie be at the courthouse?"

"License, maybe? Why?"

"Cade or Wright would handle licenses. Block says Mackie is in trouble and should be thrown out of town. He's never been here before, has he?"

"Not that I'm aware. I'll ask around. Betty George had a heart attack. Looks like they'll have to close down production anyway."

Evie whistled. "How many people knew she had a bad ticker? Someone really doesn't want them here, do they?"

"My thought exactly. Stay away from them. Talk to Pris about wedding cakes and appetizers and let Gracie hem your dress when school is out."

Evie made a rude noise and hung up. Twisting the silver ring on her left hand, she sighed. She'd never make an obedient housewife.

Jax knew that.

Observation, not planning, was her strength. She wandered down the stairs into the crowd and found the production crew in the parking lot, loading the animals into a truck. Iddy kept an eye on proceedings, so Evie felt safe enough. It was broad daylight. What trouble could she get into?

Off to one side, an older woman in blond curls similar to Betty George's stood weeping and wiping at her eyes with a tissue. Slender, dressed elegantly in a sheath dress that looked better on her than it would have on frumpy Betty, the woman appeared on the brink of collapse. But no one noticed or seemed to care. Her aura was fraught with sorrow and worry and carried few of the darker shades of most of the film crew.

Shrugging, Evie wandered over to hand her a packet of Kleenex from her tote. "Hi, I'm Evangeline. You work with Miss George?"

The woman nodded. "I don't talk to the press. See them over there." She nodded at Wright and Brice Kennedy shouting at the technicians.

"I'm not press. I was with the medics helping Miss George." That was pretty much true. She was there. So were the medics. "I understand she had a heart attack, which is understandable, under the circumstances. Are you Ray Anne? Do you need transportation to the hospital?" That last question was pure inspiration if this was Betty's wardrobe and makeup assistant, which seemed likely.

The woman sniffed, wiped her eyes, and returned the Kleenex packet. "I am. She goes nowhere without me. You can take me to her?"

Praying Betty's friend and assistant wasn't a saboteur, Evie nodded and named the hospital in Charleston. "You might want to call and ask when she can have visitors."

She'd like to kidnap the assistant, throw her into the Subaru, and pick her brain, but real life had limitations. The Subaru was back at the house, and the woman might not have enough information to last an hour drive. And Jax would kill her.

Given a task, Ray Anne brightened and brought out her phone. While she hunted for the hospital, Evie watched Mackie's assistant herd the crew into various vehicles. Roy O'Bryan, the aging cowboy, entered a limo with Brice Kennedy, the director, presumably heading back to the city.

Iddy was helping the surfer boy, Darren, and a couple of men in their mid-forties wearing cameras, to load the animals into a truck. Sandra probably would have overseen that had she been alive.

While Ray Anne waited on hold, Evie nodded toward the animal handlers. "Who are they?"

Betty's assistant wrinkled her delicate nose. "Blond one, Darren, he does the microphones. Baldie, that's Steven Nancy, he operates the camera. One that looks like hoodlum, Parker, works with Nancy on film production. The extras, I don't know." She returned her attention to the phone as someone answered.

Very small crew if the film and sound people were now handling animals. They all looked grim.

Clicking off her phone, Ray Anne tucked it away, her shoulders slumping. "They cannot tell me anything. Only family may visit. I am her only family, but not by marriage or blood."

"That will keep out everyone in the crew and the news people. Is that good or bad?" Evie realized she was leaning against the Hummer and straightened.

The elegant assistant made a moue of distaste. "Possibly good if she should not be agitated. But Betty likes company. She will be lonely."

She was talking as if Betty was already well enough to sit up in bed and chat. Evie had a notion that wasn't happening soon. Running out of inspiration, Evie called to Iddy as her cousin finished loading chickens and goats.

Before Iddy arrived, she asked Ray Anne, "If you want to go back to the trailer, my cousin can take you. I'll work on getting you in to see Betty when she's ready for visitors. You may have to say you're her sister. The two of you look enough alike."

"Lie?" Ray Ann looked unhappy about that. Even her aura dimmed.

"It's good to know honesty still exists. It's my job to help, so I can lie for you. This is Idonea, my cousin. She was hired to take Sandra's place. Did you know Sandra?"

Iddy had her keys out, ready to go.

Ray Anne looked nervous but determined. "Sandra was a nice girl in a bad business. Will her family come to take care of her horse and dog? I still have her suitcase and would like to give it to them."

Evie bit her tongue to keep her jaw from dropping. No one had asked for Sandra's suitcase?

Thirteen

CADE CALLED UP MENTAL IMAGES OF HIS OLD-FASHIONED DEN OVERLOOKING THE
Pacific and the bar built into the paneling. He imagined kicking back in his leather chair with a whiskey and watching this zoo fall over the bluff outside his sliding glass doors. It was a satisfying image, but he wasn't given time to appreciate it.

"Looks like your uncle will have to pony up," Wayne Wright said as he sidled over to watch the last cage packed into the truck. "No star, no production."

Imagining what that would do to his uncle, Cade ignored the knifing pain in his gut. He pulled out his phone and found the research files on the production crew Evie's team had sent him. "Insurance goes to investors and only covers what's already been paid out," he informed the cocky assistant. "No production, no salaries. Mackie has spent every red cent already. Looks to me like you're a little overextended as well. Maybe you'd better start looking for a new star."

Mackie's lawsuits had the producer owing money to half the world. Wright. . . appeared to have some expensive habits. Cade suspected drugs and gambling, but Evie's team hadn't had time to find proof.

After today, the production really should be shut down. It was too early in California to call his uncle and advise it. . . again. But for the sake of all the little people Mackie owed, as well as his uncle, Cade resisted closure. If he could keep the film rolling, he'd have more time to discover what had happened to Sandra. The local police didn't have a chance with this Hollywood lot of paid performers.

"That's not how it works!" Wright protested. "They got to pay us!"

Cade shoved his phone in his pocket. "Nope. Knowing Mackie's track record, the company tied up that contract so tight air can't escape. Cash cuts off the second production shuts down. Mackie is responsible for debts owed."

Cade walked off knowing his pocket wouldn't hurt, but everyone here would have to find their own way home. If anyone had a suspicion of who was sabotaging the project, that ought to jolt them into talking. He'd let Wright spread the word.

The text from Evie about Sandra's suitcase had him hurrying across the parking lot for the motorcycle he'd borrowed from the crew. Before he could hit the engine, he had a call from Brice, the director.

"Hire that vet for Betty's part. We'll have Roy do all the talking. She can just magic the animals."

"No way in hell am I putting anyone else in harm's way." Cade shoved the phone in his pocket and started the engine so he didn't have to hear Brice calling back.

How the hell was he supposed to prove any of this was sabotage? Unless someone showed up on the security video emptying the propane tanks. . . . He needed to find the cameras covering the balloon's prep, but it looked to him like the ground crew would have been responsible for checking the tanks. They had nothing to do with Mackie.

He was still swearing when he rolled up to the farm and saw Iddy cuddling the traumatized rooster. Cuddling. A rooster. The damned thing had nearly torn his hand off, yet rested in her arms like a kitten.

At his arrival, the vet carried the fowl back to the barn, Ray Anne following on her heels.

Suitcase, right. She'd been waiting for him so he could take charge of the evidence. They should probably call the police, but if the dimwits hadn't asked for it in the first place—

Or Ray Anne hadn't told them. Cade hurried to catch up. No reason a hairdresser couldn't be a saboteur. What about Betty? She must have known about the suitcases. But she wouldn't sabotage herself.

"Have you heard from Sandra's parents yet?" Iddy asked, tucking the rooster back in its pen. She patted the collie that resisted leaving Sandra's horse.

Guilt tugged at Cade every time he saw those loyal animals waiting for their owner's return. He unclenched his molars to answer. "Her parents live in a condo. Her mother is undergoing chemo. They can't take the animals. They're trying to find a buyer for the horse. They said they've found a collie rescue group for Classy." Cade could practically hear Sandra's cries of anguish.

"Where on earth did she plan on taking them if her parents couldn't?" Iddy asked sensibly enough as they passed the bull pen.

"She said she had a girlfriend who would take them," Ray Anne offered, unlocking the trailer. "We thought that was where she'd gone."

"She didn't happen to mention the friend's name?" Cade waited in the doorway as the women entered the tin shack. It was almost as claustrophobic as the one Iddy lived in. Three people were two too many. "Use a towel to hold those handles," he warned when Ray Anne reached beneath the table. Although, by now, the suitcase had probably been handled so much even Sandra's prints would be wiped.

Obediently, the hairdresser grabbed a kitchen towel to haul out a battered blue suitcase and a duffel for Iddy to take. "Betty might know." She began to sniffle again.

Standing outside, Cade texted the question to the research experts. Could they find out the phone numbers on Sandra's phone? He'd have to find out if Betty was coherent and visit her.

"Word is, production is shutting down," Iddy murmured, using the towel to hand over the luggage. "Can they just leave everyone stranded?"

He'd been the one to tighten that clause, putting the screws to Mackie. The people results hadn't occurred to him. He really was turning into a mean asshole. Thailand couldn't come too soon.

"Afraid so," he told her. "Mackie was supposed to stay on budget, which includes transportation. He cut corners on all budget items—like return trip tickets—to fund upfront expenses. All I can do is warn him and my uncle when budget is exceeded. They're the ones who have to act. Mackie has been promising he'd find more funding. Unless they can find a replacement for Betty. . ."

They both looked at Ray Anne, Betty's look-alike. The oblivious hairdresser didn't notice but patted her tears with a tissue.

"How much would it matter if someone takes Betty's role?" Iddy whispered, stepping outside with him.

"Not a lot. She's a known name, but this is a documentary. The people who watch it for the animals aren't movie buffs." Cade glanced back at the crying woman. "We can't call a hairdresser an animal expert though."

He'd already said he wasn't sending anyone else in harm's way. But Ray Anne and a lot of other people were already in a bad place if they were stranded here. . .

Iddy closed the door and sat on the step, studying the bull pen and the animal truck being unloaded. "I don't know how these things work. Could the script be rewritten so Ray Anne can say things like 'according to experts. . .'?"

"And these experts would be?" Cade barely got that off his dry tongue. One woman had already gone to her death because he hadn't stopped her. . .

He paced restlessly, seeing no good end to this drama. Mackie's problems almost made his family's troubles seem easy.

"They're farm animals." Iddy gestured dismissively, not showing any concern for the danger of the film's production. "Any farmer is an expert. Ask me questions, and I'll offer my expert advice."

Damn, he'd known they were heading that way. This show really needed to be shut down. He didn't want any more casualties. . .

This wasn't just about what *he* wanted. Just because he wanted to wash his hands of the whole mess didn't mean others shouldn't have an opinion.

He sighed, knowing what his uncle would say. The family depended on him and this production. The entire cast and crew depended on him to get paid and sent home.

If he'd wanted lives to depend on him, he'd have been a fireman. A cop. A soldier. He was beyond tired of being responsible.

"It's late enough in California that your father should be functional. Let me cross examine him before we do anything." Cade didn't look forward to the conversation.

She waited warily, apparently expecting immediate results.

"Go check on your animals and office. I want to look at this morning's film before I make any decisions." He didn't expect to see much, but he needed time.

She frowned, then recalling the suitcases at their feet, nodded agreement. "Do we take these to the sheriff?"

Given a better task than calling Slate Cooper, Cade picked them up using the towel and his handkerchief and carried them to the barn. "Call your ghost hunting cousin. Let's see if Sandra has a reaction to us opening these up."

Garcia, you're a coward a voice in his head cried. *Ghosts don't talk! You're procrastinating.*

Damn sure hell he was. When he did a financial analysis, he wanted all the facts lined up before making a decision. He didn't see why this detective business shouldn't be the same.

He just couldn't believe he was including ghosts as a line item.

IN HIS SANE OFFICE, WHERE WRITTEN LAWS RULED HIS WORLD, JAX RUBBED HIS BROW and shook his head at the speaker on his phone. "Nope, no, uh uh. Hold on until I get there with the sheriff. You are *not* a detective and any tampered evidence can be thrown out."

Trying to impose real world regulations on Evie. . . was probably as futile as imposing them on her hacker team.

On the other end of the line, Evie didn't argue, although Jax suspected she had three impatient men breathing down her neck. He really didn't like that the hairdresser had withheld evidence. "Don't touch *anything*, understood?"

He glanced at his watch as he hung up. Noon already. Loretta was out early today. He texted Gracie asking her to take the kid home with her. He didn't think this would be a fast process.

The sheriff was in court but said he'd send someone over to collect the suitcases. Poor man thought Evie's team would actually let them go unopened. This would take some fancy footwork—or the team would never call him again. They wanted to be legal. They wanted justice more. He was the fulcrum balancing their two needs. Nice to be useful occasionally, he supposed.

He stopped at Pris's café and ordered lunch boxes to go, hoping to appease the angry mob. She had a nice crowd and said Dante would deliver them shortly. That meant Jax wouldn't exactly be arriving with bribes, so he took a sack of cookies to wave under impatient noses.

One of these days he'd invest in his own car, but after driving his former XKE, he hadn't figured out how to adapt to a family car. He hopped his Harley and saved gas instead.

The whole team and then some had arrived by the time he rolled up. Iddy's Tahoe, Evie's Subaru, R&R's van, Cade's bike—saving gas wasn't happening. The cop car pulled up right behind him—and Philomena stepped out. Evie wouldn't be happy. Jax offered the surly deputy a cookie.

"I can't be bribed," she told him, taking one anyway. "That evidence is going back with me."

"No one said otherwise. How's the investigation going on the balloon incident?" That got him through the gate to the barn before she barked again.

"What investigation? Some clown didn't refill the tank. Miss George didn't know how to switch to the full one. End of story." She stomped into the dimness of the hot barn.

That was the reason Evie and crew stood waiting. The police were overworked, underpaid, and lacked the imagination of a good TV script. Jax got that —but the law was still the law.

Except when ghosts intervened. Roark and Reuben were stoically standing on the suitcase and duffel—as a howling wind roared around. *Inside a barn,* Iddy went from stall to stall, calming the spooked animals.

"Sandra wants her luggage," Evie offered in explanation, hopping down from a table. "Cookies! You brought cookies. I think I love you. What kind?"

Her conversational hopscotch made Jax laugh when he wanted to snarl. "Every kind. Can't Sandra simply tell you what's in the luggage?"

"Sandra doesn't like talking. She's an action kind of gal. Iddy and Cade had to jam bars through all the stall handles or your precious evidence would have been trampled into dust." Evie bit into a chocolate chip and chewed as she waved at the deputy. "Hey, Mena. Come to watch the poltergeist?"

"I came to get them suitcases before y'all tamper with the evidence." The deputy proceeded toward the two towering, muscular men twice her size protecting the luggage.

"Give her the duffle first, guys. Let's see what happens." Evie leaned against a stall contentedly eating her cookie.

Jax knew that look. He ought to warn the cop. Mena wouldn't listen.

"Do we get fed first?" Reuben asked, holding out his hand.

"Pris is sending lunch shortly, to go with the entertainment." Jax handed the cookie bag to Cade, who withstood the weird breeze to distribute them. Jax leaned on the stall next to Evie, the smallest person in here, ready to grab her if she exhibited any sign of blowing in the wind.

Or given the amount of ghost energy, prevent her from dropping like a rock once the spirit drained her. He'd seen it happen and didn't want to repeat it. He was terrified that one day, a ghost would suck the life right out of her.

Cookie in hand, Reuben stepped off the old gray duffel.

It flew straight at the deputy, smacking the skinny woman in the head as if swung by an invisible arm. The contents poured free and flew around the barn.

"Hoot, here we go!" Evie cried.

As if they'd prepared for just this circumstance, Cade dropped an anvil on the suitcase and everyone else scattered, chasing after whirling clothes and toiletries and forcing them into an empty feed bag.

"Have fun explaining this," Jax called at the stunned deputy. "Let them take a look, and we'll testify that a storm wind blew the contents out before you could secure the evidence."

Wearing gloves—proving they'd prepared—R&R began sorting through the duffle's contents.

"Take notes, Jax," Reuben called. "Three pairs of shorts, five T-shirts."

"All spandex," Evie added, irrelevantly.

Leaning on the stall next to Evie, Iddy took another cookie and bumped Evie's shoulder. "If you got it, flaunt it. It's Hollywood."

"Here we go," Roark shouted. "iPad, da battery run down. I'll connect it to the charger."

While downloading his spyware, no doubt, but Jax chewed his pecan bar and kept his tongue occupied.

"You ladies have anything to say about the toiletries?" Reuben asked politely, gathering odds and ends into a cosmetic bag.

"Duffle was obviously her carry-on," Iddy said.

Evie examined them with a shrug. She wasn't much into makeup.

Mena took a look and whistled. "That's some damned fine stuff. Must be nice." She sniffed the various bottles and powders. "All normal. No drugs. You recording this, Jax?"

"We all are," he affirmed. "You're on candid camera." He nodded at the rafters.

She frowned at the concealed camera, then at him, then accepted the extra protection. Mena had an attitude, but she also had brains and knew how to use them.

"We can ask Ray Anne about the cosmetics," Iddy suggested. "Maybe the studio offers them at a discount."

"Or Betty sold them to her and charged the studio, not that I'm a cynic." Evie returned to Jax's side.

Stall doors rattled. The horse kicked the box. And the poor collie looked confused. Sandra evidently wasn't happy with the discussion.

Jax was pretty certain any film of this scene would never make it into court.

"Sandra, if you don't like what we're saying, tell us why. Use your words!" Evie cried at the swirling wind.

Cade leaned against the mare's stall and patted the collie. Iddy returned to performing her mind magic to calm the animals.

"She's saying the old biddy *gave* them to her. I'll take that to mean Betty. Ghosts don't recall names. Everyone, better pull out your battery chargers." Evie slapped hers on her phone.

Philomena checked her phone, cursed, and at a gesture from Reuben, hooked it up to the barn cord. "That ain't evidence. Now let's carry that other case out to my car where it can't blow nowhere."

The barn door slammed shut. A hay bale leaped from the loft, just missing Cade, who dodged backward.

"Let's see what else Sandra has to say," Evie said dryly. "Roark, stand back."

Grinning, the fool Cajun removed the anvil.

The aging suitcase flew into the air, slammed against a stall, and shattered before the deputy could grab it. Jax gave her credit for even approaching haunted luggage.

More clothing spilled out and flew about the floor. The collie yipped and raced over to the broken suitcase. She wrestled out a rubber dog toy and settled down with it.

Jax leaned over and using a T-shirt, picked up a slender leather notebook. Its pages riffled as he did so.

Fourteen

"ARE WE HAVING FUN?" THE DEEP, SLIGHTLY POSH VOICE CALLED AS THE BARN DOOR opened, allowing the sunshine to illuminate flying underwear and shoes.

Iddy glanced over at Pris's big Italian count carrying sacks of lunch boxes and wondered if she would ever be hungry again. Using one of Sandra's dirty shirts, she lured the collie away from the open suitcase so Philomena could examine the contents. This scene with a frustrated, angry poltergeist twisted her insides into knots. To be murdered and helpless to do anything. . .

She'd known Evie saw beyond the Veil, that sometimes spirits talked to her over Ouija boards. But she'd never seen her cousin dealing with a ghost that flung suitcases and hay bales. . . and kept secrets.

"Check the suitcase seams," Evie called as Jax half-carried her out the door Dante had just entered. He grabbed two lunchboxes, and they vanished from sight.

Apparently, Evie's battery was as drained as their phones.

"I'da done that on my own," Mena muttered, running her gloved hands over the shattered suitcase's interior.

Dante handed her a lunchbox. She ignored it to pull at a loose thread.

While the deputy was exploring the suitcase, Roark and Reuben were apparently snapping pictures of notebook pages.

After consulting with Dante, Cade took two of the boxes and carried them over to where Iddy was staying out of range of ghosts and cops and things that went bump in the night.

"This one's Portobello." He handed her one marked with a V.

"Unless it contains dog bones, I'm not interested." Iddy hugged her elbows as Philomena crowed in triumph and removed an envelope from the bag's lining.

Cade peered inside his sandwich. "Mine has beef. Can the dog have that? I'll eat your mushroom. I can't remember breakfast."

"Eat your beef *and* the mushroom. I have dog bones in the Tahoe. I don't suppose those are airplane tickets in that envelope?"

"Airlines don't give paper tickets anymore. You need to eat." He broke off a piece of banana and pushed it between her lips.

Because it was in his hands, she accepted it. Despite everything, Cade still smelled of male musk and shaving lotion and a scent all his own. Obviously, she was one of those stupid women who needed a male to lean on in times of trouble. She hadn't realized that about herself. She did, insanely, feel safer with his big body shielding her from a spirit's wrath. She took another bite and kept her gaze fastened on Mena and Evie's team as they opened the envelope.

A stack of hundreds fell out. The wind died down, leaving the money safely in the detective's hands.

"ATM cash," Cade commented, producing a bottle of water and uncapping it. "They spit out hundreds instead of twenties these days."

"Where does one spend a hundred-dollar bill?" Iddy tried to remember if she'd ever seen one. Her receptionist handled payments. Did people pay their bills in cash?

"Never tried. I'm a plastics kinda guy. It's too easy to lose track of cash. The production company does direct deposit so that's not her paycheck." Cade chomped into his sandwich and watched in silence as Mena tucked the envelope into an evidence bag and held out her hand for the notebook.

Dante had followed Jax and Evie out once lunch had been distributed. An archeologist wasn't of much use as a detective, and with the twins underfoot, Pris probably needed him back at the café. Iddy figured she ought to pay attention to how love tamed even the biggest of men. Except she wasn't as strong as Pris and couldn't read male minds.

Classy dropped her rubber toy and barked at Mena as she packed the duffel and suitcase and carried them away.

Iddy dropped down to reassure the dog. "She's still sensitive to how Sandra feels. I'm picking up an impression of sadness right now. Classy is reacting to that but doesn't know how to comfort someone she can't see."

"Give me your keys, and I'll fetch the dog bone." Cade handed her the lunch boxes in exchange for the keys.

"You're not fooling me," she told him, just to assert herself. He didn't care about the animals. "You want to pick R&R's brains."

The duo was headed out after Mena, seemingly empty-handed except for the food. But they'd seen or handled everything Sandra had left behind. They had what they needed.

"I'll tell you anything I hear." Proving her point, he jogged out to pick brains.

Iddy slid down the stall door to sit with the poor abandoned collie. "I wish you could tell me what happened here, girl. Sorry I don't speak dog."

She played tug with the rubber toy, and the collie perked up, mock growling and shaking its head to hang on.

Cade returned with a smelly dog bone. Iddy received a brief flash of recognition—the collie remembered a man who came bearing bones and the toy—not Cade, but a wiry, middle-aged man smelling of a cologne she didn't recognize. The image disappeared once Classy took the bone and sniffed Cade.

"A man gave Sandra's dog this toy and a smelly bone like this one." Iddy exchanged the treat for the rubber toy so she could examine it. But it was simply a toy that could be purchased in any pet store.

Cade took a seat on the floor beside her and examined it too. "If only dogs could speak?"

"She'd be about as good at names as Evie's ghosts, I suspect. To animals, we're just a collection of perceived senses. With training, Classy might learn her name or someone else's, but it's not ingrained. I imagine them calling each other 'hound bitch smells of rabbit' and the like."

"Smelly feet who brings hot dogs," he suggested in amusement.

Iddy offered a smile at his attempt to humor her and picked a carrot stick out of her lunch box. She should probably be more open-minded about men. They weren't all her father. "What did you learn from Evie's guys?"

He held up his phone. "They sent me the images they took of the book. Cryptic numbers and letters. They'll run a code search, but Sandra wasn't that complicated. I suspect she simply noted when she got paid, by whom, and how much."

Iddy glanced at the screen. "BG could be Betty George? BK. . . ?"

"Brice Kennedy, the director? They're all dated prior to Wednesday. They may have been giving her cash to run errands. She never did drugs that I know of, but she was fully capable of picking them up for others. Or running to the liquor store for Betty. Not sure what else they'd be paying her for."

"They'd pay her in hundred-dollar bills?" Iddy was still stunned at the sight of those crisp bills.

"Standard Beverly Hills tip. But those in the suitcase were crisp out of a bank.

She had some crumpled Franklins in her pocket according to the police report—which I assume Evie's team hacked somehow?"

Iddy reluctantly nodded. Reuben and Roark were intelligence and computer experts, trained in foreign countries where privacy was a passing dream. "So, Sandra wasn't robbed when she was killed. I guess we knew that. Someone doesn't read murder mysteries."

"Someone panicked. They hit her over the head with some as yet unidentified object, panicked, rolled her in a blanket. . . which probably indicates they were in her room. Since the house is a rental, we don't have a clear idea if she might have been hit with a lamp that's gone missing or anything like that. Then, after they rolled her up, they either had to carry her out on their own or ask for help. No one is telling tales." He finished off his sandwich and started on hers.

Iddy wrinkled her nose in distaste. "There should have been blood splatters. Heads bleed."

"Didn't think about that." He opened up his phone to search through the files Evie's team sent him. "Coroner's report still out on weapon. No blood splatter anywhere so far. Angle of blow indicates she may have been crouching when hit, petting the dog?" He slid the phone back in his pocket. "The others said she stormed out. If she was killed outside—finding blood in the mud after a storm or two, on a farm this large, is impossible. But the blanket was a weird choice."

"Looks like Sandra had cash in her jeans and a packed suitcase—maybe she carried the blanket out with her? Which might mean she really was planning on leaving that evening, if we believe Ray Anne. And we have no reason to believe she was lying, just that she's mostly stupid for not wondering why Sandra didn't return for her suitcase and animals if she went to stay with her friend." Iddy crumbled her cookie before realizing what she was doing. She nibbled on the remains.

"A tangled web we're not qualified to unravel. I'm afraid it's time to call your father. Are you ready?" He scrolled through his contact list.

"Do I have to be here?" Iddy squirmed uncomfortably. Cassy laid her head on Iddy's knee to be petted.

Cade didn't answer but acknowledged the reply on the other end, pushing the speaker button. "Cooper, how much have you heard of the situation here?"

"More than I want," the deep male voice growled. "Sandra was a good kid. I told her to stay out of that mess."

Stewing, Iddy wondered if he would have answered had she called. If he even knew she was involved.

"Want to let me know why you sent Mackie to this backwater?" Cade asked, not sounding friendly.

Her father hesitated. Iddy rubbed Classy's ear. If her father had sent Mackie to Afterthought and also knew Sandra, could he be blamed for the trainer's death? Just in her head, probably.

"He was looking for somewhere cheap to film, and it don't come much cheaper than Afterthought."

Cade snorted. "There's a whole wide world of cheaper easier to reach than here."

The voice on the other end sounded resigned. "Look, Mackie never did me no favors. Him and some of his people are rotten to the core, but he thinks we're too stupid to figure it out. He needs to be stopped. If you did as I told you, you should understand by now." He hung up.

He'd told Cade to look for her. Interesting. Her father had sent Mackie here for her family to tackle. Somehow. For some reason.

"Well, at least he didn't call us interfering witches." Iddy finished off her cookie crumbs and stood up.

"Slate is close-mouthed. He knows my uncle, not me. I need to call my uncle next, see if he can pry out more information, but the next choice is whether to shut down production or continue without Betty. You should go back to your office for now." He stood with her, dusting off his jeans.

Yeah, tall, dark, and sexy would be back in Hollywood in two shakes of a lamb's tail. She needed to remember that. Refusing to be depressed by a father she never knew and a man who would never be hers, Iddy nodded and headed for the door. To her surprise, the collie followed.

Well, excellent, she wasn't giving that poor dog to a shelter.

ONCE ON THE MOTORCYCLE, CADE DIDN'T STOP IN AFTERTHOUGHT. HE CONTINUED on into Charleston and the high-end, but not luxury, hotel Mackie had settled on. Having to actually visit the production had to be crawling up the fat man's rear end. The insult of living like a normal wealthy peon instead of the 1% was probably giving him ulcers.

It certainly hadn't improved the producer's temper. Mackie flung a bound script at Cade the instant Wright let him into the suite.

"Any fool who can read can take Betty's place! She had to do just one damned thing—go up in a balloon—and she couldn't even do that right." Mackie stormed back and forth in front of the windows overlooking the courtyard below.

Cade caught the script and settled, uninvited, into a chair. "How is Betty? Has anyone checked on her?"

Surprisingly, Brice Kennedy, the director spoke up. "It was a mild warning. She's awake and wants us to send for her own physician."

"That's understandable. Does that mean she thinks she can continue?" Cade wasn't much on reading body language. He preferred numbers. But he hadn't survived this long without paying attention. Brice was unhappy with whatever Betty had decided.

"She says she's perfectly fine and wants to sue the balloon crew. Will our insurance go up with her as a liability?" Brice returned to scrolling through his notebook computer.

"I'll call my uncle. That's his decision." Cade contemplated Mackie's bar but resisted. He needed his head clear and almost wished he had his weird detective team here to tell him who was lying and who was feeling guilty.

The way Mackie paced the suite, he should be losing pounds by the minute. Guilt? Or frustration?

Wright had holed up in a corner with the drink Cade wanted, even though it was only early afternoon.

Brice's usual composed demeanor looked ruffled, but he hadn't quite lost his shit as the other two had. Brice Kennedy had developed into an in-demand director. Cade figured he had another film lined up already. The rest of Mackie's crew were a tight-knit band of scoundrels. Cade didn't know why Kennedy had bothered taking a job with this low-budget production.

"Did you talk to the vet?" Kennedy asked, thumbing through notes and making notations.

"She's doing animal surgery this afternoon. She's on call for delivering calves every night. She has a life and more business than one person can handle." Cade had learned all this over the past few days from almost everyone but Iddy. She didn't talk much about herself. "She cannot keep set hours If you don't want Betty back, how about hiring someone local?"

"The vet?" Mackie screamed, turning on his director. "That tall, skinny, brown thing? We need a blonde who won't tower over Roy and make him look pale in comparison."

"Shirley Temple is dead," Kennedy said dryly. "You need an animal expert. The vet is qualified. I told you Betty is too old. Let's cut our losses and leave."

Cade waited for Mackie—the producer, the money man—to reveal the state of his finances and what would happen if they shut down.

Mackie poured a bourbon and continued pacing.

"Can we film without a female lead?" Wright asked, almost timidly, from his corner.

Mackie ignored him too. His Hitchcock pout more protuberant than usual, he sipped his drink and waddled the floor.

"Perhaps someone could explain why we're filming in the middle of nowhere instead of back in LA where we could find a dozen Betty George's?" Cade asked. That had been his point in coming here. He needed to see and hear Mackie's explanation. His gut said the reason had everything to do with Sandra's death.

"Whim," Kennedy answered, tossing back water like beer. He gestured with his bottle. "Slate Cooper said the town mayor would bend over backward for us. Betty and Sandra were eager to visit friends and family, I think. We ran the numbers. The town photos showed they had exactly what we needed. We didn't have to rent an expensive studio lot or use union labor for the extras. Logical decision."

None of that would have stirred Mackie from the comforts of his estate and drinking buddies.

Cade crossed his arms. "Mackie? You didn't cut a deal with the devil because of Cooper and a couple of women."

The producer reached in his pocket for the cigar he no longer smoked, growled, and poured more bourbon. He gestured with his glass. "The mayor of the damned place is a flaming queen. Hire it for all I care. But we're finishing this film."

"Nice, Mack. Larraine Ward has gone out of her way finding everything you requested and under budget." Cade gritted his teeth and pulled out the big guns. "What are the cash withdrawals on the production account? People tip in twenties here, not hundreds. What was Sandra doing for whom?"

Fifteen

"Next time, take me with you." Evie slammed a salad bowl on the dinner table. "I could have read their auras and known who to question about what."

Cade didn't acknowledge that demand. Evie wasn't a real detective. Even Iddy knew no one would have allowed her in Mackie's suite.

Iddy set out the quinoa casserole she'd ordered from Pris and soothed Evie with her suggestion. "We should gather the whole production crew in the barn. Then maybe your ghost will talk."

"Yeah, I like that." Evie brightened and finally took a seat. "I'd like it even better if Mean Mena could take Betty's role in the film. She'd have had the ground crew groveling if she'd been the one stranded in that balloon."

"One's as likely as the other," Cade responded gloomily.

Iddy noticed that he'd been fretting and furious since returning from the city. Apparently, his uncle had added insult to injury by insisting on raising the insurance if Betty continued working.

"If they're pushing Betty out of the role, shouldn't they hold auditions for her replacement?" Iddy dished salad onto her plate.

Like Cade, she dismissed the excuses Mackie had given for filming here. Her father would have had to learn hypnotism to persuade a producer to Afterthought. Since Mackie was mostly staying in Charleston. . . maybe there was something there?

And Mackie's claim to knowing nothing about the hundreds in cash going to Sandra didn't sound likely, although apparently Kennedy and Cade also had access to the account, as well as an accountant back in California, who paid the bills. Of course, anyone could have used an ATM to pay Sandra. The money leaving the production account could be legitimate expenses. That was Cade's bailiwick. She didn't know how Evie kept track of all these details. Maybe ADHD worked for a detective.

"An audition is actually a good idea." Cade yanked out his phone and began texting. "I'm still not entirely buying the ghosts and goblins, but if we can keep Mackie on edge, his tongue might loosen."

Not preening over getting one right, Iddy dipped her garlic bread in olive oil and continued her thoughts. "I don't know the other men on your crew, but I'd like to know which one was feeding Classy dog bones. Thieves do that when they want to stop a dog from warning their owners. It's possible Classy saw some of what happened that night."

"Thieves also drug or kill dogs," Jax warned. "Sandra might simply have had a friend on the crew."

"What do you think it means when two people have the same red in their bubble?" Trying to look casual, Evie's eleven-year-old ward slathered her greens in salad dressing.

Iddy was pretty sure she didn't want to know the answer to this distraction. Loretta was a perceptive kid.

Sure enough, Evie grinned and glanced at Iddy and Cade. "If it means the same as their auras, you're too young to understand. Just watch out if a boy comes near you if he's projecting red."

If she could have reached Evie, Iddy would have kicked her. Instead, she ignored the byplay and stuck with the topic. If Evie was insinuating she and Cade had the hots for each other—animal attraction meant nothing. "Would it be possible to bring all the crew together with Mackie? Could the town offer some incentive—a key to the city?"

"At the courthouse?" Evie asked, diverted from her teasing. "I don't think Block's spirit will be as helpful as Sandra's."

"Let's not insult perfectly nice people by introducing them to Mackie." Apparently not receiving a reply to his text, Cade laid his phone on the table. "His employees have to take his crap. No one else should."

They needed Nick and Gracie's creative suggestions, but Gracie was working on the wedding gown.

Cade's phone finally beeped, and he scanned the text. "Brice Kennedy is desperate. They'll film the bull scene with Roy tomorrow morning at the farm, and if we can round up suitable candidates by tomorrow afternoon, he'll bring in

Mackie and the film crew, and they'll test the goat scene. The screenwriters are adapting to 'an expert's advice' but he's hoping for a real expert."

"Not me or Asia," Iddy declared. "We have our hands full."

"Besides, Mackie wants blond and short, like Betty. We might pass off Ray Anne as a stand in, but even wearing wigs, you and Asia do not qualify." Cade grimaced as he tucked away his phone.

"Ignoring the hint of bigotry . ." Evie dug hers out. "I'll ask Aunt Val. Pity our mothers aren't movie star material. They pass themselves off as experts on everything."

Cade looked intrigued at the idea of their mothers playing Betty's part—there wasn't much difference in their ages. Iddy shook her head and whispered while Evie talked into her phone. "Don't even think it unless you want a farce. Think Evie in triplicate, with gray hair and thirty extra pounds."

He studied Evie. "What about Evie in a blond wig?"

"She has the attention span of a gnat. Memorizing the script won't happen. Improvisation is what you'd get."

"And production would never finish, got it. Don't suppose you know any blond experts?"

"You might as well ask Classy. Call my father. If this is his big idea, make him pay." Iddy dug into her casserole before she said worse. Tomorrow, she'd sit on the other side of the table. She couldn't think straight when he was near.

"Aunt Val said she'd call around," Evie announced. "It's short notice to drive over from Atlanta, but the job would look good on resumes. The animal expert part has to be faked though."

"Have you read R&F's report yet?" Jax asked, turning the discussion to facts. "So far, using the phone and iPad, they've found a couple of possible connections between Sandra and people on this coast. They're digging into them now."

"If her parents live here, then she must have gone to school on this coast, right?" Iddy asked.

Cade shrugged. "She did, but that was nearly twenty years ago. As far as I'm aware, she never even attended class reunions."

"Probably couldn't afford it," Evie said pragmatically. "And if she went west with dreams of being a star—"

"She followed a boyfriend from college," Cade offered. "He landed some TV spots. She met people with animals. She really did have a knack for handling them. I don't remember her mentioning anyone back here."

"Iddy's dad sent Mackie to us for some reason." Evie sipped her tea and frowned. "Did he expect us to consult the tarot? Read the horse's mind? Set fire to his beard?"

Iddy snorted. "If only Mackie had a beard. . . Mom could sell him amulets. Should we bring in Pris to read everyone's minds?"

Evie waved her fork dismissively. "Pris is gestating. Let her bond with the baby. An amulet for speaking the truth maybe?"

Pris was pregnant. Iddy had not known that.

Apparently, Loretta hadn't either. The kid lit up like a Christmas tree. "Is that the extra bubble? Cool! Will that make me an aunt?"

"Second cousin, biologically, probably, but she can call you aunt, if that makes you happy." Evie studied her about-to-be-adopted daughter. "Knowing when someone is pregnant might be really cool or truly terrible. You may want to keep your lips sealed until you know which."

"You know it's a girl?" Iddy asked. The family conversation was easier on her stomach than murderers.

"We're Malcolms. They're almost always girls. But yes, her aura indicates female colors."

Iddy could almost feel Cade digesting all this weirdness and mentally packing his bags. Maybe she should throw all her family's madness at him at once, so he'd flee back to California—as her father had done.

"Gather the family when the auditions start," Iddy suggested, malice intended. "Let the bad vibes begin."

Cade looked a little dazed—but didn't object.

JAX LINED UP PHOTOS OF THE SALARIED FILM CREW ON THE CELLAR WALL. IMAGES seemed to help Evie focus. He hung a photo of Sandra beneath the line up and began attaching yarn from the crew to Sandra. "Ray Anne, and presumably Betty, knew Sandra was leaving because they were hiding her packed suitcases. We should probably ask at what point Sandra brought those out, since no one in the house noticed."

"Darren, the two Steves, and Wright saw her walk out empty-handed after the fight over dishes." Reuben called up text on his computer. "They all had pretty much the same story—she got mad, walked out, and some time later, they saw a truck leave."

"But it wasn't a company truck," Cade pointed out. "We only have one pickup and it didn't go anywhere."

Jax ran lines to the four men anyway. "We know she didn't leave with the truck. Sometime after that altercation, she died. Did she call someone to pick her up? Why was the truck there? If it was there to pick her up, why did it leave without her? And how did her phone end up on the interstate?"

Evie hit pool balls, listening, and presumably processing. Her cousin had escaped for an animal emergency. Cade had purchased a bottle of fine bourbon earlier and was washing out the glasses in the cellar's old bar, leaving the bottle out for sharing.

While they pondered the truck, Jax and Roark helped themselves. Evie and Reuben stuck to ice tea.

"Do we have the list of Sandra's phone calls that day?" Giving up on the truck, Cade sipped his drink. "Or is that classified?"

Roark printed out a list and gave it to Jax to hang beside Sandra's image. "Classified, but I have my ways. She didn't call any of da crew. She had Betty and everyone right dere if she needed talk or transportation. Her calls were all outside da film people. The day she died, she talked to a place dat boards horses. We only reached a receptionist who says she's never heard of her."

Cade leaned over to study the list. "She *received* calls from Parker—who was in Charleston all day—the horse boarding place, and an unlisted number. Have you traced that one?"

"Burner, not registered anywhere. The cops can't get past her phone code to read any text. We're taking this from pings off local cell towers." Reuben grimaced in frustration. "If they'd just learn to trust us, I could crack that code."

"Not happening," Evie called cheerily. "Even though Troy *knows* we provide good info, he sticks to procedure. His job is on the line."

"And what did Parker have to say?" Jax asked, scribbling notes to attach to his yarn.

"He says he was just reporting on the feed she wanted delivered. Does that sound like she was leaving?" Roark sipped his bourbon and studied the suspect board.

"Yup." Evie whacked a ball into a pocket. "There's plenty of feed there. Sounds like she wanted to make certain the animals received the right food even after she was gone."

"She was particular about brands," Cade acknowledged. "That's a reasonable assumption, except she should have asked *me* if more feed was in the budget. That could mean she didn't want to be questioned."

"All right, so we need to find out who the truck driver was and find someone at the horse boarding place who talked with her. Did the iPad turn up anything?" Jax gave up on the wall and joined Evie at the pool table. He really wanted this case over before the wedding, but they were going nowhere fast.

"She didn't have a password on the iPad and didn't have it connected to her phone. She apparently only used it with Wi-fi. There's a document folder on Mackie's lawsuit, with newspaper clippings and links and whatnot. Mostly, she watched action movies, got lots of email from clothing companies, just the usual." Reuben scanned his computer screen, reading off the iPad's contents.

"Do any of the women suing Mackie have an east coast connection?" Evie asked.

Jax watched in amusement as her rough, tough, action team dropped their jaws and spun back to their computers.

Unmoved, Cade inquired, "What made you ask that?"

"I think Mackie has been in the local courthouse. I assume he doesn't stoop to running his own errands so he needed to visit someone personally, like a judge or attorney."

Jax whistled. "I'll ask around tomorrow, see what I can find out."

Their guest wasn't satisfied. "Mackie has a team of lawyers in LA and another in New York. Why would he need to go to a tiny courthouse in Nowheresville, South Carolina? Who told you that?"

Jax sipped his fine bourbon and let Evie answer, just for amusement.

"A ghost told me," she said pragmatically, smacking another ball into a pocket. "A crooked ghost who thinks Mackie is a bad apple. Takes one to know one, I guess."

Sixteen

JUST BEFORE LUNCH ON WEDNESDAY, EVIE'S PHONE RANG AS SHE SLID INTO THE Subaru. Digging it out of her pocket, she ticked off possible callers. Loretta was safely in school. She'd already talked to Pris about the reception food and Gracie about the gown. Jax should be safely in his office. Finally retrieving it, she glanced at the screen—Iddy. Her cousin should have been at the farm, bull babysitting.

"Bull didn't gore anyone?" she asked without preamble after hitting the answer button.

"I had to give him a small dose of sedatives. He really didn't like old Roy." Iddy spoke crisply, as if in a hurry. "I have to get back to the office and help Asia. She had to do a Caesarean on a cat and the office is spilling over in preemies. She's in a panic, and I don't want to lose her already, so I have to call in our volunteers. But keep an eye on Roy. The bull smells blood when he's around."

"Ouch, not good, on both counts. Don't tell Loretta about the preemies." Evie snapped on her seatbelt thinking Iddy would make a far better mother than she ever would. "Anyone else to be wary of?"

"Betty is here, looking pale and acting paranoid. She and Mackie had a major brawl, screaming and accusations and all. Guess she got word that she's off the film. She's sulking in her trailer now, and Mackie has retreated to the farmhouse."

"I should bring popcorn," Evie said, unconcerned by human wrangling. She wished she'd been there to hear Sandra's take on the excitement. But she'd promised Jax not to run her batteries down too much, so she was waiting for the auditions. "Where's Cade?"

"In the farmhouse with Wright and Mackie, presumably arguing over money. Gotta go. Stay in the loft and out of range. I expect pitchforks before dawn." Iddy clicked off.

Pris had already called about delivering lunches to the farm, so Evie stopped and loaded up. It made a good excuse for her to be on the set. She'd find a hiding place in the barn while everyone was scarfing sandwiches.

The Mad Café was predictably mad at lunchtime. Dante helped her load up the car. She could tell by his aura that he needed to talk, and she could guess why, so she lingered. "You and Pris planning on returning to Italy after my wedding?"

She loved the way a confident man could be reduced to panic by mundane concerns like women and babies.

He slammed the wagon's door shut and leaned against the car. "I thought we were. She's training a cook in her recipes. But she's acting weird. Do you know why?"

"Yup." Evie tried hard not to laugh at the poor guy. What did intellectual scientists know about human nature? "You and Pris are a pair. Neither of you communicate. I'm not sure how you ever got each other in bed. At some point, you had to talk, right?"

He looked uncomfortable. "Not necessarily."

She did laugh then. "OK, He-man, move past Neanderthal to the stage that talks. Tell her how you feel about her and what you want. Ask her what *she* wants. Simple questions. You can do it."

"I'll have to drag her out of the kitchen first. The twins need to start school in the fall. We have to decide *something*." He straightened but still looked harassed.

"Then maybe you should decide how *you* feel before you talk. Send the kids over to us and take a night off. You're family. We look after each other." She climbed into the front seat while he crossed his arms and frowned.

He nodded curtly and returned to the café, a man with a future to decide. Stupid Pris, not simply telling him flat out.

Playing scenarios of how she'd tell Jax she was pregnant, if she ever was, Evie amused herself rather than worry about what she'd find on the farm. She had no stake in this film, but she thought Cade might have more than he admitted. And Iddy. . . needed a good man like Cade.

She and Iddy were vast worlds apart in many things, but Evie had practically hung haloes on her older cousin when she was a kid. Any person who could talk to her pets was a saint in her books. It had been Iddy who had first given her a job as a dogwalker, so Evie could pretend to be useful while looking for who she wanted to be.

With all her brains and education, Iddy deserved more than a run-down trailer and working herself to death.

She stopped at the veterinary office and dropped off lunches—Iddy had been hired by the film company, after all. She was crew too.

Asia, the new grad, was in the front, wearing a white lab coat with a colorful scarf wrapped as a turban over her short kinky hair. She held a baby pig and stroked its head while talking slowly to a worried young man who appeared to understand her thick speech just fine. Evie left the lunches, waved, and continued on her path.

Who would have thought a year ago that she'd be paid for her favorite pastime—being nosy? Was there a career description called Professional Observer?

Reuben and Roark had no excuse for being on the set today, so she was on her own. She couldn't convince all the big strong men in her life that she was pretty invisible to most people. She had to work at being noticed by wearing outrageous colors and T-shirts and letting her orange hair explode. Today, she had her hair pinned under a ball cap, wore frayed cut-off jeans and a denim shirt over her pink T-shirt. She strolled down the drive, arms loaded with bags, and no one even stopped to help—invisible delivery person.

The bespectacled man she thought was Brice Kennedy, the almost-famous director, stood in the paddock, arguing with Roy O'Bryan, the old but still handsome cowboy actor that Iddy had warned her smelled of blood.

The goats were running free, climbing on hay bales and leaping over the fence with no one paying attention to them either. Evie held her bags up high, away from nipping teeth, and walked in the front door after only a brief knock.

Cade noticed her immediately. Smart man. He'd be good for Iddy. He quit arguing with the bandy-legged little man with the shady aura and strode over to help her. "Did you leave lunches with Iddy? I ordered enough for everyone. She's working too hard."

Evie smiled in delight. "Glad you noticed because that was my first stop. I figured the Hollywood types didn't eat anyway."

"No beauty queens here. This crew will scarf anything free. The budget's too tight to offer a catering truck for the people showing up for auditions, so I figured we should stuff our faces before they arrive." As if to prove his point, men began crowding around, grabbing the sacks, and heading off in different directions.

Evie tried to put a name to each person. Unlike ghosts, she was fairly good at names, although she preferred nicknames. The ephemeral essences she dealt with seemed to relate better to emotions or character than to meaningless appellations. Wayne Wright, the production assistant, was the banty rooster. He elbowed his way through the crowd to take a sack down the hallway, presumably to Mackie, who wasn't in sight.

Parker, the long-haired, graying hoodlum and film director, took his box outside. He didn't seem very sociable. The three men staying in the house, the surfer and the two Steves, plopped down on the sagging couch and debated some game they'd watched. The director and the actor hadn't followed her in, so they had to still be outside arguing. Would they notice if she slipped into the barn?

Ray Anne entered through the kitchen door and brightened at sight of Evie. "You come with me and see Betty. She is doing much better."

"Good to hear." Evie patted Cade on the arm. "If I vanish, you'll know where."

He looked a little taken aback, but the poor clueless man was worse than Dante. He'd learn, eventually, if he stayed long enough. His colors were shifting, as if he might be going through some changes.

She followed Ray Anne back to the little trailer, where Betty sat outside on the step. The late April heat was probably building inside the tin can trailer. Window air conditioning couldn't defeat the humidity.

"I'm glad you're feeling better," Evie called cheerfully, carrying her own lunch. "Ray Anne was really worried about you the other day. I would have had two heart attacks and fallen over the side if I'd been up there in that wind."

The small blonde actress put on her best face and smiled graciously. Her aura said something completely different, but Evie got that a lot.

"Altitude sickness," Betty said dismissively. "There's nothing wrong with me. These old fossils simply behave as if women are made of feathers."

Evie was pretty certain altitude sickness required a few thousand more feet than the height of the courthouse, but she wasn't here to argue. She was here to hide in the loft with ghosts. "That's how we southern girls wrap men around our fingers—they'll do anything to keep us from weeping and fainting. So much simpler than arguing."

Ray Anne looked worried. Betty actually brightened a little. "Mackie doesn't notice any female over the age of twenty-five, but Wright, now. . ." She frowned again. "But that bastard Garcia says the insurance company wants more money, and the budget won't allow it. They're bringing in sweet young things who aren't union and will work for nothing."

"But you're the animal expert," Evie said cheerfully. "They have to pay you for your expertise. Talk to Mr. Wright, tell him he can film you sitting in a chair, surrounded by books, looking professional. I bet that doesn't need insurance." She was totally making that up.

But Betty already had her phone out, and Ray Anne was smiling again.

"I want to say hi to the horse." Evie tucked her lunchbox under her arm and spoke to Betty's assistant. "Want to walk over with me while Betty negotiates?"

"The horse misses the dog," Ray Anne said, taking one last look at her employer to be certain she didn't mind. "And maybe it misses Sandra? It makes sad sounds."

"We're trying to find the place where Sandra meant to take the mare. She brought it all the way out here for a reason." Evie stepped into the dim barn and oriented herself. Sandra's ghost didn't immediately appear. The animals weren't pounding on their stalls. It seemed safe enough.

They settled on hay bales to nibble at Pris's quiche and fruit salad. She was going all out for the film crew that had probably made her reputation in one day. They even rated plasticware today.

"Sandra had a girlfriend with a farm," Ray Anne reported, tasting the salad. "We thought that was where she went the night she disappeared, to fetch a horse van."

"But she didn't tell you her friend's name? The only number we can find says they've never heard of her." Evie kept a wary eye for auras in the dust-motes dancing in the sunlight through the open doors. She couldn't eat and hang onto pitchforks at the same time.

"Zoe, maybe?" Ray Anne screwed up her broad brow in thought. "We didn't talk much."

Zoe. She needed more. "Oh, I thought maybe you were the friend who gave her some of those cosmetics in her bag. I drooled in envy," Evie blithely lied. She'd managed mascara a few times, but she usually poked herself in the eye and came out looking like a raccoon.

"Betty gave Sandra samples for running errands. Companies give the studio cosmetics all the time as advertisement, you know? She felt sorry for Sandra, who lost all her money and jobs because of one lying man." Ray Anne's face shuttered. "I should not talk like this."

Evie shrugged and picked up her quiche slice with her fingers. "We all know about lying men. I heard she lost her ranch. A lying man almost scammed my aunt out of everything she owned last year." That was actually almost truth, except Pris had stopped the scam with the help of Evie's team.

Ray Anne nodded vigorously. "Men are scum. Mackie is being sued by almost every woman he's ever worked with. And I hear another is about to join the suit. Sandra said this one has evidence that will put him behind bars. We are all hoping Mr. Kennedy will take over the studio when he is gone."

Evie itched to text Jax with this news but she refrained. Sometimes, talking to people was almost as good as ghosts, and this way, she learned names. *Sometimes.* "I don't read Hollywood news. Any famous people I might know involved in this suit?"

"No, not really, I don't think so. Wannabes and newcomers mostly. Everyone else knows what he is and keeps their distance. That's why only old ladies like Betty will work with him." She looked worried again. "It is not good to send new ones to audition."

Oh, feces. Evie had set up Aunt Val's wannabes with a predator. Duh, Evie, she should have known that. "Well, they'll all be out here and surrounded by people, so that's all right."

Ray Ann shrugged. "He'll find a way to take them in the house. They should not pull Betty from the part."

"Any of the men willing to keep him from doing that?" Evie wished she was a trained investigator. She had no idea how to interrogate except by gossip.

"Maybe Mr. Kennedy. He and Mackie fight all the time. Betty will be there. I should go back to her." Ray Anne stood, wiping lemon cookie crumbs off her tailored linen.

"You take care of yourself now, y'heah?" Evie said absently. Ray Anne waved acknowledgement and wandered off.

With the barn empty, Evie stacked hay bales in front of the phone charger plug near the front entrance, found a stool, and settled in, safely hidden, with her phone fully charged. With this much battery power, it should be interesting to see if she could video with her phone while talking to a ghost.

She had texted R&R and Jax with her meager information by the time she heard the first voices headed her way. She peered through the crack in her bales.

Before she could identify the men, the pig pen opened and the chickens flew from their roost, squawking. Betty George was no animal expert if she'd been the one to install all the animals in the barn instead of outside, where they belonged. Although Evie thought she recalled that Sandra had been responsible for the setup.

"I will not be blackmailed by the likes of those jackals!" a deep male voice semi-shouted.

Evie admired the way he could say it without actually shouting. An actor?

"All they can do is bring the news crews in. Good publicity." She was almost certain the dry irony came from the stooped and bespectacled director.

"I want this kept undercover until this countersuit is in motion. I'm tired of being the victim. I don't like bringing all these strangers onto the set. Just take the first one who looks the part and doesn't stumble over her lines." A rotund shadow nearly filled the wide front entrance of the barn.

"Or isn't afraid of ghosts or sheep or. . ." The dry voice let that sentence dangle as he entered the dim interior to the bleating of ghosts and cackle of chickens. "Betty wants to remain the official expert. We can sit her on a hay bale and let sheep nibble her toes."

"I want that damned woman off the set!" Definitely Mackie shouting.

Before Evie could react, a rake flew off the wall, followed by the pitchfork. The toolbox opened and a hammer and screwdriver joined the aeronautical acrobatics. Caught by surprise, the men ducked and dodged.

Sandra must have been some action figure when she was alive. That was a lot of coordination and strength, if not the world's greatest aim.

Evie winced as the hammer whacked Mackie in the head.

Seventeen

"*Tio*, you are mad to have insured this film." Cade paced on the far side of the front paddock, out of range of the people gathering for the audition. "Mackie is paying no attention. Someone is attempting to sabotage the production. Betty is refusing to walk away. She has her lawyer and agent screaming bloody murder. And now they're bringing in locals to play Betty's part. We're already over budget."

Mackie had staggered in earlier, yelling about liability issues and flying hammers. Cade had verified there was no blood, he didn't need an ambulance, and left Wright to placate him.

Cade was ready to believe in Sandra's ghost if he bought into Mackie being attacked by flying hammers. More likely, Betty hid in the hayloft and flung hard objects at him.

"Just do what you can, *hijo*." His uncle used his best reassuring salesman voice. "It is a very short film. Keep them out of trouble for another week and a half, and we'll be fine."

Cade snarled. "I'd have to tie them all up. Betty and Wright have been tippling already, and it's just past noon. Kennedy and Mackie appear ready to kill each other. I'm not a lion tamer or circus ring master. If anyone else dies, it is on your head."

His uncle sounded a little more worried. "Surely, that will not happen. You just find out what happened to Sandra."

How the hell was he supposed to do that if the police couldn't? Rely on ghosts and psychics? How much did he really owe his uncle?

A lot. Growling, Cade shoved his phone in his pocket. His father would have lost the farm, and his siblings would have ended up in foster care, had Uncle Enrique not stepped in. Cade hadn't even graduated high school when his father literally drove off a cliff.

Clenching his molars, he watched all the excited wannabes climbing out of their various vehicles. He muttered obscenities when a news van rolled up, and Brice Kennedy went out to meet it. Who wanted media following this fiasco? He'd never understand this business.

Iddy drove up in her truck. He was afraid she'd see all the vehicles and flee. His insides surprisingly churned in rejection of that thought. He needed another sane person here. He loped toward the drive and caught sight of the damned runaway pigs at the same time as Iddy did. She blocked the drive and climbed out.

"How are the pigs escaping?" she asked in exasperation, rooting in her truck for whatever she needed to lure them out of the garbage can they'd overturned.

"Same way the goats escaped from behind locked doors earlier, I assume. I made Darren help me round up the goats, and he's no longer speaking to me. Maybe this is his way of getting revenge."

"Domestic pigs don't herd." She produced a couple of long wooden paddles from the truck and handed him one. "They don't see well, so they don't travel far. That trash can doesn't belong out here. Someone tipped it over and let the pigs follow it." She sounded half irritated and half amused.

Following her lead, Cade slowly rolled the can toward the paddock, shooing the three little piggies with temptation and the paddle she handed him. "Give me a wild stallion any day," he muttered.

She laughed at his ill humor. It almost brightened his grim mood.

"May I help?" One of the newly arrived wannabes wandered over. Wearing rhinestone-studded denim—shades of Sandra—and red top clinging to bounteous curves, she rolled the can and made smooching noises the pigs followed.

"You've handled swine before," Iddy said appreciatively.

"Oh yeah. You can take the girl out of the farm and all that." Dyed blond, wearing expertly applied makeup, she wasn't on the farm these days.

"I'm Iddy Malcolm, the wrangler for this production. You here for the audition?"

Cade could almost hear the speculation in her voice. Cars were starting to line up on the drive blocked by her Tahoe. She ignored them in favor of leading the pigs to the safety of fences. The lady had focus—and a serious lack of respect for time and film production.

"Zoe David, glad to meet you. I heard about the audition and thought, since I know animals, I might be a good fit." She made more kissing noises and unabashedly waved a chicken bone under the lead porker's nose.

Zoe? Wasn't that the name Evie had just texted them? The one Ray Anne thought might be Sandra's friend? How many Zoes would there be around here?

By now, the pig parade had attracted an audience. Most of the cast and crew settled on the porch to watch and cackle. Parker, the film director, pointed his camera. Even the news crew was filming. Mackie stepped out for a moment, turned purple, and stormed back inside, slamming the door. *Interesting.*

Not to be outdone, Betty strolled down to join them—and put her face on the news. Cade figured she was operating on liquid courage when she held out her hand for Iddy's paddle.

Grinning, the incorrigible vet handed it over. "I'll move my truck. If you'll wave that smelly wrapper, this little piggie will follow you anywhere." She jogged off, leaving the movie star holding a paddle and the remains of someone's ham sandwich.

Surfer boy Darren was the only one with sense enough to open the gate, so maybe he wasn't harboring a grudge. Cade kicked the can through and nudged Piggy #3 to trot after it.

"Pig stalker," Wayne Wright called from the porch. "Where's your hat, cowboy?"

Cade had heard it all long ago. He'd learned to ignore verbal bullies. He was big. He could wring the neck of a tame chicken like Wright with one hand. Busting his nose had no appeal. Mackie now— He'd stay away from Mackie, or he'd probably kill the filth.

After moving her vehicle, Iddy jogged back, and a stream of new arrivals hunted for parking. Evie's Aunt Val obviously cast a wide net.

"Do I have a vote in who's hired?" Iddy asked, a little too perkily.

Betty apparently heard. She frowned briefly then plastered on a smile. "I'll cast my vote with yours, Miss Malcolm. We experts should stick together."

Carrying his lunch box and noshing on the contents, Roy O'Bryan joined them. He snorted but didn't comment. "Mackie wants to start the auditions. Kennedy is setting up the shoot in back. Writers got you sitting on a fence, Bets. Better go on back." He gestured with a plastic fork.

Betty handed Cade the smelly wrapper, chirped a cheery farewell, and set off through the barn. Roy trotted on her heels. A couple of the contestants and Parker followed, although he'd turned off the camera. Rhinestone Girl waved and trotted in their wake. Scowling, Wright climbed off the porch and brought up the rear, keeping the sweet young things away from Mackie?

"Ego isn't pretty," Iddy murmured as Cade nudged the last pink rear end through the gate and slammed it.

Cade had the strongest urge to kiss Iddy—the only down-to-earth sane person currently occupying his planet. With some of the idle crew still watching, he resisted.

Finishing off a sandwich, Darren ushered the remaining wannabes through the house—where Mackie was.

Cade nodded after them. "I have to keep Mackie away from the wannabes."

She grinned. "You tackle the old goat. I'll look after the young ones. Are they still in the barn?"

"Unless your ghost let them out. This crew usually avoids the animals. They're all yours to wrangle." Cade abandoned her to the real animals and set off to deal with the human ones.

He didn't need the complication of a woman like the vet. She positively screamed *marrying kind* and *never leaving town* kind. He'd worked hard for going on twenty years. He'd raised a family already. Once he finished this job, he was finally seeing the world.

Inside the farmhouse, Cade saw no sign of Mackie. He asked one of the Steves, who nodded at the hall to the bedrooms. "He's claimed Sandra's room. He's yelling at people from there."

Cade strode back, heard the producer hollering and no one talking back, and left him alone with his phone.

He wanted to see if anyone else had a reaction to Zoe, so he continued through the kitchen and out on the back porch.

The other wannabes were milling about, trying to follow Kennedy's directions as to what order they should line up. The back of Cade's neck prickled, but he couldn't pinpoint a reason.

Wayne Wright, Mackie's assistant, wasn't in sight. Maybe that's what bothered him. He didn't trust him any more than he trusted Mackie, which was not at all. Wright had followed Betty through the barn. . . But Roy, Parker, Zoe, Iddy and a few others had trailed right behind them. He'd thought they were headed out here.

Fighting a sense of wrongness, he jogged down the steps, past the milling contestants and the bull, and entered the barn just as a gun shot rang out and Betty started screaming. A second shot barked.

Cade went down before he knew what hit him.

~

BETTY SCREAMED HYSTERICALLY AS CADE'S BIG BODY CRUMPLED TO THE HARD ground. Iddy wanted to scream with her. As if his collapse was a signal, the tableau in the barn unfroze.

Parker, the cameraman, tackled Mackie's bandy-legged assistant, knocking him flat, sending Wright's gun skittering across the barn dirt. Zoe stomped on it.

Iddy ran to Cade. She didn't realize she'd stopped breathing until she saw him move. Dropping to her knees, she thwarted his effort to sit by shoving both hands against his broad chest. "Don't. I need to stop the bleeding. Lie still."

She could hear one of the terrified wannabes calling the police. Good, at least someone in this clown production had a little sense. "Tell them we need a doctor," she shouted.

Blood poured from Cade's shoulder. She wasn't wearing her white coat. She didn't have her bag. She used the front of his shirt to hold over the wound while she frantically glanced around in futile search of a medical kit. She could feel his heart beating his blood right out of his body. She knew how to do this with a dog. She'd never worked on bullets in people.

Evie popped out from behind a haystack wearing a sleeveless denim vest buttoned over nothing. She held out the pink T-shirt she'd been wearing. "I put it on clean this morning. Will this do?"

Her cousin looked a little worse for wear. If what Iddy had seen meant anything, the ghost was running her ragged. At least Evie wasn't completely drained—yet. Iddy gratefully accepted the offering and added it to the compress she had formed with Cade's shirt tails. "Make the fools run in the house for a first-aid kit or bandages or anything!"

She was pretty certain Evie was texting her team, but they weren't trained medics. They wouldn't be far down the road, so Iddy hoped they'd take over whatever in heck was happening here.

As if he heard her thoughts, Cade muttered, "Don't let anyone leave!"

Yeah, like that was happening with this lot. She couldn't count on any of them. Cade was the only reliable person on the whole damned farm, and he was down for the count. Ding-dong-*dang*.

"Kennedy," Cade squeezed through teeth clenched in pain. "He'll cooperate."

"Betty," Iddy shouted. "Shut up and call Kennedy in here. Don't anyone leave!"

The Zoe person had handed Parker a leather harness to use in tying up Wright. Iddy had the notion that Wright wasn't entirely responsible for his actions. She'd have to ask Evie what she saw. . . some other time. Right now, she was trying to breathe and not panic.

"I'll live," Cade murmured huskily. "Quit looking like that. You'll frighten the goats."

She tried to laugh and couldn't. His blood poured through two shirts. She pressed harder, using the heel of both hands.

She lost track of events about then. Kennedy ran in the back door. Evie's team ran in the front. Sirens roared down the highway. Evie returned, wearing someone's overlarge denim shirt over her skin-revealing vest and carrying a first-aid bag. Iddy had her open it and ignored the rest of the commotion.

Without Betty's screaming, the tense crowd seemed unusually quiet. Iddy peeled back the shirt bandage and dumped disinfectant over the wound she could see. She didn't think the bullet had gone out the back. She took the gauze bandages Evie ripped open for her and pressed hard, swearing under her breath. Cade sung some foolish counting chant under his breath, apparently trying to numb excruciating pain with nonsense.

"One potato?" she asked, trying to distract herself. "Is this how you teach your kids to count?"

"Sister, when she was small. She didn't like numbers."

He passed out then, and she started hyperventilating.

Evie dragged a half-naked Reuben over to help with taping Cade up. So that's where she'd got the denim cover-up.

They had the bleeding slowed down by the time the sheriff arrived with a local physician. Afterthought had no hospital, just a clinic and a medic working with the volunteer fire department. The doctors made emergency calls in place of ambulances.

"The bullet is probably still in him," she told the GP. "I only had dirty shirts to staunch the wound."

The doctor ordered Reuben and Roark to lift the patient on a stretcher and carry him back to his SUV. "I'll take a look at the clinic and let you know if he needs surgery," he said curtly before following them out.

Iddy wanted to race after them, but she was a vet and no more. She buried her face against her crossed arms braced on her knees and tried to control her breathing. *One potato, two potato. . .*

Evie patted her on the shoulder. "Our mothers are headed to the clinic. They kept us alive all these years."

Iddy nodded. "I know, I know." She conjured an image of her mother swinging an amulet over Cade when he woke and almost smiled. Evie's mother would be sprinkling the room with sage and rubbing compounds into the bandages. He'd freak. "We probably ought to rescue him."

"Doc won't let them into the surgery room. He's good for a while. Better talk to Sheriff Troy. He's looking seriously unhappy. You know how he gets when I tell him the ghost did it."

Iddy did let out a laugh then. "Poor Troy." Filling her lungs with musty barn air, she made herself stand and study the situation she'd been ignoring.

Wright was still trussed up on the floor, rolling about and muttering that he didn't do it—even though Iddy was fairly confident he'd been the one holding the gun that went off both times.

Reuben was staring at his phone, possibly studying video from the cameras he'd planted on the ceiling. Roark seemed to be hunting bullet holes, guided by Zoe, who helpfully acted out the whole scene. Reuben corrected them, pointing at a post over by the mare's stall.

Wright could have shot the animals! They weren't acting out for a change, but Iddy strode from stall to stall, petting, handfeeding, testing to make certain the commotion wasn't disturbing them. From their minds, she received an odd sensation that Evie's ghost was doing the same.

Sheriff Troy had Mena with him, and they were both taking statements. No longer screaming, Betty was happily following Zoe and acting out the whole scene.

Zoe was the one the sheriff should be talking to.

Swearing he hadn't been filming, Parker handed his camera over to Mena anyway.

"Where's the news crew?" Iddy whispered, returning to Evie's side.

"Wright closed the door when he came in, remember?" Evie sat on a hay bale, looking pale, and munching a cookie for energy. "Parker had to unbolt it to let the sheriff in. Someone outside must be blocking reporters. Are you okay now? Can you tell the sheriff what you saw Wright do so he won't think I'm nuts?"

Iddy nodded. "I'll try. How are you feeling? You're looking a little stronger."

"I had the phone plugged into a charger," she said triumphantly. "I think Sandra fed off that instead of me. Or the phone helped keep me charged. No clue. I'm good."

"May I return to conducting these auditions?" Brice Kennedy said stiffly after his interview with Troy. "I'll need the rest of the participants if you're done with them."

Troy waved a dismissive hand. "I have everyone's name and number. I'll let you know if I need more."

Iddy supposed this wasn't exactly a murder investigation. Everyone had seen Mackie's right-hand man with the gun.

She trotted over to tell Troy not to release Zoe yet.

Iddy hoped R&R's video had caught Wright pointing the gun and shouting at Zoe to get the hell off the property—before Evie's poltergeist whacked him with a crowbar.

By Wednesday evening, Cade had been installed in the servant's bedroom off Evie's kitchen. That meant the whole Malcolm parade had gathered there to argue over the best care for the patient.

Jax was attempting to juggle three conversations at once and keep brooms from flying, when the Victorian's brass knocker banged loud enough to be heard over the shouting. Abandoning the futile quarrel, Jax headed for the front, wishing for the umpteenth time that Evie would allow him to install a camera over the door. She'd warned him the ghosts would just mess with it, and idiot that he was, he believed her, even though he knew she was fully capable of messing with him for her own purposes.

That was probably one of the many reasons he loved her. He loved a good puzzle and a challenge, and Evie was the best one ever. He'd never quite made the transition from war in Afghanistan to a desk job in a law office. With Evie, his life could be both exciting and useful, although there were times when safety was still an issue.

He peered out the side windows but didn't recognize their visitor—a big man, as tall as Cade, a native brown, black hair graying at the temples. . . The black hair hung down a broad back in a thick braid. Jax had a feeling the women wouldn't like this surprise.

He opened the door anyway. Ever curious, he waited.

"Slate Cooper," Iddy's father growled. "Is my daughter here?"

"And your wife and Caden Garcia and probably the circus if you wait around. Are you sure you want to come in?" Never let it be said that he was unadventurous.

"No, probably not. But Garcia's uncle is about to cut my throat, so I'm here." He grudgingly stepped in and looked around the eccentric foyer. Nick, the Brit antique expert, had assured them that the armoire serving as a hall closet was a priceless collector's item, even if it was covered with sticky notes and a bulletin board.

Ahead of them, Loretta had been testing stair rail decorations for the wedding. The scuffed and battered mahogany was hung with ivy, magnolias, ribbons, and anything else his about-to-be daughter could find in the attic.

To a visitor's right, an arched doorway opened into a parlor cluttered with the most gawdawful collection of tables and chairs any hoarder could gather.

To the left, the library looked almost sane these days. The walls were a plain cream instead of wallpapered in orange foil like some of the bedrooms. Evie's sister had added airy midcentury modern shelves between the front windows and crammed them with books Gauzy curtains now covered the old-fashioned panes. The library table. . . was currently covered in wedding projects. Perfection did not happen here.

Cooper grunted. "I always imagined a hoity-toity lace-and-flowers place, with polished silver everywhere. The old lady never let me in."

Probably rightly so. Jax never had heard the whole story and didn't ask now. Thirty years ago, Evie's Great-Aunt Val probably still lived here. She was a terror. "You want to wait here while I fetch Iddy? Cade's been told to rest. He had some blood loss." And a chipped bone and a torn muscle, but those were Cade's tale to tell.

"I'd rather cut my own throat then go back in that nest of biddies. If Cade can't come out. . ." He sighed in reluctance. "Send Iddy or her mother. One hex at a time."

"Hide in the library." Jax nodded to the cluttered room. "Close the door. Maybe lean against it. I'll see if I can pry one loose without the others. I make no promises."

Evie was waiting for him before he even reached the kitchen. "They know. You can't hide anything from the *Tres Madres*. I threw them out the back and threatened to call Troy if they come in the front. You might want to move the wardrobe in front of it. Bring him back here and I'll stand guard with an ice pick."

"You have an ice pick?" He really didn't need to ask. The house had everything anyone had invented in the last hundred years or more. He leaned over and kissed her. "I'll be right back."

He returned to the front, threw all the bolts he'd installed because everyone had a key, and knocked on the library door. "They're on the warpath. Is that culturally insensitive?"

Slate opened the heavy panel and shot him an unhappy look. "They knew?"

"They knew. You can't do anything in this town without the coven knowing. The wind probably whispered your arrival. Black clouds flew across the horizon. The raven circled. Evie threw out the mothers. I've bolted the front. Evie's guarding the back. Give me a minute to see what Iddy and Cade want to do."

What he'd really like to know was what Cade's uncle held over Slate Cooper to make him fly across the country to check on him. Jax texted R&R with questions.

CADE WATCHED IN DETACHED SURPRISE AS IDDY'S MOTHER HURRIEDLY HANDED HIM A healing amulet and charged out in a flutter of gray hair and billowing tunic. Evie's mother departed immediately after, leaving an herbal candle burning, and the other aunt stopped her incantation, apparently to join her sisters in. . . warfare? Evie spoke sharply from the kitchen.

Paying no attention to the drama, Iddy paced his tiny bedroom with the Siamese cat on her shoulder and the schnauzer puppy on her heels.

"Did I say something wrong?" His head still wasn't completely on tight after blood loss and anesthesia. His shoulder throbbed, but he didn't think that should impact his thought processes.

Black hair as lovely as a raven's wing spilled over the vet's shoulder and down her breasts as she offered a wry smile. "They know who's at the door. If I'm reading La Chusa right, we have an unwelcome and unexpected visitor."

His murky brain couldn't process the connections until Jax arrived.

"I've stored Slate Cooper in the library. I can send him away if you prefer, but Cade's uncle sent him. He wants to talk to one of you."

Cade didn't wonder how Slate could have arrived so quickly. Mackie had a private jet and his uncle Enrique had the producer by the balls.

"My uncle is next of kin. The doctor's office called him." Cade winced as he sat up a little straighter. Knowing Iddy's feelings about Slate, he studied her. "Your dad, your call. I don't know him well."

She shrugged. "He's a liar and lacks integrity, but he's not dangerous to anyone but my mother."

"Your mother and aunts appear strong enough to blow him into the next state." Cade wasn't coping well with this weirdness. If he could set them all on a spreadsheet and sort through everything he'd seen today—he'd probably have to commit himself to an institution. "Bring him back here?"

She frowned but didn't flee. Instead, she held the Siamese up to her face, studied it, then set it on his pillow. "Psycat will scare him if he's obnoxious."

Right. One more line item on his chart to the madhouse. He really needed to talk about what had happened in the barn. He just didn't know if he should talk to Jax, the women, or a psychiatrist.

Jax returned with a large man in his late fifties. Hollywood was filled with characters who looked like they'd walked off an old Western movie, so Cade had never thought twice about Slate Cooper. Seeing through Iddy's eyes now. . . He saw the man who had given Iddy her good looks and height, but probably none of her character traits.

"Cooper." Cade acknowledged his entrance, although his visitor was more interested in Iddy.

"Your uncle is disinclined to believe whoever he talked to here. He says this is all my fault, so I'd better see if you need to come home." Slate reluctantly turned his attention from his daughter to Cade. "You want to shut down Mackie?"

Yeah, he wanted to shut down Mackie but not because of himself.

Iddy answered before he could. "You don't ask a surgery patient questions like that until the anesthesia has completely left his system."

Cade liked that excuse. He had this weird notion the barn shooting was only partially about Mackie. He couldn't shrug his indifference without shooting agony through his shoulder and back, so he just frowned. "Mackie needs to be permanently shut down. Enrique is delaying the inevitable."

"No, he's not." Since no one offered him a chair, Slate loomed in the doorway. "Mackie's here because he's hiding another lawsuit. He plans on countersuing the plaintiff for defamation. If he wins, he'll have grounds to throw out the class action suit."

"We need Jax to translate," Iddy said in irritation, perching at the foot of his bed and petting the puppy.

The cat practically wrapped around Cade's good shoulder. "It's okay, I understand what he's saying." Although it lent a whole new perspective to events that he wasn't in any condition to sort out. "How was Sandra involved?"

"She knew the plaintiff. They're friends. I thought I was doing a good thing by telling her she'd find sympathetic supporters for her friend's case in Afterthought. It's close to her home and her friend. Between us, we pulled a few strings, turned Mackie this way."

"That doesn't explain why my uncle agreed to insure this madness. What did you think Sandra could do? Stop Mackie's countersuit? She might as well try to stop a tank." Cade still wasn't making connections.

From her frown, neither was Iddy. So maybe her father was fuzzy, not him.

"I can't speak for your uncle, but a whole lot of us want to see Mackie hoist by his own petard. That can't be done if he's holed up inside his fortress. We wanted Sandra safe if she insisted on working for him. Mackie was looking for a small town where the big reporters wouldn't go. I knew your mayor was hungry for film crews, so I suggested here." Slate shrugged his massive shoulders. "I was wrong."

"My family didn't know Sandra was here," Iddy pointed out. "Did you give her our names? Communication helps."

Cade admired how she managed to criticize without actually laying blame. He should set her on his uncle. "For what it's worth, Sandra always worked her own side gigs. Helping a friend, getting Mackie to move her animals, those were just gravy. She was making money off almost everyone on the set and probably didn't want outside interference."

"Yeah, I got some of that. Maybe she pulled your uncle's strings." Slate shrugged and studied his daughter.

Cade entertained a woozy hallucination about the schnauzer responding to Iddy's mental command when it jumped down to sniff Slate's expensive heels and squat. Iddy snapped her fingers and stopped the puppy with a simple, "No, Morrigan."

Apparently, he was the one with anger issues, not the vet.

The braided big man moved his boots away. "So, I can tell your uncle you'll live?" He backed toward the door.

Cade heard Iddy's raven cawing in the kitchen. Not all the windows had screens—apparently for a reason.

"I'll live," Cade agreed. "I may not be on top of Mackie every minute. And after learning about this new lawsuit, I may quit and feed the whole business to reporters. Tell my uncle he'd better start talking to me pronto."

Iddy stood. "La Chusa tells me my mother and aunts are setting up an ambush in front. Let Evie show you how to leave through the back. You'll have to return for your car later."

"La Chusa?" Her father glanced over his shoulder, presumably at the raven in the kitchen Cade couldn't see.

"Your call whether you want to listen or not." Her river of hair rippled with her shrug.

"Where are you staying?" Cade asked, too wiped for a family fight.

"Hadn't planned to." Slate nodded at his daughter. "Look after your mother."

He walked out. They could hear him in the kitchen with Evie, and from the sounds of it, Loretta.

"How can I hate an imaginary figure?" Iddy asked, not following to say farewell.

"Hate's corrosive anyway," Cade assured her, while wondering how any father could abandon a daughter any man would be proud to claim.

Looking weary, she nodded, and Cade had the insane urge to comfort her, not that he could with his shoulder wrapped like a mummy. He'd brought all this down on her. He ought to be like her father, acknowledge his faults, and bow out.

He knew his brain was fuzzed when he realized he didn't want to leave.

Evie popped into the open doorway. "Battle planning required. Zoom or I bring everyone in here?"

That's what he needed to get out of this sentimental funk. Cade threw back his covers. "Beer. Food. Kitchen."

Iddy flung a shirt at him before he realized he was in pajama bottoms—not his—and nothing else.

"You're on painkillers and antibiotics. No beer."

There was a good reason to rebuild that wall between them. No one had told him what to do in decades.

"Coffee," he countered, pulling on one sleeve and draping the other over his shoulder. "Lots of coffee. I want this case nailed so I can get on with my life."

The cat and dog snarled and left the room. Charming. He would not believe that was Iddy's opinion of him.

Nineteen

"YOUR DADDY'S BUBBLE IS SHRIVELED AND BLUE," LORETTA SAID SYMPATHETICALLY AS Iddy tossed her raven out the window.

"Too much pride and vanity in his aura," Evie concluded, fixing fresh coffee to ease them through an explanation none of them would like. "Not a bad man, just one who can't entirely be trusted to do anything that doesn't benefit him."

"Narcissist. Tell me something I don't know. Are the Tres Madres still lurking in the bushes?" Iddy opened the cookie jar.

Evie knew she wouldn't find anything. If sugar was required. . . She removed cookies from the freezer. "Yup. Do we invite them in?"

"No way." The love of Evie's life appeared with R&R in tow, responding to her text. "It's been too long a day to set fire to visitors now."

Leaning wearily against the wall, their patient narrowed his eyes at that remark but remained silent. He'd learn. Eventually. Or maybe not. Exactly what Cade accepted of their family eccentricities, he wasn't communicating, even through his aura.

Evie tossed frozen cookies on a sheet to heat. "Loretta, run on up to bed. You still have school tomorrow. I'll save a cookie for your lunch."

When the kid looked ready to protest, Evie pointed at the door. "Bridesmaid, remember? Red dress, blue boots?"

Loretta grinned, grabbed a frozen cookie, and dashed out.

"Red dress, blue boots?" Iddy settled on a counter stool.

Interestingly, so did Cade. Even unshaven and looking as if he'd been run over by a Mack truck or a Mackie, he was an impressive specimen. They'd thrown a lot at him. A lesser man would have packed up and fled for the peaceful luxury of a hotel in the city.

"Don't tell Gracie, but I'm not into matchy-matchy," Evie explained. "I told Loretta she could choose her own bridesmaid outfit."

"I don't have to wear green?" Iddy sipped the coffee Evie poured for her.

"Not for me. You'd look good in red too." Evie gave Cade her largest mug and pushed the sugar at him. "You'll need energy to survive this."

He grunted and doctored his coffee.

Reuben, Roark, and Jax settled in the booth to show each other the day's videos, attempting to make sense of the senseless.

"OK, Cuz, spill. What exactly happened in the barn that we couldn't see?" Iddy took a bite of cookie and waited with an air of defeat. "Who really shot Cade?"

Evie poured tea for herself. "Sandra did it. You saw Wright stupidly pull a gun on Zoe. I have no idea what that was about. But when he did, Sandra turned a livid red and really walloped his arm with that crowbar. I don't think I've ever seen a ghost strike, but I suppose, if she has the strength to juggle pitchforks and hammers, she can whack an arm Wright isn't strong."

The men in the booth studied the video and nodded. "Flying crowbar and the gun diverts from Zoe to shoot wide," Jax said, scrolling back and forth.

"And then Cade makes the mistake of entering, and Wright freaks and the gun goes off again. Did Sandra do that?" Reuben studied his phone.

"I'm guessing she wore herself out with that first hit," Evie said apologetically, glancing at Cade. "She faded. Wright was shooting at ghosts."

He sipped his coffee with a frown. "So, if I'm believing Sandra saved Zoe, I'm also to believe she didn't care if Wright shot me? Or she didn't care who got hurt?"

"Well, her aura was pure fury. She wasn't exactly operating on rational. Don't expect logic from a vaporous energy operating on leftover resentments. Now, will someone tell me who this Zoe is?" Evie checked the cookies.

Reuben called up a file on his laptop. "Zoe David, owns the boarding farm Sandra called."

"The number where no one admitted to knowing her?" Iddy finally spoke.

"One and the same." Reuben continued reading from the file. "Zoe David, wannabe movie star a few years back. Landed a role in one of Mackie's productions. Quit and walked off but mysteriously had the cash to make a down payment on the farm when she arrived here."

After distributing hot cookies, Evie slid in beside Jax and peered over his shoulder at the file he was reading. No pictures. "How do you go about seeing who is filing a suit against Mackie?"

"Heard that, did you?" Cade asked. "Does anyone know where Zoe went after I was hauled away?"

"She gave a statement to the sheriff and left. Her aura was pretty agitated. Since the gun was aimed at her, she had to have seen the flying crowbar." Evie nibbled her cookie and tried to recall the would-be victim's colors, but she'd been watching Sandra.

Roark read from a file he'd undoubtedly hacked from Troy's computer. The sheriff had never attempted to block the hack, so Evie figured Troy trusted them.

"According to her interview with the sheriff, Zoe says she has no idea why Wright ordered her to leave. She thought he might be deranged. She'd merely been talking to Betty and trying to see the goats they'd be filming."

"I assume the scene wasn't filmed, and Betty's replacement wasn't hired," Cade said gloomily, chomping on his cookie, then examining it to see what he was eating.

"Chocolate chip zucchini," Evie called from the booth. "The squash vines took off and it's not even summer yet."

"Loretta is growing a garden," Iddy explained when he only looked baffled. "It appears she has a green thumb."

"Zucchini cookies." He studied it a second, then finished it off. "I am officially on another planet."

"So is LA," Jax pointed out.

"Zucchini sushi," he muttered. "LA does sushi."

"Better make your point quickly," Iddy warned. "I think Cade's fading fast."

"They filmed the scene using Betty," Reuben told them. "She autographed headshots for the disappointed wannabes."

Cade rubbed his brow. "Do we know anything else about Zoe?"

"Not yet. I have people hunting for a lawsuit against Mackie. I'm adding her name to the keyword search." Jax snapped off half Evie's cookie and nibbled it. "Add cranberries next time. Pretend a bucket of sugar and butter is good for us."

"I ground pecans into them, very healthy. How do I warn the film people to stay out of the barn?"

"Tell them Sandra is haunting it. They're superstitious and stupid enough to believe you," Cade cynically suggested.

Evie threw the other half of her cookie at the back of his head. He didn't even look up.

"If no one goes in the barn to feed the animals, I'll have to go out twice a day to do it," Iddy complained. "I'm not sure you're paying me enough to risk assault by ghost."

"Take me with you." Evie finished her tea and thought about it. "When you're up to it, Cade, you should probably go too. Maybe she'll be frustrated enough to try speaking. She's done it once, although hurling insults and curses isn't helpful."

"Aren't you supposed to interrogate *people* instead of ghosts?" Cade didn't look happy.

"Sheriff will do that, although I'd like to have a long talk with Zoe if the opportunity opens. I didn't have a chance to study her aura." Evie hadn't paid attention to a woman with colors too pragmatic for rhinestone jeans—not until Wright yelled at her anyway.

"Hire Zoe." Iddy carried her cup to the sink. "Call her Betty's understudy. Let her feed the pigs. Sandra must like her."

"She would need accommodations. No budget for understudies." Cade finished his coffee. "Insurance has to cover budget overages. I need to call my uncle and tell him to shut down this debacle. Again."

"He won't, not if he's determined to stop Mackie as my father seems to be insinuating."

"Mackie just let a suit into his hotel suite," Reuben reported, watching his laptop. "Looks like a lawyer to me. You recognize him, Jax?" He turned the screen around.

Evie rubbed Jax's shoulder the instant his aura flared. They'd bugged Mackie's suite? Her guys were going to get arrested one of these days. Maybe they were just looking at the hotel security feed. Was that any better?

Jax studied the image and grimaced. "Yeah, he used to work for my old law firm. This guy is a shark. We fired him for sending an opposition witness back to Cuba. Whoever is Mackie's target doesn't have a chance."

IDDY TOSSED IN HER BED IN EVIE'S SECOND FLOOR GUEST ROOM. SHE GLANCED AT HER phone—after midnight. Maybe she should read a while. Maybe the room was too spacious after her trailer. Evie and Gracie had stripped the awful 70's wallpaper and painted the walls a soothing, misty, gray-blue. Nick had chosen some of the better antiques from the attic to fill it. This was probably how normal people lived.

She wasn't normal, she conceded. She gave in to the mental pull of Psycat and

Evie's puppy and recognized Cade tossing as restlessly as she. He might be feverish.

Getting up, she pulled on the thin robe she'd packed in her one bag and sought Evie's medicine cabinet. Finding acetaminophen tablets, she carried them downstairs, turned on a light over the kitchen sink, and filled a glass with water.

She didn't know how the animals had insinuated themselves into Cade's room, but the door gave when she pushed on it, as old doors sometimes did. She rapped lightly, but no one answered. Morrie yipped softly in greeting.

If she thought of Cade as a surly bear, maybe she could do this. Of course, she'd probably have to tranquilize a bear.

Jax and Evie had finally replaced the child-size twin bed with a regular double bed. Cade more than filled it. Since he was sleeping partially upright, his feet didn't hang over the edge, but it was a near miss.

The instant she tested his forehead, his eyes opened. Thank heavens the kitchen sink light only cast shapes and shadows. "You're feverish," she whispered. "I brought something to help. When did you take the last pain pill?"

"I didn't. I don't do narcotics." He wasn't wearing a shirt and sounded grouchy.

Iddy told herself she was studying his bandage for leakage, but it was difficult to avoid the brown muscled torso it was attached to.

She'd obviously been celibate too long. She held out a couple of tablets and the water glass. "You're better off taking the painkillers, but these will bring the fever down and help you sleep."

Psycat leaped off the bed and padded out. The puppy snuggled happily into the covers piled at the bottom of the bed. Cade was sleeping under a light sheet. Danged good thing she didn't have a light in here. Watching him in the kitchen earlier had her salivating more than Evie's cookies—which was probably why she wasn't sleeping.

"You don't have to nurse me," he said crankily, taking the pills and swallowing before he took the glass.

"The animals worried about you." She hid her smile, knowing he wouldn't appreciate her humor or her comment.

He grunted but didn't argue. "Are they not allowed upstairs?"

"You've met Evie. Do you think she has rules?"

She couldn't read his expression. She gingerly settled on the bed in the region of his hip.

"You believe she's seeing Sandra's ghost?" he asked, as if that might have been what had kept him awake.

Admittedly, knowing a former lover was haunting a barn couldn't lead to pleasant dreams. "I believe that we cannot live without the spirit of life. The more sophisticated the life form, the more animated the spirit and stronger its energy." She'd never bother explaining her beliefs, but she knew animals had spirits just like humans except less complex.

"Fish don't have lively spirits?" he asked in what actually might pass for amusement.

"Exactly. Ants are probably more complicated, but they have a symbiotic relationship with the nest, like bees—the original Borgs, perhaps. They're not human." She hoped he understood scientific terms better than spiritual.

"So, you're saying Sandra was a complex life form, and it's possible her energy can exist without brains and lungs?" He shifted so their hips almost touched.

She preferred to believe the move was accidental, even though it incited thoughts of what was below that sheet—*pajamas*, she told herself. "I'm not Evie. I don't know what she senses or sees. I believe, like any energy, the spiritual energy that animates us simply changes form after our bodies die. I don't think any of us are qualified to say what that form is. It could be a vaporous cloud for all I know. But apparently sometimes—the energy doesn't completely transform."

In the dark quiet of midnight, Iddy found it easier to articulate her thoughts.

"I don't like it," he said resentfully. "Dead should be dead. And if it's not, we should all be able to communicate with the recently passed. I sure could have used a little advice from my parents after they were gone." He found her hand on the mattress and rubbed it absently.

Human touch helped her speak as she usually didn't. She grasped his fingers. "You lost them young?"

"Mother when I was ten. Effectively, my father died then, too, but he managed to physically exist until I was ready to graduate high school. Maybe his spirit went with her before his mind did." He sounded more sleepy than cynical.

She touched his forehead with her free hand. "Rest. Your body requires it to rebuild. The world will wait until morning."

"If someone murdered Sandra, they could be killing someone else right now. How can anyone rest like that?" He slid his pillow down and shifted for a comfortable position.

"La Chusa is watching," she whispered, squeezing his hand.

And so were all the creatures of the night, although he wouldn't believe her. When his hand relaxed, she opened the door to let Psycat back and returned to bed, but not to sleep.

The animals could watch, but they couldn't stop a killing.

$$Twenty$$

THE NEXT MORNING, REFUSING TO LIE IN BED ANOTHER DAY WHILE MACKIE AND HIS crew ran rampant, Cade struggled into a pair of jeans and half a shirt before searching for help in the kitchen. Gritting his teeth at Iddy's lemon-scented proximity as she eased his arm into a short-sleeve shirt, he consoled himself with the knowledge that at least Wright was behind bars.

That didn't distract him from the memory of the slender vet coming to him in the nightmare hours when he questioned every belief he'd ever had. He was pretty certain she hadn't been a dream, but this morning, she displayed none of that tender affection. She was all business. She buttoned his shirt while talking into her earbuds, giving Asia instructions for the day.

Asia could hear on the phone? Voice to text, probably.

He poured coffee. She popped a whole grain bagel from the ancient toaster and offered him half. Lacking avocado, he slathered cream cheese and pesto on his. She nibbled hers dry while she talked.

Judging from the remains in the sink, Evie and Loretta had eaten their cereal and headed for school. He could hear Jax showering upstairs. It wouldn't hurt to learn a little more from the vet—if she'd just get off the phone.

She finally clicked it off and pulled eggs from the harvest-gold refrigerator. Maybe he should gift Evie with a new one in exchange for her hospitality— although stainless steel would look soulless in these colorful surroundings. Behind plates of colorful roosters, the walls were a deep rich red. The red-blue-yellow-green theme carried through curtains and placemats and anything else a kitchen/breakfast area might need. A rainbow kitchen, right. Or in Evie's case, perhaps it was an *aura* kitchen.

"You need protein. How would you like it?" Iddy asked, waving both eggs and bacon at him.

"I can't ask a vegetarian to fix meat." He took the package, debated how he'd open it with one hand, and shoved it back in the fridge. "Eggs any way you like them."

"Various breads in the box over there. Help yourself. The eggs won't take long." She buttered an enormous griddle and cracked half a dozen onto it.

"You don't have to cook for me. I can go to the diner." He ate out most of the time, but he was almost enjoying this opportunity for intelligent company instead of his usual solitary meal.

His memory of home-cooked meals was of siblings complaining that he never fixed what they liked, that they'd lost their homework or hair ribbons or the guinea pig, and demanding he pick them up when they knew he couldn't.

"I don't have time for the diner. This is faster and a lot quieter. Over easy?" She held up the spatula questioningly.

He'd popped bread in the toaster. "That's fine. Those are the prettiest fried eggs I've ever seen. How do you do that?"

"Low heat. You should probably rest another day, but you're not, are you?" She flipped two eggs onto one plate and four on another.

He appreciated that she understood he needed lots of food. The eggs were slightly juicy, just the way he liked them. He refilled her coffee cup and managed to carry his plate and cup to the counter. "Look, I'm a big man. I have quarts more blood than most. I'm not keeling over easily."

"You don't need or want nursing, I got it." She set her plate down at the counter next to his. "But I've spent a lifetime feeling pain and wanting to fix it. Fortunately, human minds are too complex for me to read, but that doesn't stop me from noticing the limp, the wince, whatever, to know you're hurting. Just think of me as a serious empath, if that helps."

He'd seen enough Star Trek to understand. He just didn't like it. "I'll try to keep my distance so you don't suffer."

"Y'know, there was a time when I'd punch someone's arm for that." She took a healthy bite of toast and eggs and chewed before continuing. "But I've learned to accept that humans bite when anxious, just like animals."

He grunted as that hit home. "I'm not good at apologies. I'm not any better at being fussed over. Let's move on to how we keep everyone out of the barn."

She lifted her cup in salute. "Good start. We need Evie for this discussion. She'll be back in a minute. What time will they start filming?"

"Kennedy and his crew won't arrive before ten." He checked messages on his phone. "Looks like a quiet night at the OK Corral. They've given up on replacing Betty. She's offered to pay the extra insurance out of her salary."

"Not a good standard to set but better than being fired, I suppose. I wonder if someone deliberately sabotaged that balloon to get her off the set?"

Cade sipped his coffee and thought about it. "I've questioned the balloon crew. We've reviewed video of the event. It doesn't appear as if anyone else was in that balloon except Kennedy, Darren the sound man, and Betty, after the crew lit the burners. I should think one or the other would have noticed if they tampered with the tanks. The switch to an empty tank had to happen earlier."

"Knowing Betty wouldn't know how to switch from one to the other?"

"Exactly. She bragged she knew how to fly a balloon and the balloon crew stupidly trusted her."

"Wouldn't the film crew know better? Could Kennedy or the sound man be sabotaging the film? Are you sure you can't talk your uncle into shutting them down?" She cleaned up her plate.

"After what your father said yesterday, if I registered it correctly, I'm thinking there's a conspiracy to end Mackie's career. I can't imagine Kennedy or Darren being in on it, but I bet my uncle is. Enrique is a hard-headed businessman. He will work toward the greater good only if there is something in it for him." Cade had accepted that as a teenager, when he'd given up sleep to work his uncle's insurance office job around his school schedule in return for keeping a roof over his family's head. "If Mackie is blackmailing him. . ."

"Do you know any reason he could?"

Cade shook his head. "It could be anything. They've worked together a long time."

"So, you think my father is telling us that Sandra was on a mission to help her friend Zoe to sue Mackie? And your uncle was helping her?"

"If we believe Slate, who you claim is a liar." He got up and poured more coffee just as Evie breezed in.

"If you're talking yesterday's visitor, I think he was being honest enough, if not telling us everything." Evie washed her hands at the sink and foraged bacon from the refrigerator. "Want some?" She held the package up to Cade.

"If you're fixing some for yourself, yes, please. I need to buy your groceries. I don't eat light."

"Neither does Jax or his mooching friends." Evie pulled out a frying pan. "We just throw whatever we have at the grocery account. Communal living at its best."

"Only works when you trust everyone," Iddy corrected. "We all rely on your ability to see character."

Evie shrugged. "You shouldn't. Perfectly honest people can do horrible things in the name of some misguided cause."

"Instead of biding by the law and letting justice prevail," Jax concluded, joining them, smelling of fresh shower—

Which Cade badly needed and couldn't have until the bandage came off tomorrow. "All very nice and well, but Mackie, my uncle, Sandra, and apparently Slate Cooper don't operate on judicial wavelengths."

"And apparently someone else doesn't either, unless you think one of that lot killed Sandra." Iddy stood and washed off her plate. "I need to run into the office. I'll be over to check the animals after that."

"Everyone at the farm has murky auras." Evie flipped the bacon. "I wouldn't let any of them in this house, but that doesn't mean they killed Sandra."

Cade wanted the bacon and more toast. He wanted to follow Iddy more. He thought quickly under stress. "I can't drive like this. Wait for me and let me go with you."

The vet gave him a long, thoughtful look. Was she using her *empathy* to know he was playing for time? He ate his toast rather than attempt to look innocent.

"I need to brush my teeth. I can answer a few emails while I'm waiting. Eat your bacon, big boy." She strode off.

Yup, she had his number.

Evie chuckled. "Just keep playing surly bear, and you have her hooked."

He didn't want to hook anyone, did he? Depending on the definition of *hooked*, he supposed.

JAX WAITED UNTIL THEIR GUESTS HAD DEPARTED BEFORE NUDGING EVIE TOWARD wedding plans instead of ghost hunting. "It's Thursday. If we don't go over to the courthouse together with the marriage license application and ID stuff we'll have to postpone your Beltane date."

She settled next to him in the booth and leaned against his shoulder. "Do you really want me talking to Blockhead while we stand in front of the probate clerk and pledge allegiance to whatever?"

"No choice." He crunched his bacon. "I'd rather you talked to the courthouse ghost than go back out to the farm with men waving guns."

"You own a gun. Half the men in town own guns. If I had a choice, I'd pour salt and sugar down all of them. I'd conduct an uprising. . . Women and children dismantle all the guns, throw their parts in the river or ocean or down the toilet. . .”

“If you can manage to organize all the women in the world to do the same thing on the same day, let me know, and I'm right there with you.” Jax sipped his coffee, knowing keeping Evie on task required a bent mind. “In the meantime, we need to go to the courthouse.”

“Where there are probably more men carrying guns than in Sandra's barn. When the law requires everyone to have mental stability and military training, like you. . .” She kissed his cheek. “. . .to use firearms properly, I'll have a lot fewer ghosts to talk to.” She slid from the booth.

Former mayor Block had been shot in the courthouse by an unstable wannabe gunslinger. Jax got where she was coming from. He didn't have to like it. “We can't get married without a license. I can go online in another county, but that could take weeks.”

Before he could press, Evie's mother sailed in the back door bearing donuts. “Did I miss everyone? Sorry. Evie, can you take over the shop at noon? I really need to buy supplies.”

“And gossip with Gertie, I know, but I can't promise anything. I was just about to tell Jax I'd meet him at the courthouse to sign up to get hitched at noon. If you're trying to distract me from Cade's case, you'll only distract me from wedding plans.” Evie grabbed a chocolate donut from the box before Mavis could tug it away.

Jax accepted that Mavis had sailed in here with that message on purpose to pin her daughter down. He would have one spooky mother-in-law.

“I'll send my receptionist over to the shop at eleven, while I'm there to cover the office. You can go to lunch then, but you may have to help me hogtie Evie and carry her to the courthouse at noon.” Jax cleaned up his plate and slid out after Evie.

Mavis wrinkled up her nose. Her graying hair hadn't had time to come loose from its bun this morning. Today, her red caftan was sleeveless and adorned with countless beads and an amulet or two. That probably wasn't a good sign.

“There's a very bad cloud over that farm today, and the cards show danger.” She slipped off one of her amulets and hung it around Evie's neck. “It's not enough. You should stay at the store or walk the dogs.”

“Turned all my dog-walking clients over to someone else, sorry. What if I persuade someone to go with me to visit Zoe? I'd like to get her back out to the barn so Sandra can see her, but maybe another day.”

Impressed, Jax almost bought that spiel, until he realized Wright had been gunning for Zoe yesterday. “Do you really want to wear a bandage like Cade's to our wedding? Let him talk to Zoe. Let me find out about Mackie's lawsuits. Iddy can talk to the animals. You've done all you can do until you have more information. Spend the day checking off to-do items on your wedding checklists." As if she had such a thing.

Jax hugged and kissed her despite her crossed arms and pout. "I have a client in at nine, gotta go. Don't go anywhere without your team."

"There's a killer on the loose, lawyer man. Someone has to stop him," she called after him.

"We can't adopt Loretta until we're married," he called over his shoulder. "You really want to disappoint her by getting yourself killed?"

She had no answer for that. Jax had to pray she'd be sensible and stay home today—until noon.

Twenty-one

EVIE HAD HER MOTHER'S BOX OF DONUTS ON THE SEAT BESIDE HER AS SHE DROVE UP to the farm. Someone had finally hired security—they stopped her on the drive. But her beloved didn't have Cade under his thumb yet—she was on the approved list. Security waved her through.

Iddy's Tahoe was here. She'd be in the barn. It ought to be safe enough.

Evie didn't feel the least bit guilty ignoring Jax's anxiety and her mother's warnings. She knew they loved her. They just couldn't figure out how to store her in a bubble. Actually being useful by talking to ghosts was the most fun she'd ever had, even if it still hadn't earned her much respect.

At least she respected herself more these days. That was more important.

She'd texted R&R about visiting Zoe and the boarding farm. They recommended bringing Cade. Cade was in pain and shouldn't be subject to whatever rough roads led to the farm. He needed time to heal.

So, here she was. She carried the donut box into the barn as a peace offering.

She didn't see Cade or Iddy, but Sandra was looking—dispirited—attempting to pat her horse. Huh, *there* was a reason to call Sandra's friend.

"Want us to ask Zoe if she'll take your mare?" Evie set down the donut box on her hay bale stack and waited to see if Sandra would respond.

The aura flickered with surprise, then fear. She seemed to look over Evie's shoulder—before she evaporated. Dang.

Evie swung around to see Betty stepping from the goat pen.

"You're talking to Sandra?" the actress asked—a good question since the mare had belonged to the dead woman. "You're the one they say talks to ghosts?"

Evie didn't like admitting that to strangers. They got weird ideas and wanted her to connect with their rich dead grandfathers to locate a will or worse.

"Dead people don't talk." She produced her phone, inconveniently in her pocket. "Sandra's parents own the horse now."

Betty nodded sadly, but then, she was an actress, after all. "I wish I owned a place where I could take it. She loved that horse. Do you have her dog?"

To Evie's relief, Iddy entered then. Betty's aura just didn't. . . focus. . like it should. Perhaps she was genuinely sad, or acting messed with her emotions, producing a cloudy aura. Evie checked her chakra to see if a heart attack was imminent. A dark shadow in the region of her heart, but given her recent medical emergency, not unexpected.

"I have Classy," Iddy declared, rummaging in the donut box.

"How's Cade doing?" Evie changed the subject before Betty could question more.

"He's arguing with the director, so fine, I suppose." Iddy turned to the actress. "Were you interested in adopting Classy? She's moping around. I'm hoping whoever takes the mare will take the dog too."

"Have you called everyone in that little book Sandra carried with her? Surely there's someone who will adopt her pretty dog." Betty eased toward the rear door Iddy had just entered.

"Only little book the police found didn't have names. Was there another?" Evie asked. Sandra's bags had been in Betty's trailer. Had she searched them for the book?

Betty's aura reflected a hint of relief. "Oh, I thought it might be an address book, silly me. I better get back on the set." She smiled, waved, and strolled away.

"Are all actors that weird?" Evie asked as Iddy fed the horse a carrot.

"Everyone in the production is weird, says the pot calling the kettle black. They're just a different kind of weird. Are you seeing Sandra anywhere?"

"She disappeared when Betty arrived. I had a feeling she was trying to warn me, but I don't know why. Maybe I'll be banned if Betty calls me a freak who talks to air?" Evie glanced around, hunting for Sandra and finding nothing.

"Maybe Sandra wants you to warn Betty. Someone has already endangered her. She probably should have quit then. Wouldn't a normal person figure if someone tried to kill her, she ought to leave?" Iddy found an apple fritter. "They're hauling the sheep downtown, for reasons well beyond my understanding. No one raises sheep in this heat. It ought to be entertaining."

No, it wouldn't. But if Evie followed the crew downtown, she'd at least be near the courthouse at noon. That ought to count for something.

"All right, I'll take my bribe and leave. When do you think Cade might be ready for a road trip?" Evie reclaimed the donut box.

"He won't take painkillers. My Tahoe had him wincing with every bump. Borrow a limo." Iddy checked on the pigs and chickens, stalling for time, waiting on Cade, Evie assumed.

"We should take Mackie and his limo, make a day of it. OK, I'll see you in a little bit." Evie headed for the Subaru.

On her drive into town, she made a mental list of everyone who had been at the house when Sandra was murdered. She probably ought to include Betty and Ray Anne, too, even though they were in the trailer. So that was two women, the two Steves, surfer Darren, and gun-toting Wright. And maybe whoever drove the truck away? And why had Mackie's assistant not been with Mackie in Charleston? She really needed to organize her suspects. But if Wright was behind bars, she had one less to worry about.

LATER THAT MORNING, IDDY LET THE COLLIE NUDGE THE EWE PAST A COLORFUL display of pansies at the hardware store. If she'd trained these sheep, she would have them eating out of her hands and could lead them herself. Sandra had apparently used her dog.

Up in front of the wandering pack of woolly animals, Betty and Roy were speaking their memorized script for the sound crew. Iddy ignored their inane patter about farmers leading their flocks to market during the Civil War. Afterthought wasn't built until the early 1900s. No one farmed sheep even then. Wool and ninety-degree heat and humidity were a bad combination. Cotton had brought in more money.

But apparently cotton wagons weren't as entertaining as sheep dropping dung down the brick sidewalk.

"I refuse to be a pooper scooper," she told Cade when he strolled up with his usual frown.

"In this heat, the place will be fragrant before noon," he acknowledged. "Maybe we should let Wright have the job. They let him out on bail this morning."

Iddy thought half a dozen foul words before allowing herself to speak. "Evie says he didn't mean to shoot you, but surely the sheriff didn't buy ghostly accident?"

"Not up to the sheriff. Judge offered bail. Mackie paid it. I've told them legal fees don't come out of the film's budget. They're not happy." Cade nudged a wandering lamb back to the road with his boot.

"You want him to shoot you again?" she asked.

"Wright and Mackie are chafing under restrictions as it is. If they had a choice, I'd never be hired in the business again." He said that with a degree of satisfaction.

"Who would want to be hired in this business?" In disgust, she watched Betty attempt to pet a woolly head. The ewe tried to eat her hand. "At least whoever rented the sheep had enough sense not to rent the ram."

"That would be Sandra. Now that we know about Zoe, we need to have a talk with her. The two of you connected, didn't you?"

"She knows animals better than Betty George. That's all I can contribute. If Sandra got herself killed for helping Zoe with her lawsuit, and Wright held a gun on her, then I'm guessing it isn't really safe for Zoe to return."

"But Evie says she needs to see her aura while we talk. How much of that do I buy?" Still frowning, he didn't look at her as he asked.

"All of it and more," Iddy assured him. "Evie does not talk about her skills. We've watched our mothers attempt to help people and get scorned as charlatans in return. The younger generation simply keeps our mouths shut and does what needs to be done. Except for Evie, we don't have to sell our services the same way our mothers did."

She nodded at one of the smaller animals. "That lamb on your right smells food every time that door opens. Catch it before he wreaks havoc."

A rush of cool air hit them as the lamb's weight opened the automatic door. Classy cut off the wanderer. Cade grabbed it and set it back in the street, bleating protest.

"I trust they edit out that part." Marching down Main Street in a sheep parade was a waste of Iddy's precious time—but it had gained her an assistant and a big fat check come payday, so she couldn't complain. Too much.

"Not convinced," he told her. "Animals stray. But I believe some people simply have the ability to connect with animals better than others."

She shrugged. "Go with that. I don't have much faith in my mother's amulets or Aunt Mavis's weird predictions because I don't believe our fates are written in the stars or whatever, and I don't really understand what it is they do. Our abilities are open to interpretation. Even Evie has difficulty understanding what she sees. But if you believe some people connect better than others, believe she connects with people."

He processed that and finally nodded. "All right. I'll see if I can reach this Zoe, and we'll all go out to visit."

With the scene filmed, the director called for the herd to be returned to the truck. Cade strode off, a busy man with much on his mind—and a shoulder that really hurt.

Evie wandered over to keep Iddy company. "Have you seen Wright or Mackie anywhere? Jax said they let the little creep out on bail."

"They don't need to be here for filming, so I assume they're holed up in an air-conditioned hotel. Why?"

"Wright was there the night Sandra died. Mackie is his money tree. I'm assuming that little gun trick yesterday was Wright's way of protecting the source from whom all wealth flows. Therefore, ergo sum, if Sandra threatened to join or help Zoe with a potentially damaging lawsuit, would he not attempt to stop her?" Evie ran her hand through her already tousled hair.

"Ergo sum?" Iddy asked in amusement, willing to be diverted from sheep that rightfully did not want to be herded back to the truck.

"I'm trying to learn to speak Jax. Is it working?" Evie shoved a sheep rear end with her sandal to move it in the right direction.

Iddy mentally coaxed the herd with thoughts of yummy pellets. They all fell in line and trotted toward the truck at dangerous speed. OK, that was amusing too. Roy and Betty had to dodge the near stampede.

"I'd say leave lawyer speak to lawyers," Iddy recommended. "But you could be on the right path. From what I gather, Sandra was strong and probably taller than Wright. He'd have to approach her from behind with something long, then catch her by surprise. Do we have a coroner's report yet?"

"Preliminary. Wide blunt object caved the back of her skull. The angle of the blow indicates she may have been crouching. My guess would be a shovel, but the ones at the barn were used to dig up her body and have been pretty contaminated." Evie stood aside as the collie herded the sheep into the truck.

"The sheriff tested them. Wouldn't they have blood traces even if washed?"

Evie shrugged. "I'm not into forensics, but there would probably be blood in the grave they dug. And everyone's prints would be all over the handles."

Iddy let the crew slam the door on the truck and checked her watch. "I need to head to the office and give Asia a break. Aren't you supposed to be at the courthouse?"

"Is it noon already? Whoops. OK, just watch out if you go to the barn. Mom says it should be avoided today." She dashed off toward the courthouse.

Iddy had to check on the animals at the barn this evening. She'd worry about her aunt's warning then.

Starting to walk away, she watched one of the extras who'd been scooping poop hurry to the truck with shovel in hand.

Had the shovel always been in the truck?

She texted Evie's team with the question and stopped at Pris's café to order lunch.

Cade was already there—*as was Zoe David.*

Twenty-Two

CADE HAD THE URGE TO EXPLAIN TO IDDY WHY HE WAS HANGING OUT WITH SANDRA'S best friend and hadn't mentioned Zoe was in town. He didn't. He owed no one any explanations. Yeah, he much preferred the vet's all-natural lanky good looks and blunt honesty to Zoe's theatrical dyed blond performance, but his personal preferences had no place here. This was business.

He didn't speak, but Zoe did.

She lit up. "Oh, you're the lady doc! I heard you put in a good word for me yesterday, until the bumpkin here got shot."

There was another reason Cade didn't speak. Zoe was a Sandra clone.

"They shouldn't have you carrying lunch," Iddy admonished, speaking to him and not acknowledging Zoe's gushing, which pleased him on some primitive level. "Have Dante bring out the delivery. I'm taking a to-go box to Asia."

That she was coddling him didn't tickle him quite as much. Was she actually sensing his pain or guessing? But she was right. He didn't need to suffer for the clowns. "I'll pick up your tab. Staff gets paid food. It's in the contract."

She didn't argue but turned to Zoe. "My cousin wanted to talk to you about yesterday, but she's over at the courthouse filing for a wedding license. Will you be around long?"

"I brought my horse trailer. I've talked to Sandra's parents, and they agreed I should take the mare. Losing Sandra has been hard on them. Do you know when they can have the body?" Zoe's plastic smile disappeared with her concern.

He'd already called the parents and confirmed this. What he needed to do was learn interrogation before Zoe vanished again. "I'll check, but apparently the sheriff has to use the services of an out of county department, so the process is slow. We'll load up the horse when I deliver lunch."

Cade watched the light on Iddy's face abruptly shut down. After her warning, he didn't need to be a mind reader to guess why. "Only. . . Wright is out on bail. You probably shouldn't go near the farm."

He'd guessed right. Iddy smiled in relief. Ha, he was getting good at this psychic nonsense. It just required paying attention.

"I'm part of the staff," Iddy explained. "They don't notice my existence. If you'll trust me with your trailer, I can load her for you."

Cade didn't think it was possible to not notice Iddy's existence. She had a very odd view of herself. But he wouldn't discourage her problem-solving.

"I'll leave you here with my SUV, and we can meet in the city parking lot after lunch." Iddy cast him an uninterpretable look. "Cade can stay and keep you company. He shouldn't be loading horses."

He snorted at this. "You won't have anyone else to help you. Roy only plays at being cowboy. I'll go with you." He signed the bill for the lunches and delivery.

The woman behind the counter who Iddy called cousin wore her hair in purple stripes today. She gave him an odd look that would have him believing in mind readers if he stayed much longer.

As if she really were feeling his pain and not looking happy about it, Iddy pulled out her phone. "I'll let Evie know we're heading to the barn. Maybe the license thing won't take much longer, and she can meet us there. She won't like it if we take Sandra's horse without her."

"Why?" Zoe asked, naturally enough.

Not explaining ghosts, Cade made a dismissive gesture with his good right hand. "She's become real attached. You wouldn't happen to want the collie as well?" Cade aimed for the door before the topic became too convoluted.

"I could, I suppose." Zoe took the to-go box he handed her. "I have room and they probably shouldn't be separated."

"I left the collie with the Tahoe and one of the crew." Iddy followed them out. "You and the dog can get acquainted while Cade and I drive out to the farm. There's a nice little park down the road from the city parking lot. Classy is well behaved. I have a couple of her toys in the back." Iddy's phone buzzed as they turned the corner.

"You won't need either animal for the next week of filming?" Cade had to ask.

Iddy all but growled at him. "I haven't read the script. What do you think?"

He hid a smile. "I think you'd kill me if I said we needed them at all." He accepted her curt nod as acknowledgment that he was right once again.

She checked her buzzing phone and waved it. "Jax is about to kill us for telling Evie about this. The clerk is moving like molasses, and they haven't eaten. He planned a special lunch. And now Evie is about to bolt."

"Tell her we'll wait," Cade advised. He wasn't entirely certain why they should, but he did hire Jax and Evie and her team. He supposed he ought to listen to the professionals, such as they were.

Iddy's father had hinted that he should do more than listen, but he was too cynical to trust easily.

"I really have to take lunch out to Asia and check in at the office anyway. Should we all go there? It's air-conditioned." She turned to Zoe. "My office is only a few miles from the farm. It's on the way."

"Sure. We all have to eat. Let your friend enjoy her official engagement day."

The vet's office was filled with whimpering dogs, hissing cats, and a few caged rodents waiting in the reception room. Attempting to feed a tiny kitten, the receptionist looked harassed, and Iddy passed the girl her uneaten lunch before disappearing in the back with the other box and the collie, which seemed to prefer Iddy to anyone else.

"No wonder she's so skinny," Zoe said, checking out the contents of her box. "I bet she never has time to eat." She tore into her sub sandwich.

Having watched Iddy lose her appetite and refuse to eat the previous day, Cade made a trade with the receptionist and took the vegetarian box back to the clinic part of the building. Iddy was examining a bleating calf. He caught Asia's attention and held up the box. "Make her eat." He mouthed the words carefully.

Beneath her exotic headgear, the assistant's big brown eyes widened, then she nodded.

Cade called the café and added another box to their order to be dropped off on the way out to the farm. The cousin's café was quick. A teenager arrived with the order not long after. Dante had apparently tired of playing delivery boy.

Cade had second thoughts about sending a kid out to the farm where idiots with guns roamed. He told him to leave the delivery with security and tipped him for the lot. The kid strolled off, smiling. At least he'd made someone happy for the day.

"Sandra said you were a tightwad. Doesn't look like you have a problem spending other people's money." Zoe wiped her mouth with a brown paper napkin.

"People need to eat. Those who work hard deserve reasonable recompense. Sandra didn't need *or* deserve thousand-dollar boots." Sandra had had some notion he was rich enough to treat her like a movie star. He'd had to disabuse her of the notion.

He leaned against a wall and tore into his sandwich so he didn't take up space in Iddy's limited office seating. A place this busy really needed to expand.

"Huh. So, you *deserve* to work for Mackie and your fancy beach house is *reasonable recompense*?" She bit into a peach and let juice dribble down her chin.

The woman had a bee up her butt, for certain. Cade shrugged it off. "My cabin is on a bluff, not a beach. It's almost a hundred years old and belonged to my grandfather. The ground's so unstable, even the land is worthless. I couldn't get a mortgage on it when I needed the money."

He resented the questioning but realized this was an opportunity to turn the conversation around. "I assume Sandra worked for Mackie to ship her horse and dog here. Was she quitting the business?"

Zoe eyed him warily. "We were going into business together. Hollywood wasn't working out for her. If you're on Mackie's payroll, you wouldn't understand."

"I'm working for my uncle to keep production under control. Mackie is getting my financial services cheap. Do you know why Sandra decided to ditch the job before it even started? She was being paid well."

"Why should I tell you anything?" she countered, checking out her chocolate cookie.

"Because I want to shut Mackie down as much as you do." He dug into the French fries—sweet potato with spicy seasoning he couldn't identify.

"Yeah, right. Mackie is trying to spy on me. It won't work. I have him dead to rights, and he's gonna pay this time." She drank her water with a grimace of distaste.

"He doesn't think so. He's hired a shark from Savannah to take you down, whatever it is you think you're doing. You don't have enough money to make Mackie pay."

"What, you think he's gonna hire someone to kill me like he did Sandra?"

Iddy emerged from the clinic, feeding one of the preemies. Cade and Zoe were shooting eye daggers at each other in her lobby. Well, she could understand the desire. Cade didn't possess an ounce of nuance. He said what he thought and did what he must. Most of the time. And right now, he was in pain and worse humor than usual.

She laid the satiated kitten in the flannel-lined box at the desk. "Evie's on her way," she told them. "I don't know how long this will take. You be okay waiting here, Zoe? Evie wants to talk to you."

"Why?" The other woman crumpled her lunch wrappers.

"She's trying to find out what happened to Sandra. You'll see when you meet her." Iddy really didn't want to go to the barn after all the warnings, but the mare needed green pastures and more agreeable company.

"Zoe thinks Mackie hired someone to kill Sandra." Holding Zoe's truck keys, Cade stood and opened the door. "She won't tell me why."

"Mackie has spies," Zoe said mulishly. "I'll be fine here. Just bring me Sandra's horse and tack. I'll be out of your hair."

They left her with the sweet potato fries and a reception room full of pets.

"Tack," Iddy said the instant the door closed behind them. "Didn't Sandra fling a saddle at you? Is that hers?"

"Yup." Even though he was the wounded one, he opened the passenger truck door and assisted her into the high cab.

He stopped to check the trailer hitch before climbing in. He had to adjust the driver's seat for his longer legs.

Iddy wanted to smack him, but he was already hurting. "You're planning on steering this rig with one hand?"

"Yup. My one hand weighs more than your two." With that nonsensical announcement, he started the rig. "You ever driven one of these?"

She fastened her seat belt. "I want a smaller van for the Tahoe. I'm debating whether to buy that or expand the clinic with Mackie's blood money. Talk to me of tack. How much did Sandra bring? Where is it stored?"

"Why the interest?" He used both hands to bring the trailer around to the exit.

His pain was practically killing *her*. "I carry drugs in my bag. I'm going to shoot you with tranquilizers when we're done here. You're ruining those stitches."

"Am not. And you're avoiding the subject. Why tack?"

"Don't know. The emphasis seemed strange under the circumstances. I don't remember the saddle as anything special. Zoe ought to have her own if she's boarding horses. If it had been me, I would have asked for the mare's special feed. The mare doesn't seem high-strung enough to only accept Sandra's tack. Is there a box somewhere with horseshoes and whatnot?" Iddy didn't know why she was pressing the subject. It just seemed important.

"Huh. Didn't look. Good point." He winced as the old truck hit a pothole. "Wonder if the sheriff searched the box?"

"Probably not unless someone said it was hers, and who in that menagerie would know? To them, it's just a bunch of smelly old leather that came with the barn. I better text Evie's team." She sent a warning to Evie and Jax as well. Jax would not be happy.

They rolled up the drive, flashing ID at security before backing the trailer up near the paddock.

"Why didn't they have security earlier?" Iddy asked. "Sandra might still be alive."

"Mackie used the security budget for his hotel expense." Cade pulled hard to line up the trailer. "Which means Zoe might have a point about him hiring someone to kill Sandra. No security meant anyone could have been here that night."

"How is he paying for security now?"

"I told the accountants to take it out of his share. He hasn't figured it out yet."

Checking the mirror, Iddy could see the film and sound crew hovering over Betty and Roy as they strolled along, checking the paddock's fence. She rolled her eyes and jumped down without Cade's help.

Wright ran out to wave them away. "Stay out of the shot! Get that thing out of here."

Cade glared down at the smaller man. "Get outta my face, asshat. You don't know how much I want to punch you."

Realizing his error, Wright hastily backed up. "I didn't mean to shoot you! It was an accident."

"That's the only reason you're not pulp in the dust right now. But it still damned well hurts, and I'm not moving that trailer again until it's time to leave. What the friggin' hell were you doing carrying a gun on the set? They have license laws here! If you think production is paying your fines, you're fooling yourself."

"A man has a right to protect himself," Wright insisted, turning red in the face. "They took my weapon! What happens if someone tries to shoot me?"

"They get arrested. Don't do things that will get you killed. It's not as if you'd have time to pull the thing out of that holster before you were dead anyway. Now tell them to take a break so we can bring out the horse." Cade strode toward the gate, apparently not climbing the fence today.

Iddy thought she ought to be impressed by the machismo, but her father had attitude and then some. Posturing was meaningless. She was more impressed that Cade didn't pound the little man into the ground with one fist. She hoped Wright didn't see that as weakness, or he'd be buying another gun and shooting Cade again.

She didn't wonder why Wright feared being shot. Anyone that obnoxious had probably been threatened a few times.

Apparently with nothing better to do once Wright paused the filming, Betty and Roy and the crew trailed into the barn in their wake. Iddy couldn't see ghosts, but the cold eddies on a hot day told her Sandra was watching.

"Better check to see no one else is carrying a weapon," she murmured at Cade as she crossed to the mare's stall.

"Security is supposed to be checking." He stood between her and the rest of the company, texting, presumably to his hired guards.

Iddy entered the stall and found the tack box beneath the feed bin. She'd had no reason to look before. The saddle hung on the wall, right where Cade had left it days ago. Didn't look like the sheriff's men—or Mena—had touched either box or saddle. She couldn't ask Cade with his bad shoulder to carry it all. She checked the weight of the box—not too heavy.

Carrying it out, she handed it to him. "Let's put the tack in the truck first," she murmured. "Less chance of tampering."

She went back to get the saddle when loud voices erupted further down the barn.

"Can't you frigging assholes do one damned scene from beginning to end? A kindergartener could have read those lines by now! Get back out there and let's can this scene before we all melt."

Carrying the saddle, Iddy watched a big man with a big belly waddle through the back door. The dusty air turned frigid.

The bespectacled, skinny director, whose name Iddy could never recall, blocked Mackie's path. "It's hot. We're taking a break. Your babysitter is moving out the horse. You didn't have to be here. Go back to the hotel."

Babysitter, nice. Iddy cast Cade a glance but he was strolling toward the door without acknowledging the argument. Iddy figured it was wise to follow suit.

Before she could escape, the mare broke from her stall, screaming. Iddy instantly dropped the saddle to turn and focus on the terrified animal.

Instead of hitting the ground, the saddle flew across the barn to hit Mackie upside the head as if it had been hurled by the winds of fury.

The big man collapsed like a ton of bricks on the dirt floor, sending up a cloud of dust.

"I DID NOT DO IT," IDDY WHISPERED OVER AND OVER, SITTING ON A HAY BALE WITH her head in her hands.

Having entered at the flying saddle incident, Evie knew her cousin hadn't done anything. Iddy wouldn't strike a fly anyway. But there was nothing natural about the way that saddle had flown across the barn. Try explaining that to an outraged crew and the cops.

Jax had followed Evie in and instantly called R&R. The team had arrived before the sheriff and the doctor. While Cade captured the mare, Jax and Roark helped the crew muscle the unconscious Mackie into the house. Reuben cased the joint for ropes and tackles. Evie knew he wouldn't find any.

Once the sheriff arrived to interview everyone, Evie patted her older cousin's shoulder. "Sandra's antics are getting seriously old," she whispered in sympathy. Iddy just shook her head.

"This barn needs to be off limits from now on," Cade shouted. "Sheriff, can we move everyone outside?"

Interesting. Was he accepting they had a temperamental poltergeist on hand? The cowboy's aura was pretty confused.

Evie studied the angry spirit hovering near the terrified mare. Sandra wasn't ready to go. Leaving Iddy, she strode over to the horse, pulling out her phone and pretending to talk into it. "You really need to use your words. What do you want us to know?"

Sandra's aura drifted to the saddle and appeared to kick at it. *Evidence.*

Thrilled that the spirit was finally communicating, Evie wandered past Sheriff Troy to kick idly at the well-worn saddle as the spirit had done. Surprisingly, after tying up the horse, Cade joined her. They both studied the missile that had brought Mackie down, not daring to touch it unless Troy told them they could.

"Sandra says it's evidence," she whispered. Then talking into her phone again, she asked, "Who killed you?"

No answer.

Evie tried again. "Is this evidence against the person who killed you?"

Sandra only seemed puzzled. If she'd been struck from behind, perhaps she didn't know who had done it.

"Ask her who was waiting to take her away," Cade suggested, sounding as if he'd rather his tongue be cut out than ask.

Sandra kicked at the saddle again, but she'd lost most of her energy with that last mighty heave. *Darren,* she whispered, her colors flickering with confusion before she vanished.

"Darren?" Evie whispered to Cade, putting her phone away.

"Surfer boy?" He sounded incredulous, before he looked thoughtful. "He had access to the company pickup, but everyone says it never left the lot."

Jax strolled up in time to hear this exchange. "He could have *promised* to take her when she was ready to go. That doesn't mean he was in the truck that left. We need to talk to him. For all we know, the driver of the truck killed her."

"We need to open this saddle." Cade turned to speak with authority. "Sheriff, this saddle is part of Sandra's tack, as is the box. I think they need to be examined professionally."

"Cade's listening to me," Evie whispered to Jax, pleased with this breakthrough. "Now fetch Iddy and tell her no one can charge her with anything."

"You want me to lie?" But without further argument, he strode over to her cousin.

Looking unhappy, the gray-haired sheriff joined them to study the saddle. "It should be fingerprinted."

"All our prints are on it. Everyone here will tell you it flew by itself," Cade insisted. "You can believe Evie and ghosts, or talk to the crew about special effects or whatever you like, but *no one has examined Sandra's tack.* A woman who is suing Mackie is waiting down the road to take Sandra's personal possessions, so these will be gone shortly unless you hold them as evidence. I doubt Mackie is dying from being hit on the head, so unless you want to charge a ghost with assault, let's find Sandra's killer."

"This belonged to the murder victim?" The sheriff kneeled down to check the saddle for hooks or ropes or anything to explain flight, then shook his head.

Evie felt kind of sorry for him. "Maybe it was mass hallucination," she suggested helpfully.

Troy snorted. "Tell Mr. Mackie that and persuade him not to press charges." He undid the tack box first, peering inside. "Any of this look unusual?"

Evie called over to her cousin, who was refusing Jax's assistance. "Iddy, you're the expert here. What should be in this box?"

Betty and Roy crowded around to look, as did any of the rest of the crew still in the vicinity. To Evie, the box contents looked like a lot of old junk.

Looking pale beneath her bronzed complexion, Iddy reluctantly strode over to study the box. Kneeling down, she removed each item, naming it. "Curry combs, bridle, hoof pick, saddle soap, fly mask. . ."

Underneath all that, Evie thought several metal items looked capable of smashing skulls. Troy didn't appear interested.

But there was a knife capable of severing spines. Wearing gloves, Troy hefted that, checked it thoroughly, then turned to the saddle. "Now look at this thing and tell me if there's any place she could have hidden anything."

Evie leaned into Jax. She knew nothing of saddles, and Sandra had vanished. She had the uneasy notion if they didn't find what the ghost wanted, she'd be back to wreak havoc.

"It's a basic western saddle. Not too many places for concealment." Cade crouched beside Iddy. He pointed at the high back. "Tacks on the cantle might be pried open." He flipped the saddle to show the bottom padding.

"The stitching is loose," Iddy noted. Using a cloth, she took the knife from the sheriff and pried the thread. "Not much you can conceal in here."

"Hold right there." Jax released Evie and crouched down to lift the loosened padding. "Sheriff, never let it be said that this evidence has been tampered with. See that black square? Microchip. You should be the one to pull it out."

Dismay and shock rippled through their audience, Evie noted. Roy and Betty's auras were murkier than usual, but they seemed as surprised as everyone else. Darren showed a little more interest and pushed forward. The boyfriend's aura wasn't exactly brilliant, but there was a streak of vengeance that didn't look pretty. One of the Steves, the cameraman, had his phone out, taking a video. The saddle search wasn't exactly treasure hunt material, but he seemed fascinated. Brice Kennedy, the director, narrowed his eyes—and his aura—as he watched.

"Well, now that we have that worked out, may we take the horse? Zoe is waiting." Evie said that as loudly as she could without sounding insane. She didn't know how much energy Sandra had or if she'd retreated to wherever spirit energy went.

Ah, there was the tattered aura, clinging to the pretty roan as Iddy untied her.

Evie pulled out her now-dead phone and whispered into it, hoping the ghost heard her either mentally or aurally but never really knowing. She suspected it was all about focus, of which she had little. "You can let go now, Sandra. Zoe will take care of your animals. Unless you can tell us who hit you, your job here is done. Would you like to move on?"

Zoe knows, Sandra said inside Evie's head. *Help Zo.*

Evie opened herself up. The spirit appeared to visibly brighten for a second, and then she was gone.

Evie felt a ton lighter for passing her on.

Jax was there to catch her when her knees crumpled.

JAX HAD DRIVEN EVIE'S SUBARU TO THE BARN FEARING SHE WOULD OVERDO HERSELF. He was starting to recognize the symptoms when she was ready to send a spirit to the next plane. But he couldn't always be there to catch her, and that ate at him.

The sheriff hadn't objected when he'd carried her from the barn.

"Zoe," she commanded before he drove past Iddy's animal hospital.

Since Iddy and Cade were turning the horse van into the parking lot, Jax complied. He wanted to talk to Zoe too. "Will reading her aura exhaust you more?"

He didn't turn off the car until she shook her head negatively. Evie was stubborn, not stupid.

The blond bombshell ran out of the office building to examine the van as soon as it stopped. She held out some treat through the bars of the trailer for the horse to take and was talking to it when Jax and Evie approached.

Cade introduced them, not repeating any of what they'd just seen and done. He was about as recalcitrant as Iddy, who'd gone to fetch the dog.

Evie leaned wearily against the truck cab. "Sandra was going to you the night she died, wasn't she?"

The tough-looking blonde set her jaw and concentrated on the horse but nodded. "Said something came up, and she'd explain when she got there."

"Did you come here to pick her up?" Jax tried not to sound like he was interrogating her, but the sheriff really didn't know who Zoe was. And for her own protection, they needed to keep this quiet.

Zoe looked puzzled. "No. Sandra knew I couldn't let any of Mackie's crew see me. It was stupid of me to show up the for the audition, but I just couldn't stand it, y'know? If I could have left flowers where she died, I would have, but I thought the least I could do was pay my respects. We were very quiet about her knowing me. Why do you ask? Did someone say I was here?"

"No, we're trying to piece together what happened that night. We thought she was planning on leaving, but we don't know how."

"She had a boyfriend here, or some sucker she'd wheedled into believing he was her boyfriend." Zoe shrugged.

"Darren," Evie murmured. "She said Darren was helping her."

Zoe wrinkled her brow. "Sandra told you that? Which one was Darren?"

"Surfer dude," Jax said, diverting the conversation from Evie and ghosts. "You said Sandra wheedled men into doing what she wanted?"

Zoe let the subject drop to answer his question. "Sandra tended to play both sides against each other. Her family never had money, but she grew up around kids who did. She'd learned to play them."

Cade snorted and spoke before Jax could. "She played everyone. How much did you tell her about your lawsuit? Did you know she was carrying evidence, is that why you wanted the tack?"

Zoe looked wary. "Sandra was pretty close-mouthed. She just said she had acquired something I might find useful. Since no one has asked me about anything except the mare, I figured it hadn't been found."

Jax didn't want to badger the witness, but they weren't in a courtroom. "Did she tell you if she hid it or where to find it?"

Zoe shook her head. "Not precisely. She might have looked like an airhead, but Sandra tracked anything and anyone who might make her money. She had notebooks full of who did what to whom and how much they paid her to keep quiet or to run as go-between and for what. I assumed there might be something in there and gave up hoping I'd ever see it."

"We can show you images from her notebook, but it's all initials and dollar amounts," Jax told her. "Would any of that mean anything to you?"

Zoe shook her head. "That's just Sandra keeping tabs on who owed her what and when. Now if you found her camera. . . She had a tiny one she got from one of her boyfriends. She took lots of videos that she'd produce if anyone argued about what they owed. That's why, when she offered to pay me to take her in with evidence she said would help my case, I believed her."

"Even knowing she wasn't to be trusted?" Cade asked.

Zoe shrugged. "She's good with animals. She'd have earned her keep. And I needed a friend who understood. Going up against Mackie is a scary business." She looked sad, as if just realizing that Mackie might be the reason Sandra was dead now. "I can't believe the creep would do this."

Jax couldn't offer sympathy, but he did offer hope. "The sheriff has what might be the evidence she was holding. Have your lawyer apply to him. And Mackie just hired a shark to countersue you, so I hope the evidence is strong."

Zoe's jaw stuck out stubbornly. "Mackie *raped* me. I went to the hospital and got a rape kit. He can't deny DNA evidence."

"He can and will," Jax warned her. "Your lawyer has to know he'll declare it was consensual."

"Mackie films everything," Zoe declared. "I was hoping Sandra may have got her hands on his videos."

Twenty-four

Cade couldn't sleep. Images of Sandra bleeding in a bullpen and Zoe being raped by a monster and Iddy crying in helplessness danced behind his eyes when he closed them.

He'd called his uncle and ordered him to shut down production. His uncle had sent an email in return showing his financials and what would happen if he had to pay off the investors. It wasn't pretty. He'd known it wouldn't be.

He had a healthy investment account of his own. He'd planned on using the income to live on while he explored the world, working with non-profits, looking for his next venture.

If he sold his investments, they would cover his uncle's losses, but it meant starting all over at the tedious financial grindstone he'd only just escaped. He'd borne the burden of his family for twenty years. His last sibling was out of college, and the family farm was paid for and profitable again. He'd yet to have a taste of freedom.

His choice now was the same one he'd had as a teenager—support his uncle and the family he employed, or be selfish and walk away. . .

A soft knock on the bedroom door relieved him of finishing that thought.

Carrying a mug, Iddy let herself in. Tonight, she was wearing a bronze silk robe over a high-necked nightgown that prevented him from seeing her tawny skin. But the robe tie cinched to a slender waist, revealing the tempting sway of her unfettered breasts as she settled at the foot of his bed.

She offered the mug. "My aunt's herbal sleep remedy. There's not enough breeze through that window to cool you so I added ice."

He took the mug and sniffed it—definitely herbal and not alcohol. "I didn't leave a light on. How did you know I was awake?" And could she tell her presence had just reduced him to his sex-deprived adolescence? Nothing like being hurtled back in time to enhance frustration. He sat up and bunched the sheets around his hips.

"Your shoulder hurts," she said simply.

After today, he might have to take her empathy declaration more seriously. How had her cousin known to tear open that saddle? And that was the second time the saddle had taken flight through no visible means. He'd been there to see it take off this time. He knew Iddy hadn't done it. *Poltergeist.* Right. Well, if anyone could return as a malicious spirit. . . it would be Sandra.

He was beginning to understand why Slate Cooper had left this town.

"If I take a pain pill, will you sleep?" In the quiet dark of this spooky house, he was ready to believe anything.

"I will, eventually." She brushed her long braid off her shoulder. "I just keep trying to fit pieces of the puzzle together and nothing works. Mackie is a dreadful man. Why isn't anyone besides a ghost trying to kill him? Why kill Sandra? Betty? You?"

"I don't think Wright meant to kill me. He might *want* to, but he hasn't the guts or the aim." Cade had done his best to block out Wright's weird behavior that day. Mackie's assistant wasn't normally unbalanced, but he had practically been flailing while he held that gun.

Sandra again? Had Sandra's ghost really unbalanced Wright? He needed to solve this case before he lost his mind.

"Doesn't make me feel better," she murmured. "I wish you'd persuade your uncle to shut down the production, but it would disappoint the entire town. The mayor is crowing that we're making the Sunday Charleston entertainment section. She's expecting an influx of tourists filling our coffers."

Cade sighed—and then there was that. "Stopping production would cut your paycheck and Asia's. It's not an easy choice. Have you heard how Mackie is doing?"

"He hit his head when he went down. They're holding him for observation. I'm trying not to think bad thoughts." She started to stand.

Cade set the mug aside and reached to stop her. The instant the pain shot through him, he knew his error, but he didn't want her to leave. "Stay. You help me focus on facts. I want to believe this is all a form of sabotage, but I can't fathom how it's done."

"Who would gain from sabotage?"

At least she wasn't trying to convince him of ghosts. "Unsure," he admitted as she sat down again. "Mackie has multiple enemies. But I can't see any of them sabotaging a production without a profit motive. Everyone stands to lose if the film isn't made."

"Do we assume he came here specifically to hire a local lawyer to stop Zoe? Stopping production wouldn't stop that, would it?" She plucked restlessly at the sheet, not looking at him.

He wasn't wearing a shirt. Too damned hot and it irritated the bandage. Was he making the unflappable vet nervous? That didn't ease his boner. Not for the first time, he cursed the angry wound preventing him from pulling her closer.

He had to drag his mind back to the question. "He only needs to be here if they're going before a judge, I suppose. Everything else can be done online. The film budget is paying his travel expense."

"Is he the type to hire thugs to harm or threaten Zoe?"

Cade considered that. "If he's planning on suing her for defamation, he must think he has information against her. I still can't see why that requires his presence unless a courtroom is involved. He can leave anytime, I assume."

"And insurance would cover investment losses if he shut everything down, but he wouldn't get paid, right? So, if it's sabotage, Mackie may be the target, but that's pretty weak. And I can't see why killing Sandra would stop the production since you so easily replaced her."

Easily replaced only because he offered his own salary as insurance that the extra expense would be covered, but she didn't need to know that. Besides, if his experience had taught him anything, it was how to nickel and dime every line item. Sandra's death deserved to be avenged.

"Sandra's death and sabotage could be two different things. I don't think we can easily solve this," he admitted, now that his thoughts weren't whirling. "Maybe the microchip has the answers."

She nodded, then surprisingly leaned over to brush his mouth with hers. "Thank you for thinking of others besides yourself. I know you'd rather be elsewhere, but this job and Asia will change my life. I have you to thank."

He didn't want gratitude. Using his good hand, Cade held her head and brought her in for a more satisfying kiss. The contact was explosive, as he'd known it would be. This woman was a lit firecracker.

She pulled back first. "I don't do casual," she warned, hastily standing and retying the robe belt he'd loosened. "I'm tied to this town, and you're not. Good night."

Cade closed his eyes and groaned as the door closed behind her. Why did women make sex so damned difficult?

He knew why, but it was hard to think when all his brains had gone south. He drank the herbal she'd brought him. He was fairly sure the sugar wasn't part of any medicinal formula.

What would it be like living in a town where the women talked to ghosts and animals and relied on herbs and amulets—as if this were the seventeenth century?

A town where a fashionista mayor had the ability to summon film makers to bring in much needed revenue?

And had that kiss been the result of Iddy's *knowing* of his desperate lust? How the hell did any man live with a woman like that?

WITH LESS THAN SIX HOURS SLEEP, IDDY WAS BARELY DRESSED WHEN HER PHONE rang. She punched answer on her way down to rummage for breakfast. Morning sun spilled through the front door.

"You should probably get down here before your mom kills your dad. Don't think the town needs more murder headlines," Pris said, not sounding too urgent.

"Can you throw cold water on them?" In exasperation, Iddy turned toward the front door instead of the kitchen.

She hadn't slept much after that encounter with Cade. She really didn't need this now. Why on earth was her father still here?"

"Tempting," Pris acknowledged. "But I have customers. Bring a bucket and lure them out." She hung up.

It didn't make sense to drive the Tahoe a few blocks and then have to walk from the city parking lot. Iddy just jogged down the street, plotting how to kill her parents. She hoped her aunts weren't involved yet. It was before eight, after all.

Aunt Mavis's Psychic Solutions shop was still dark. That didn't mean she wasn't next door at the diner, buying donuts. Iddy jogged by without being flagged down.

Afterthought wasn't large. Pris's café was a block down from the courthouse. Good location for all the lawyers and jurors and whatever to stop in for coffee and a quick snack. If her parents killed each other, they'd have lots of witnesses.

To her surprise, the director—Brice. . . Brice Kennedy, she remembered his name now—was already setting up a scene for the day's shooting. She probably ought to keep track of the production schedule and which animals he was harassing today, but she had the video link in her phone and relied on that. She hadn't checked it at this hour. They usually didn't work before ten.

She wanted to take a look at the corral his help was building, but she dutifully entered the café to throw verbal water on her parents. Maybe Pris would give her coffee.

Although Iddy's mother was the tallest of the Tres Madres, Slate still towered nearly a foot taller. Undaunted, Felicia waved her fist under his beak of a nose and had him backed up against the café wall.

Let it be duly noted who the abuser was in this relationship, Iddy thought wryly.

Also taller than her mother, Iddy simply walked between the combatants, grabbing her mother's raised fist and pushing her toward the counter. "People are trying to eat. Take this outside with the other mindless animals."

If either of them felt pain, it was emotional, and Iddy didn't register it. Her mother tore her arm away, straightened her colorful tunic over her bright red leggings, and picked up a paper coffee cup from the counter. "This is not your fight, Idonea."

"There are three people in this family. Of course it's my fight." Iddy caught her mother's wrist again before she could fling the cup. Glancing over her shoulder, she glared at her dad. "You spent the night together, didn't you? Then told her you were going back to La-La Land. So, go. Don't come back."

"That's harsh, Idonea. I still have business here. Where's Cade?" He brushed down his fancy cowboy shirt where angry fingers had apparently wrinkled it.

"With any luck, getting some much-needed rest. Let him alone. I'm a big girl now. If you need information, try me." She marched her mother toward the door.

"Except for one thing, Macho Men don't need women," her mother said scornfully, not fighting Iddy. "Your Cade is another just like him. Don't fall for that trap. Find a nice polite accountant who will come home every night and leave his work at the office."

"Cade is an accountant." Slate shouted after them. "He just has a lot of fancy titles to hide the fact."

"And I'm the one who doesn't leave my work at the office," Iddy pointed out as they reached the sidewalk. "Stereotyping is senseless."

Her mother pulled her arm away and sniffed disdainfully. "You've been warned. I can't save you from heartbreak. But I can tell you that your father is conspiring with that man." She nodded at the director taking notes on his tablet and talking into his headphones at the same time.

"Kennedy appears to be the only sane man of the lot, besides Cade. One hopes they're conspiring for good. I'm hungry. I need to go back and grab breakfast. Why don't you flirt with Mr. Kennedy and find out what he's doing?"

"Huh." Diverted, her mother watched the bespectacled director. "He's skinny. I bet he doesn't eat enough."

"He probably eats scripts and nibbles small animals. Have at him." Iddy swung around and returned inside, where her father was rescuing his order from the counter.

Pris handed Iddy a sack that smelled delicious and pointed at the kitchen door. Iddy got the message. Keeping her parents apart had been a sport in their younger years.

Iddy took Slate's massive arm and steered him around the counter. "Who are you spying on and why?"

"None of your concern." As they strolled through, he glanced around at Pris's busy kitchen. At least Dante and the twins weren't here at this hour. "Looks like you girls turned out okay without fathers around."

"We might have turned out better if we'd had two parents to understand us, but we look after each other. And I won't be diverted. I met Zoe yesterday. If you know her story, I'm hoping you're working with her and not against her."

"Stay out of this, Idonea. None of it is pretty and a lot of people will be hurt if you interfere in what you don't understand. Tell Cade I'll be in touch with him later." Emerging in the back alley, he strode away.

She'd be better off helping her mother tackle Brice. Felicia had no trouble communicating.

Instead, Iddy carried her breakfast to a concrete bench on Main Street that her family had donated to the town years ago. It rather intimidatingly faced the courthouse, as if anyone sitting here was keeping an eye on the law. Or maybe that was her mood as she unwrapped her egg bagel and watched Brice and her mother consulting.

Her mother's amulets were mostly harmless, imbued with the knowledge she gained from her empathic abilities. Her mother and aunts had been raised in more narrow-minded times. They'd had to hide their gifts and never been allowed proper education and exploration, which had limited their abilities. That no one had been killed yesterday while Evie and Iddy wore protection necklaces didn't necessarily mean anything. They'd simply been more careful than they might have been without warnings hanging around their necks.

So Felicia selling amulets to Kennedy was simply business as usual. That he actually bought them—was far more suspicious. Which ones did he buy? That behavior provided more information than Aunt Mavis's crystal ball.

Iddy sipped her coffee and waited for her mother to quit prying, knowing Felicia would find her.

Sure enough, once Brice strode off to direct work elsewhere, her mother toddled over and sat down.

"Hollywood corrupts," she announced. "Power and greed, very bad combination."

"Tell me about it." Iddy finished her bagel.

"He's not a bad man, but he's watched too many bad men. He thinks the end justifies the means. Someone is likely to be hurt."

"Someone already has. You're saying Brice is responsible?"

Her mother screwed up her face in thought. "Possibly. He's certainly feeling guilty. And desperate enough to buy a protection amulet. I gave him a truthfulness one instead. Let Evie and Jax at him before it wears off."

Twenty-five

Evie pinned a ribbon in Loretta's hair to hold back the fringe she was growing out. "You'll have to cut the sides if you ever want these strands to even out."

Psycat curled restlessly around their ankles—never a good sign. Ever since Iddy had attempted to teach the cat how to talk, the Siamese had been sensitive to human tension. Sensitive, as *aware*—not necessarily caring—he was a cat after all.

"Larraine says she's booked her hairdresser for all of us tomorrow." Loretta bounced eagerly out of Evie's hands to snatch up her schoolbooks. "We can all go together, like a bachelorette party, right?"

Probably preferable to a bar, alcohol, and naked men, but Evie didn't discourage an eleven-year-old's innocent assumptions. "You think Gracie, Pris, and Iddy will join us?"

"Of course they will! We can all have milkshakes and brownies and have our nails done. And Aster should be there too. Do you think Pris will marry Dante? Maybe Nan should come? Would she come without her twin? We don't want boys!"

There spoke an eleven-year-old. Even brilliant Indigo children had blind spots.

Evie dumped Psycat in his favorite box on top of the refrigerator and picked up her car keys. Loretta could bike to school, but this parenting business was still new. She didn't like taking chances with this precious child she'd been given.

"Just persuading Pris out of her kitchen is enough task for now. Let's offer a general invitation and see what happens." Her phone binged with a text but Evie ignored it. For these few minutes, Loretta had her full attention.

"Betty George said she might speak to our class," Loretta announced happily as they drove toward Main Street.

"Betty George? How did you do that?" Evie almost lost her focus between the ringing phone, Loretta's announcement, and the unusual traffic.

Loretta grabbed the phone for her. "It's Aunt Iddy. Should I answer? She texted you too."

Since Iddy and Pris were like sisters to Evie, Loretta didn't differentiate them from Gracie. They were all aunts in her mind.

"Might be a good idea." Stymied by the line of cars, Evie turned away from Main Street and took a back road in the direction of the school. The phone stopped ringing before Loretta could answer.

"The text says she's at the café and needs to talk." She hit the voicemail icon and Iddy sounded a little more urgent.

"Kennedy ordered the bull brought to town. Avoid the courthouse square. Mom says he's guilty and gave him a truth amulet. Better hop over here soon."

"Shall I call Dad?" Loretta asked anxiously.

"He's still in the shower. Send him a text and call Cade." Bulls on Main Street were not a good idea, especially if car horns started blaring. Fortunately, people down here were polite and didn't hit the horn—until the bull rushed at them.

Evie steered down still another side street when it was apparent the unusual traffic wasn't going away. She hoped the bull was still penned.

Loretta left a voice mail with Cade. He might still be asleep. The traffic backup was even worse over here. Giving up, Evie maneuvered into the city parking lot. "I'll walk with you over to the highway. That may be faster."

Abandoning the car in the lot—Mayor Larraine had ordered the meters removed this spring, gaining the approval of almost every resident except the city council—Evie hurried Loretta down to the highway that became Main Street. The road out of town passed the school and the Antique Barn where Nick worked, and Gracie often stopped on her way to school. Sure enough, her sister was in the parking lot.

Traffic on the highway had slowed to a crawl and many of the cars had pulled off to let out students.

"Wow." Loretta stared at the strange sight. "Is the president coming to town?"

"Just a bull, I suspect." Evie hugged her daughter. "There's Aunt Gracie. She'll see everyone crosses the road okay."

Evie watched until Loretta was safely in her sister's care, then turned to walk into town. She punched Iddy's number on the way.

"Nice circus," she said when Iddy answered. "They couldn't wait until the kids were in school?"

"Bull got loose when they unloaded it. Surprise, surprise. They've barricaded the street. I have it cornered, but I can't hold it forever. Apparently, ropers weren't in the budget. Is Cade up yet?"

"Not when I left. I'll see if Jax is answering. You think Cade can rope?"

"With his arm, probably not. I left my car at your place. If one of them will grab the tranq gun and bring it over, I can use that. Hate to. Won't solve the traffic. But this isn't a goat I can pick up and carry off."

"Got it. Give me a minute, and I'll be with you." Evie cut off Iddy and called Jax. He answered on the first ring. "Have a situation downtown. Wake Cade, if you can. Find Iddy's keys and grab her tranquilizer gun and kit. You'll need the Harley to reach us."

"I have the keys," Jax reported efficiently. "I'll hit Cade on the way back to the bike. Give me two minutes."

She loved a man who unquestioningly responded to her insane requests as needed. The world definitely deserved a future with a few more of him in it.

She located Iddy easily enough. Her cousin was ordering men to erect fences across Main Street to keep cars out. The company's cattle truck and a limo lined either side of the road inside the perimeter of the temporary paddock. In between the vehicles and the fences, the snorting bull looked ready to attack anything that moved. The low-slung limo appeared to be its current target, stupid animal.

Then she took a good look at Iddy and realized her cousin was probably furious enough to be mentally directing the animal at a car instead of the men setting up the fence.

"Help is on the way," Evie shouted over the crowd gathering on the corner. She preferred not going closer. Iddy's mental hoodoo was fragile. Her cousin didn't need the distraction.

Iddy stood between the truck and the limo, concentrating on calming the frightened animal, presumably until it could be roped and led back to the truck. She directed one of the crew to drop a sack of feed over the fence. The bull backed off to watch.

Remembering the warning about the director, Evie glanced around for Brice Kennedy. The skinny, bespectacled man stood on a stepstool—*ordering the film crew to catch the action.*

To Evie's utter dismay, the two co-stars, dressed in tailored denim and leather and made up for the camera, lingered outside the portable fence that wouldn't stop a sheep much less a bull. These people were unequivocally certifiable and deserved their fates.

Iddy had said the bull hated Roy.

Evie instantly grasped what her cousin would not—Iddy was likely to be blamed for any disaster. She was the official wrangler, after all.

Hearing the Harley approaching, Evie eased her way over to the director. His aura was over-excited and determined as he pointed at the limo. Was there someone in there?

"That's it, that's it!" Kennedy shouted. "We want the bull attacking the car. Open that door! Betty, Roy get ready. . ."

"Open that door and you're dead meat," Iddy shouted back, crouching down to open the feed sack. "I can't hold this animal."

"It's your job to hold that animal!" Brice shouted furiously.

"What, you like your wrangler dead? And half the crew in traction?" Iddy shouted back.

"You're fired!" Brice shouted. His aura turned fiery. Huh, Aunt Felicia's amulet might be working.

"I'm the town's animal control officer and your license is revoked!" Iddy retorted.

To Evie's astonishment, Brice almost looked satisfied as he shouted "Cut!" What the fancy heck was happening here?

The shouting was enough for Iddy to lose her mental control. The volatile animal charged—directly at Iddy.

Evie shrieked, knowing it was too late for a warning.

RIDING UP ON THE BACK OF JAX'S HARLEY UNTIL THEY REACHED THE FENCE, CADE'S heart stopped in his throat at sight of the loose bull and Iddy. He was off the bike and aiming the tranq gun before Jax cut the motor. Pain shot through his injured shoulder, but letting anything happen to Iddy was beyond unthinkable.

Before he could aim, the bull charged. *Noooooo. . .*

Tossing the gun to Jax, Cade dived past the limo to cover Iddy, bringing her to the ground on top of the feed sacks.

Before the bull attacked or Jax could fire, a single gunshot brought the animal to its knees in a bellow of pain. Iddy's accompanying wail of horror and anguish silenced the mob.

Fearing she'd been struck or he'd crushed her, Cade carefully rolled off, examining her for blood. He breathed again as Iddy sat up, furious and apparently unhinged—by experiencing the bull's pain? He didn't attempt to stop her as she crawled to the bellowing animal, muttering soothing phrases. The bull struggled to stand. From the sidewalk, Jax hit him with a dart. The poor beast didn't deserve to suffer.

Neither did Iddy.

When she collapsed, too, Cade figured they were both out for the count. He didn't want to consider why he thought anything that irrational. He just gathered the raven-haired vet against him, held her in his aching arms, made sure she was breathing, and let chaos erupt.

JAX HANDED THE TRANQUILIZER GUN TO A BYSTANDER. HE HAD HIS OWN WEAPON OUT while scouring the courthouse roof for the shooter, when Evie smacked his arm.

"Where do you keep that thing? On the bike? Did you think you could shoot a bull?" She beat him with her small fist before collapsing, sobbing, against his chest.

"I'd do better with a rifle," he admitted, holding her close but keeping an eye out over her shoulder. Love provided the understanding to know she simply needed to express her horror, but he couldn't contain his protective instincts. He had to locate an active shooter.

The only person holding a rifle was Roy, the fake cowboy. Nope. No way did that compute. The angle was all wrong to start with. No smoke, no gunpowder stench. . . That had been a high-power, long-distance shot.

"Brice," Evie hiccupped. "We have to question Brice. There's something squirrely happening here."

"Yeah, I'm picking up on that." Seeing Reuben dashing over from City Hall, Jax signaled him toward the movie cowboy with the rifle.

There. . . A large form on the courthouse roof. *Iddy's father?* What the. . . ? Slate wasn't carrying a rifle. Was he looking for the shooter? Or had he done the shooting? He'd lived in this town, knew his way through the courthouse. . .

On the ground, Iddy and Cade had recovered their senses enough to shout orders about the bull. Jax was a city boy and couldn't help there. But at Evie's insistence, he located the skinny director ordering his minions and led her in that direction. Having his own personal lie detector was convenient. This nonsense ended *now*. He had a wedding planned, and bulls and shooters weren't terrorizing their guests if he could help it.

Jax used his size to shove his way between the scrawny director and his half-baked crew. "I trust shooting the bull was not in the script."

"Who are you and why do you care?" Kennedy tried to turn away.

Escaping Jax's hold, Evie circled the director, blocking his escape. She was short and cute and a sunset-haired menace no one could avoid if she put her mind to it. "That was my cousin you almost got killed. Have you ever been mauled by a bull? He can rip you open faster than a heart surgeon."

The crowd dropped back to let Mean Mena stroll up in her uniform. "I have people looking up all the charges I plan to lock your bony ass up for. We can take a little walk over to the station, or I can slap bracelets on you and order a patrol car. Your call."

Mena had been watching a little too much TV, Jax concluded, but she captured the director's attention.

"I'm not responsible for the bull," Kennedy protested. "That's why we hire an animal wrangler!"

"Who you didn't listen to," Jax pointed out. "Endangering life, property, and livestock immediately come to mind."

Mean pulled out her notebook and duly noted the charges.

"I take my orders from Mackie," Brice snarled. "He approved the script and scene, the wrangler had a copy, and I was told we had to wrap up the bull's scenes today. All I do is order sound and film." Indignantly, he handed over his tablet. "It's all right there."

"Guilty as sin," Evie said cheerfully, presumably reading his aura. "Where's the shooter? Are you sure it's the bull that was supposed to be shot?"

Jax whistled. Mena's eyebrows shot up. Reuben was already jogging over to the courthouse. The engineering professor and security expert had apparently decided the same as Jax—the courthouse roof had been the angle for the shot that hit the bull. And Jax was fairly certain Iddy's father was up there. He studied the trajectory.

The bull had been hit in the hindquarters. The limo was parked across the street from the courthouse, in direct line of sight of the courthouse roof.

A shaken Wright, Mackie's assistant, climbed out of the limo's back seat. Had he been the target? Or ordering the action? They should have left him in jail.

"Camera?" Jax called to Reuben before he could get out of earshot.

The mayor's security held up his phone and made a gesture they'd practiced in their military days. Reuben and Roark had set up their own cameras around town the minute Evie had taken Sandra's case. He was sending footage.

Kennedy grew considerably paler behind his black-rimmed glasses. "What camera?"

"Security. You didn't really think we're rural rubes, did you now? My office is one block back." Jax gestured. "Why don't we all adjourn there?" He glanced at Evie. "I assume you don't know what he's guilty of?"

"You assume rightly," she said with her usual cheer. "I'll have Pris send up yummies and a pot of coffee. Mena, that's better than whatever they have at the station."

"You and whose mother gonna 'splain that to Troy?" the cop asked.

Evie held up her phone. "Already done. The mayor doesn't want more news crews."

Mena's phone rang. She glanced at it in frustration and walked away to answer.

Jax really loved this town. He didn't need Evie's explanation but hid his grin when she whispered, "Called Mom, who called the mayor, who called Troy. I love cell phones."

"You called your mother or she already knew?" Jax didn't really care. He just wanted this over so their honeymoon could go as planned. It wouldn't if Evie was hunting killers.

"Little of everything," she said, kissing his cheek. "It's a small town and there are eyes everywhere."

Mena returned and yanked her thumb at the wilting director. "His office, now. I'm not arresting you yet, but if you want an attorney, I suggest you don't hire Jax. That was his wife's maid of honor you nearly got killed."

Twenty-six

CADE KNEW IDDY WOULDN'T LEAVE THE BULL. HE DIDN'T WANT TO LEAVE IDDY. Every instinct screamed to protect her, shelter her from whatever the hell was happening here. But she wasn't paying a bit of attention to him or his admonitions. Still, he'd felt her shake and weep, and she'd let him hold her. He knew she wasn't as strong as she pretended.

Now that the bull was being loaded into the truck, he was pretty sure the woman in his arms had reached murderous rage. But the man responsible had just been led off by the law. He wanted to hear Brice's story.

He wanted to hear Slate Cooper's story, too, but that could wait. He hadn't missed the big man on the roof. Cooper taught the use of guns along with his *sensitivity* training. Cade figured he could call his uncle and get that particular tale—but not the director's.

Reluctantly, knowing she could handle herself, he kissed Iddy's forehead. "I'm going after Brice, okay?"

Her luminous aqua eyes swept up to transfix him. "I want him chopped, boiled, and fried." Her eyes said it all. She respected his ability to do just that.

The connection was visceral, a deep-down meeting of minds and souls.

Other than sheer terror at that level of connection, Cade didn't know how to react. It had taken him years to overcome his need to coddle his siblings through tears and tantrums and ignore their pleas for what he couldn't give. Emotions got in the way of getting things done, like right now, when he had axes to grind. He needed to box up this internal pain the way he did the external.

But losing this woman would be like losing his right arm.

"Save the butchering for Mackie," he warned, attempting rationality. "Brice is only a side order of rice. Keep that bull sedated. Spend whatever you need to protect yourself and everyone else, okay?" At this point, he didn't care whose checkbook he emptied—definitely evidence he'd gone overboard and was in over his head.

Her lovely wide mouth tightened. "Got it. Mackie will owe some farmer a huge bill by the time I'm done. I think the cost overrun will show it's time to shut down. Weigh damage against money when you make the call. Go after Brice. My mother gave him a truth amulet." She kissed his stubbled cheek.

He hadn't had time to shower today. He probably stank to high heaven. He was wearing the only buttoned short sleeve shirt he'd brought with him. It was in dire need of washing, but it was all he could maneuver on without help. And she kissed him anyway. *She understood.*

He almost smiled as he set her down and walked away. And then he remembered Brice Kennedy ordering the limo door to open, and he glanced around for Wright. The production assistant wasn't in sight. Cade stopped at the limo and pounded on the window. The driver rolled it down. "Where's Wright?"

The driver shrugged. "Probably buying new underwear. This is a no-parking zone. If they're pulling out for the day, I'll drive around to the parking lot."

"Let me know when Wright shows up again." Back to growling, Cade followed the others down the street.

Jax's office was on the second floor in an old building with no elevators. Cade could hear shouts before he reached the top of the stairs. Lawyers probably saw a lot of angry clients. He understood why Jax packed a gun. Ex-military, his host at least knew how to use it.

Truth amulets. . . He didn't understand so much. Had Iddy really said *truth* amulet?

At this hour, the receptionist wasn't at her desk yet. Cade opened the inner office door on what to all appearances was a heated coffee klatch. In between shouting at each other, everyone was sipping from steaming cups and nibbling on pastries, including the uniformed cop. Shoulders slumped into a question mark, Brice glumly held his food without lifting it to his mouth.

At Cade's arrival, they shut up and just glared. Nice to make an entrance, but he figured Jax had shouted them down to watch whatever he was fiddling with on his computer.

Lacking sufficient furniture, Evie perched on the edge of Jax's desk, swinging her bare legs and sandals. Jax turned the monitor so Brice and the cop could see it. He glanced up at Cade and nodded toward the credenza where what was left of the food waited. Starving, he poured coffee and grabbed sausages blanketed in pastry. Using the wall to rest against, he set the cup on a bookshelf and dug in.

The monitor flickered grainy footage from one of the team's security cameras. Cade confirmed that was Slate Cooper on the courthouse roof with a rifle. He chewed his pastry and let the lawyer do the talking. Cooper had sent Cade and the film crew to this town for a reason. There was more here than met the eye.

"You have an excellent reputation as an intelligent, experienced director." Jax said. "Nothing we've seen this past week would lead me to believe you're the real Brice Kennedy behind that reputation."

The director winced. "I work for Mackie. This film is not my vision; it's his. It's supposed to be a quick filler before my next real film."

Figuring Jax didn't know a lot about how Hollywood worked, Cade washed down crumbs with his coffee before asking, "What was Mackie holding over your head?"

That drew a grimace. "Drunk driving accident. He claimed he was driving, so I didn't lose my license. He doesn't have a license to lose, and I paid the fines. But if it gets about that I'm still drinking. . . I could lose this next job."

If that was an example of a truth amulet working, it left a lot to be desired. Mackie had a tight-knit crew of louts who couldn't find jobs anywhere else, ones who'd been with him since his porn film days. Making a highly employable Brice one of his extortion victims didn't compute.

Cade shook his head slightly at Jax, who picked up on it with a curt nod. "Fine. Pretending I accept that, why would you set a scene with a loose bull in the middle of town?"

"Mackie wanted it," Brice insisted. "It's the action climax. We needed to send the bull back this weekend, so it had to be shot early."

"Bull crap," Cade said succinctly. "I read the original script. Yes, the bull scene was to be shot today—*at the farm*. There was nothing in the script about letting a bull attack a limo. Doesn't exactly fit the theme now, does it?"

"Mackie changed the script. Wright stupidly had the limo pull up where the cart should have been, and then the bull got loose. The wrangler was supposed to have the bull partially sedated and a rope around its legs. She arrived late and unprepared." Brice set his coffee down and crossed his arms belligerently. "I didn't want to film the scene again, so I took advantage of the opportunity, figuring we could edit later."

Evie looked as if she was swallowing bad medicine, but she must have bit her tongue. She said nothing once the cop held up her hand. Even Brice looked a little. . . startled. . . at his own explanation. Rather than pound the director into the floor, Cade imitated Evie. He ground his molars, sipped his coffee to keep his tongue occupied, and helped himself to a scone.

"It says here in this script you sent to me," the skinny uniformed cop waved her tablet, "that the animal is to attack a *fence*, not a cart or a limo. This email that went out changing the time of the scene was not addressed to your wrangler, the producer, or the producer's assistant. And 'less I have this wrong, your producer has been *unconscious* and in the hospital since yesterday afternoon and cannot approve script changes. You did not have a permit for closing Main Street. Today's permit only allows closure of a side street after 10 am. I am holding you responsible for every charge on today's debacle. We're still compiling the list, and by the time I'm done, you're looking at jail time, not just fines and losing your license. You cannot endanger lives without consequences."

Impressed at the young cop's assessment, Cade nodded agreement. "Seems like endangering lives is your specialty. That was you who released the brake on the Hummer and nearly crushed the crew at the farm, wasn't it?"

Brice grimaced. "I didn't know it would roll that fast. I figured if they were saying the farm was haunted, they'd blame it on a ghost and maybe they'd all quit. One of them *killed* Sandra! And they acted as if nothing had happened. The whole lot needed to be shaken out of their complacence."

Now they were getting somewhere. Cade glanced at Jax for permission to continue. At his nod, he tightened the screws. "The animal control officer has revoked your permit. Looks like the city is about to revoke the rest. I will have to call my uncle and tell him to cut his losses. You have succeeded in sabotaging the project, at the expense of a lot of people's pockets and time. Want to explain why?"

Let the truth amulet put that in its pipe and smoke it.

Brice managed to display a shade of defiance as he leaned back in the big leather chair and let his long legs sprawl. "Not my problem."

Epic fail on the part of the amulet. But Cade wasn't in charge of this show. He followed Jax's direction and watched Evie.

She twirled a strand of her hair and looked as if she'd slipped off to distant lands. When she returned, she simply asked, "You hired Sandra because you knew she was friends with Zoe, didn't you?"

How in hell had she come up with that?

Cade checked his watch. There was a slim chance that his uncle was awake. He texted him with that question. He didn't receive a reply.

Brice at least looked shocked.

Cade let his mind play with that scenario. After being blackmailed into working for a pervert, Brice hired a friend of the person suing Mackie? Brought

Sandra out here hoping she would do what? Sandra was mercenary and might have taken the job for her own reasons, but the director would have been an idiot to hire a loose cannon.

Had Brice hoped Sandra would help him sabotage the film? That made a little more sense, but what would he accomplish by pulling the rug out from under Mackie? That wouldn't stop the producer from announcing to the world that Brice was drinking. That was a pretty damned feeble excuse in the first place. Every damned person in the business did drugs and drank to excess as far as Cade could see.

Coming from an insurance perspective, he could be biased.

This scenario still did not compute, but it was a fraction closer.

Brice stuttered over a non-reply to Evie's question about hiring Sandra. Cade wondered if the truth amulet was on a cord around his neck and if he could strangle him with it.

Evie merely smiled and said, "You've been lying and only half-telling us the truth. Sandra said she had a boyfriend who was helping her. You're the boyfriend, aren't you?"

Whammo. Aside from the fact that Sandra was dead and couldn't tell anyone anything. . . Cade straightened and studied Brice's dour face. Sandra had taken up with *Brice Kennedy*? He had to be almost twenty years older. But he had money and was on the verge of fame and power. . .

Brice actually looked a little younger when he sat up straight and glared. "She told me she and Zoe had the goods on Mackie. It's time his reign of terror ended. If he lost money on this film, he was dead to Hollywood."

Interesting, but not the whole scenario, Cade calculated. "Were you in the truck waiting in the lot the night Sandra died?"

The director shoved his thinning hair from his face and glared. "She said she'd pushed someone a little too far, and she needed to get away. I rented a truck in my own name, drove over, and waited, but she texted me to say she didn't need me, after all. I couldn't let the crew see me, so I couldn't go in and find her. I told her I'd wait in town if she changed her mind, but she didn't reply. I had no choice but to drive off."

If this was evidence of how an amulet worked, Cade wanted to buy a trunk full. But he wanted to pound Brice Kennedy into the ground first. If the little shit had just risked his reputation for half a second. . . He might have been killed too. Cade slumped against the wall in frustration.

"You have a burner phone? Is that what she called?" Jax held out his hand.

"I couldn't let Mackie see my calls." He pulled a small flip phone from his pocket and defiantly handed it to Mena instead of Jax.

"Why the hell didn't you tell that to the sheriff?" Jax demanded.

Brice struggled, as if choking on his own tongue. Cade contemplated strangling him with the amulet again since the thought had been so successful last time. Look at him, Superstition Man.

"I didn't think saying anything would help, and I needed to make Mackie think everyone was on board with his project. The more he spent, the deeper in debt he sank. If Roy and Betty knew I'd been out there, they'd have thought I was spying on them." Brice looked a little stronger as he added, "The two dinosaurs think they're fooling everyone by sleeping in different towns. They're both married and their spouses would divorce them in a minute if they knew the trailer is their little getaway."

"Roy O'Bryan was at the farm when Sandra died? Or could have been?" The cop dived right on that one.

"I saw the Buick he usually hires arriving as I left. He had his headlights off and rolled in quietly, stopping at the bottom of the drive, but yeah, I drove right past him. Betty's personal assistant usually takes the car for an evening off to give them privacy, then returns when they call." Brice slumped again, his face wrinkling as if he'd been tortured and released.

Cade had more questions, but Jax and Evie's phones pinged. Since the lawyer took the time to read the message, Cade waited. If he was paying his uncle's expenses for this debacle, he wanted legal expertise in interrogation.

Jax whistled.

Evie pushed icons on hers. Her eyes widened in what appeared to be horror. "What is this?"

"The video on the microchip hidden in Sandra's saddle. I'd say that was the evidence she was taking to Zoe—or how she was blackmailing Mackie. Or both." Jax held out his phone for Cade to take.

They'd taken this from police files? The uniform looked more curious than confused. She probably didn't grasp what Evie's team must have done.

Rather than concern himself over how they'd done it, Cade studied the jerky black-and-white images and felt his gut tighten. That was Mackie's corpulent anatomy shoving a woman onto a bed. The face wasn't clear. The *action* was. The woman beat frantically at Mackie's shoulders until he slapped her. The large ring on the victim's fingers and her western boots were strong evidence to substantiate Zoe's case if she could produce those items.

And Sandra had this chip in her possession.

Motive for murder with a capital M—in bold face and exclamation points.

~

THE BULL PATCHED UP, THE FARMER REASSURED, AN EXCEPTIONALLY LARGE BILL AND letter of resignation emailed to everyone involved in Mackie Productions, including Cade's uncle, Iddy retreated to the comfort of her office. She retied the *I need a good home* ribbon around the ragdoll kitty, let her loose, and, while nursing one of the preemies, contemplated her next step.

She'd just burned all her bridges. Cade no longer had a reason to hang around. She wouldn't be expanding the clinic anytime soon, although if they actually paid some portion of her Hollywood salary, she might buy a cattle trailer. She waited for Asia's lunch break before facing her valuable new assistant.

When the young vet in her turban, and lab coat crawling with kittens, sat across from her, wearing a quizzical expression, Iddy sent her the text she'd prepared in advance. Asia studied her phone and Iddy's detailed proposal for partnership.

The new vet nodded once, removed the preemie's twin from a pocket, stroked it the way Iddy was stroking the other, and grinned. "I would do it for free," she said slowly, to be perfectly clear. "I love it here." She signed this last for emphasis.

Iddy almost melted in relief. She opened her desk drawer and produced a box of expensive chocolates she'd ordered for a special occasion. Despite crumbling Hollywood dreams, celebration seemed appropriate. "Welcome to the team and thank you!"

Her assistant wouldn't be working for free, just less than she deserved. But she'd have use of Iddy's trailer until they were able to expand the business.

They chose chocolates, clinked them like champagne glasses, then scrambled to catch the ragdoll before it bumped the box off the desk.

Iddy might have to live with Jax and Evie forever. It would take years to save enough to expand the clinic. But she'd have a life of sorts at last. She could spend time with Loretta while Evie and Jax honeymooned. Maybe she'd even take a vacation and find some man to distract her from her obsession with Cade.

He'd risked his life for her. But she thought he was probably the kind of man who would risk his life for any stranger passing by. Which was why she was obsessed.

She stuffed another chocolate in her mouth and went back to work with the animals who couldn't tell their owners what was wrong. Being able to communicate with simple minds calmed and reassured her, unlike dealing with human complications.

By mid-afternoon, the two of them working in tandem had slowed the steady stream of patients to a trickle. Iddy dove into catching up on neglected housekeeping, cleaning cages and preparing food for special diets. No one had called to tell her what was happening in town. She was just debating calling Evie—not Cade, not yet—when her receptionist said a man wanted a word with her.

She quickly washed her hands, straightened her hair, and donned a clean lab coat. Men didn't normally stop by to have a word with her. It had to be Cade.

The shock of seeing Mackie's assistant, the one out on bail for shooting Cade, did not improve her mood. "May I help you?" She wasn't taking Wright back to her private office.

La Chusa flew in from the window in back to settle on a perch Iddy had constructed in the lobby. The raven fixed their visitor with a beady eye, but there wasn't anything the bird could tell her that Iddy didn't already know.

"Look, we gotta finish this film. Mackie promises to pay all the damages personally, if you'll just give us the permits. We don't need to do more downtown. We'll keep it on the farm." The bow-legged man looked anxious—and nervous. He twisted his ratty Stetson in his hands.

Iddy checked that he hadn't acquired another gun. Crossing her arms, she shook her head. "My duty is to the animals, not the film. Your director nearly killed an extremely valuable animal today. It could have gored me and many others. This is not acceptable. I've asked Cade to call the owners of all the animals to pick them up. I don't care what you do about the city's permits, but there will be no more animals on the set."

She'd actually texted Cade with the request. He hadn't replied. She assumed he'd tell her this evening but was busy now.

Wright looked a little more desperate. "Mackie's awake and out of the hospital. He's demanding we keep the schedule. He can ruin us!"

Iddy wanted to feel sympathy, but she didn't. "Then I suggest you not work for men with no conscience. He'll not be working in this state again. You'll have to film back in Hollywood."

She could and would send an alert to the state's other animal control officers if she thought he'd attempt to move the operation elsewhere. She couldn't guarantee they'd respond, but she could go over their heads if needed.

"The budget won't allow us to do that! I can speed up production, have them work nights, get out of your hair. . ."

La Chusa flew down to sit on her shoulder and caw loudly, causing the assistant to back off nervously. "That sounds even worse. Good-day, Mr. Wright." She turned on her heel and stalked back to her office.

As she left, Wright protested loudly. Apparently one of her customers blocked him from following her. She would check with the receptionist to find out which one and give them a discount on their bill. She really disliked arguing.

Setting the raven on the windowsill, she left Asia with the clients and immersed herself in the puppy cages in the yard. Wriggling puppies always made her feel better.

To her surprise, Betty George strolled around to watch the puppies playing. "They're so cute. I wish I had time for a pet."

The older woman seemed harmless, but if Iddy was putting her out of a job. . . She checked in with La Chusa, who was seeing no sign of Wright, just a Buick idling in the front lot. The raven was better than a security camera.

"We should all find time for simple pleasures," Iddy agreed warily. "Perhaps there is an animal shelter near your home that would enjoy having you play with the animals occasionally."

"Maybe, when I retire," she said vaguely. "I just wanted to say I'm sorry the bull was hurt. Mackie is taking Kennedy off the film. We think he may be having a nervous breakdown. If you could persuade Mr. Garcia not to shut down production, I'm sure it will run much smoother with Wright in charge."

Ah, that might explain Wright's desperation. Being a director was probably quite a step up for an assistant producer, not that Iddy knew about these things.

"Mr. Garcia will have to persuade *me* that the production can go on without harm to the animals. Best talk to him first," she advised. It seemed simpler than arguing.

"He doesn't appear to be answering his phone." She looked disappointed. "Oh, well, I had a lovely time visiting with your niece's class today. I told them they could come out to the farm and visit tomorrow. I hope there will be animals for them to see. Hug that adorable puppy for me. I'll be in my trailer this evening if you find Mr. Garcia."

She sauntered off, a little too pudgy to pull off the movie star sway but looking good for a woman her age in tight jeans and cowboy shirt.

Even the puppies didn't make Iddy feel good after that. She dug out her phone and started making calls.

Twenty-seven

FRIDAY AFTERNOON, JAX SAT IN THE MAYOR'S CITY HALL OFFICE ARGUING FOR common sense. "Look, a woman was killed on that farm, quite possibly for the microchip sitting in the sheriff's safe. Cade has been shot, Iddy nearly gored, the lead actress almost killed in a balloon. Someone else is likely to die unless we send the film crew back where they belong."

Mayor Larraine Ward didn't appear convinced. In her sedate business attire, wearing a wig fashioned in a sleek chignon, she pursed her lips in stubborn disagreement. She'd decorated her predecessor's enormous desk in photos of the town, friends, and famous visitors, evidence of the people who had given her authority.

"How will we find that poor girl's killer if they all leave town?" she asked. "Troy wants them where he can find them. Have them hire more security to patrol 24/7. I want this town known to be friendly toward the film industry. They've already made a generous contribution to the town's coffers."

"Mayor Ward." Cade spoke before Jax could. "As Iddy said, consider the damage rather than the money. I'm sure the sheriff has shown you the clip Sandra probably died for. Do you really want a violent, unprincipled man like Mackie here?"

The sheriff was trying to locate Betty and Roy for questioning about the morning's incident, but Jax didn't hold out much hope that they'd seen anything criminal besides incompetence—and even then, they wouldn't say anything.

Their careers depended on loyalty to the industry. He'd like this case solved too. He wanted people safe even more.

"I have contacts in the business," Cade continued. "What if I put in a good word for Afterthought?"

With a little more insight into the mayor's thinking than Cade, Jax knew it was Sandra's death bothering Larraine. The mayor expected Evie's family to solve it.

"Our wedding is *Sunday*," he protested what Larraine didn't say. "If we don't send the film crew away, Evie won't stop hunting until she's caught a killer. We're likely to have a shoot out in the backyard on our wedding day. You really don't want that."

"Since I'm officiating, I'll speak for everyone and say certainly not. I'll personally hire more security for the wedding. If Evie has sent the spirit energy on, then there is no reason the two of you can't happily fly off for your much deserved getaway. Reuben and Roark are here to hold the fort in your place." The mayor stood, forcing Cade and Jax to do the same.

Larraine knew better. She simply had her own agenda and always had.

Jax muttered curses as they departed. "Have you persuaded your uncle to cut his losses? Mackie can't continue without money, can he?"

Cade snarled as if he'd bite off heads. "Mackie has other sources. He may have to blackmail and twist arms and pay interest out the nose, but he's a producer. Finding money is what he does. My uncle knows that. His investors won't be happy if they lose out on an opportunity. It's not a simple call."

"Can we get Brice Kennedy drunk and persuade him to tell us everything?" Outside city hall, Jax glanced at the evening sky. No point in returning to his office.

The director had refused to reveal anything more. Mena had threatened Kennedy with fines and jail time, but she couldn't prove he had deliberately attempted to kill anyone with a bull. Sabotage, and quite possibly revenge, really did seem to be his motivation.

"You heard him. He's taken the pledge. You want to be responsible for setting him back? We have no tangible evidence that he deliberately did anything. We can surmise he was hoping to shut down production and bankrupt Mackie. If he and Sandra were blackmailing anyone, he won't admit it. He'll be gone tomorrow, his illustrious career clouded with rumor. If Kennedy thought there was any way he could come out of this a hero—" Cade left that fantasy hanging.

Brice Kennedy had shut up after the microfilm reveal. The director had no reason to kill Sandra, but he knew more than he was saying. There was nothing heroic about covering up extortion, if that's what Sandra had been doing.

"We'd better round up security, then. Roark and Reuben can't do it all. Is your uncle pulling the plug?"

"He hasn't got back to me, which means he's polling the investors. They're cautious people, on the whole. I'd expect them to cut their losses. I just have this ominous feeling that there's more to all of this, and Kennedy didn't help. I'm conjuring conspiracy theories everywhere." Cade pulled out his phone to read his texts and looked even less happy. "The limo driver left voice mail. Wright visited Iddy. That can't be good. He's headed back to Charleston, so I can't nail him today."

"Iddy will let us know if he said anything useful. I don't like any of this." Jax cursed at Cade's conspiracy theories involving wealthy moguls. "I want to pull Evie from this case, but she won't let Sandra go."

"I need to reach Slate Cooper and pry more out of him. Do we tell the sheriff who the bull shooter was or let him figure it out on his own?" Looking worse for wear, Cade stopped on Main Street rather than follow Jax back to the house.

"You're figuring Iddy will fry your testicles if you allow the filming to continue?" Jax asked in sympathy. "Might as well tell her over dinner when she can't sic the dogs on you."

"The raven can still peck out my eyes. I'll be in the same doghouse as her father. If he's smart, he's on a jet home. Shooting a bull was the same as shooting Iddy."

Jax snorted and shook his head. "Glad you're grasping the problem here. But neither bull or Iddy are dead. She's just pissed. If she won't talk to you, talk to her family. One of them will eventually see sense."

He shoved Cade toward the house before the fool man fell over from pain and exhaustion.

CADE DIDN'T KNOW IF HE WANTED IDDY TO SEE SENSE. HE WANTED HER OUT OF THIS whole debacle. He wanted out as well. The whole weird town had him believing Iddy had felt the bull being shot, that her mother's amulets forced Kennedy to speak truth, and that Evie had talked to Sandra's ghost. And then there was the raven.

He could understand why Slate Cooper had fled.

He'd earn Iddy's scorn if he did the same. For whatever reason, that mattered. He was a grown man, unafraid of superstition. Judging by appearances, Cade assumed Iddy's father had been a callow youth when he ran off. Cade wasn't.

He was obviously suffering from blood loss to the brain. Instead of hunting down Slate or Wright or any of the other suspects, he followed Jax to the chaotic comfort of the old Victorian.

They opened the door on the hunger-inducing aromas of baking biscuits and frying chicken. At their arrival, Evie and Gracie scampered up the front stairs carrying acres of green fabric Cade assumed was the wedding gown. He felt guilty for upending Jax's wedding plans.

The front parlor spilled over with Malcolm women and children. The library door was ominously closed. Cade sought Iddy in the crowded front room first. She looked grim. Oddly, the expression looked good on her. He had the strangest notion that he should hug her. . .

She glared at her mother, and the spell broke. *Spell*. Right.

Jax jogged up the stairs after Evie.

Cade shook his brainless head and boldly entered the parlor. "What is the politically correct way of asking the reason for this assemblage?"

"Don't call it a coven or pow wow and you're good," Iddy assured him. She nodded in the direction of the library door. "My dad's in there. I think he's barricaded the door. Mom hexed it. Want to go look for a killer? It would be easier."

He almost laughed at her pragmatism in the face of obviously emotional tension. "I want to talk to him. You okay?"

She nodded. "I'm good. I quit the film. Asia agreed to stay. Betty is out scaring up goodwill using the kids, and Wright wants permits so he can take over production. I refused. So, I'm fine. How about you?"

"I've been better," he admitted. He turned to the other ladies, who had gone back to laying out cards, beading, and dealing with the children. He was starting to sort them out and assumed if the twins were here, then Pris was in the kitchen. Dante and Nick had probably holed up in the man cave. "Thank you for holding Slate until I can speak with him. Is there time before dinner?"

He didn't even feel like an idiot asking. If Iddy respected these women, so did he.

"Don't invite him to dinner," Evie's mother advised, glancing up from her cards. "He might end up dead."

"Duly noted." He didn't think she was reading that from the cards or anyone's minds. She just knew her sister. He turned to Iddy. "You want to join me?"

She shrugged and followed him across the foyer. Producing a key from her pocket, she unlocked the door. "Sometimes, magic isn't necessary."

He did laugh at that. This was probably one of the grimmest weeks of his life, and she had him feeling as if insanity was normal. The urge to kiss her had to wait. Inside, her father paced like a restless bull.

"About time you got here," Slate growled. He flung a folder spilling with photographs on the library table. "Mackie needs to go down, but I'm not having my daughter hurt in the process."

Cade sorted through the photos, obviously taken from the courthouse roof this morning. "Want to clarify what in hell is happening here?"

The photos gave a better perspective of where everyone had been standing this morning, but there had been no crime, just gross neglect and arrogance. If the industry could be sued for that, there'd be no Hollywood.

"Sandra and Zoe, Brice Kennedy, your Uncle Garcia, and a number of investors are attempting a coup de grace as far as I can tell." Slate stacked the photos again. "All they told me was that they want to shut Mackie down. They knew he was out to get Zoe and was looking for a location here. I directed them to Afterthought."

"We gathered most of that," Cade said. Sometimes, conspiracy theories weren't all wrong. "I just don't understand how Sandra ended up dead."

"Neither do I, although knowing Sandra and Zoe, they were running their own operation, and the others joined in later. Brice was supposed to sabotage the film by driving up costs, bankrupting Mackie, and blackening his name with his moneymen. When it all started going wrong, I came out here to see what in hell was happening. I've been following the crew around wherever I could, but they're all doing their jobs." He paced some more.

"But it very much appears as if Sandra was blackmailing people. Judging by her little book, they were paying her cash under the table for something." Iddy was scanning the novels on the classic mid-century modern bookshelves, but she was listening.

Cade would have expected antique oak shelves in a house like this, but nothing this family did surprised him anymore. "Do we know how Sandra got the video?"

"What video?" The big man looked as if he didn't know what to do with himself. He shoved his hands in his pockets and tried not to watch his daughter.

"Sandra had a microchip video of Mackie raping a woman in cowboy boots, which we are assuming to be Zoe. We have no idea how she got it, but chances are that someone else was aware of it and didn't want it found." Giving up on being polite, Cade settled in the ancient, cracked recliner in the corner. His shoulder hurt like hell. He needed food before he collapsed of lightheadedness. But if Slate was unwelcome at the dinner table. . .

Slate cursed, then confirmed what they'd already been told "Mackie filmed everything. My guess would be that Brice got his hands on some of the films. Don't know why he'd give them to Sandra and not keep them for himself."

"To see if Sandra could identify the women," Iddy suggested. "She may have recognized the boots."

"Or the ring. The woman wore a big stone in a fancy setting. The video is black and white. I couldn't tell what kind of stone." Cade shifted his shoulder, looking for a comfortable position.

With her back to him, Iddy said, "Idiot, you should take your pain pills. Dad, Cade needs rest. Can you pretend like you've left? I'll tell them Cade and I want to eat on the porch, and we'll join you there shortly."

"They won't be fooled," Slate said in resignation. "I can't tell you much more."

"You're here. You know these people. You saved Iddy from being gored." Cade had to put that out there. He assumed Iddy had worked out the shooter for herself. "We need all the help we can get."

"Mackie may be a rapist, but one of his crew is a murderer," Slate conceded. "If we can pin Mackie to ordering Sandra's death. . . I'm in. The kid was ambitious and greedy, but she loved animals. Someone should be held responsible."

Iddy turned with an unhappy look. "Does that mean they need to continue filming animals?"

At seeing their expressions, she slammed out of the room.

"You still want me to hang around?" Slate asked dryly.

Twenty-eight

"Iddy's got a boyfriend," Evie sang in a sing-song whisper to Pris as she leaned around her cousin to grasp the biscuit pan with potholders.

"Shame that. I was counting on her being the crazy spinster aunt with a dozen cats who dotes on the kids." Pris sorted the air-fried chicken platters. "She'll starve any man to death."

"She can't help it. I don't think she's squeamish about others eating meat. But how likely is it that Cade will stick around? His aura is an awful lot like her father's."

"Which means what?" Pris gave the gravy a final whisk and poured it into a waiting bowl.

With the last of the biscuits added to an already full platter, Evie got out Iddy's beans and rice casserole. "Which means they're restless, high testosterone, not exactly thrill seekers but needing adrenalin outlets. I don't know how Cade ended up as an accountant, if that's what he really is."

"Financial investor." Pris added chicken to the platter. "Dante looked him up. Wall Street bull rider."

"Huh." Never having had money to invest, Evie didn't grasp the comparison. The dull financial guy handling Loretta's fortune didn't strike her as an adrenalin junkie. A pity Iddy didn't have a fortune for Cade to get his jollies on.

Iddy joined them in the kitchen. "If you don't mind, Cade and I will take our plates to the porch. He's trying to convince me to let the show go on."

"You need a scene re-enacting Sandra talking on her phone, blackmailing someone, like they do in the mystery shows," Evie suggested. "Have all your suspects around and let me watch them."

"Sandra didn't use her phone," Iddy reminded her. "It had to be person to person, which leaves out our most obvious suspect, Mackie, unless we're still considering the director."

"Well, Kennedy did finally admit that he was there that night," Pris pointed out.

"True, but you said his aura says he's telling the truth, and he's just a wimp. I suppose we shouldn't discount him. His motivation is as questionable as everyone else's." Iddy carried the casserole to the table as she talked.

"Sheriff's report says blunt force to the skull, similar to a shovel. I'm going with spur of the moment rage, so yeah, anyone there that night is suspect." Evie filled a plastic plate and set it aside for Slate. Iddy wasn't fooling her with the eating on the porch bit. "I have Roark and Ariel looking deeper into everyone's finances, but they've found no evidence that Mackie or anyone is paying off a killer. Tell your dad that your mom fixed the green beans," she added when Iddy returned to the kitchen.

Not showing any surprise that Evie knew her father was joining them, Iddy grimaced. "Thanks for the warning. She uses ham hocks."

"Ham hocks?" Pris curled her nose. "How did we survive childhood without weighing two hundred pounds and being on the verge of heart attack city?"

"We walked and rode everywhere because we didn't have cars," Evie said with a shrug. "Don't be such a snob. Your Junior looks as if she'll thrive on grease. Really vibrant colors. Can we keep murderers out of her future? I want this killer gone before the wedding."

She carried the biscuits to the table as the family followed their noses and began appearing in the dining room. She wanted a quiet family meal. Or what passed for one.

After delivering the chicken and returning to the kitchen, Pris came back carrying a bucket of ice and champagne bottles. Because, of course, Aunt Val had ice buckets stored in the attic, Evie realized with a mental laugh.

"Since this will have to serve as the rehearsal dinner, there's bubbly. Who wants to do the honors?" Pris gestured at the corks.

Jax and Dante each reached for a bottle.

Having just filled his plate, Cade looked a little shell shocked. "You're all in the wedding party? Should I bow out?"

Nick, Gracie's significant other, beamed. "I'm merely an usher, and I am included. Sign on to set up chairs, and you're one of us, mate."

Evie couldn't resist checking Cade's aura—a spike of terror followed by a note she might call acceptance. Or resignation. She'd have to know him better.

"It's also a killer-catching party," she informed them as everyone but Iddy and Cade took seats. "I'll let you know how that goes while the two of you bill and coo on the porch."

Loretta started to speak up, but Evie shot her a warning look. The kid needed to learn to keep quiet about some of the things she saw. Evie was providing a cover for Iddy to talk with her father. Loretta would just be curious about the lusty color of bubbles. Evie would have to explain the facts of life later. Her mothering skills were a bit eccentric, but then, so was her kid.

Looking vaguely uncomfortable, Cade carried his plate after Iddy. Evie didn't want to hurt her cousin's chances with the gorgeous financier, but he needed to be reminded this wasn't all his show.

For all she knew, Sandra might come back to haunt her if Evie didn't find her killer.

"Leave killer-catching to the sheriff," Jax said sternly as Iddy and Cade departed. He turned to Loretta. "And you are to go nowhere near that farm."

Loretta pouted.

Evie frowned. "What brought that on?"

"Cade warned me that Betty George is trying to endear herself to the locals by inviting the kids out. I don't want any innocents in harm's way if a killer is around." Jade was wearing his protective aura like a shield.

Pieces of the puzzle clicked, but Evie couldn't fit them into the big picture. She simply nodded agreement. "It's not safe out there, kiddo. Iddy almost got killed today. We'll take you to the zoo if you want animals."

"I want to see a movie being filmed! Maybe I could learn what a killer's bubble looks like." Loretta pouted some more.

"I sympathize, I really do," Evie acknowledged. This mothering business was tough. "And if I had some way of wrapping you in a bubble so you could watch as if they were on TV, I would. But this isn't TV. Sandra died. Others have been seriously hurt. Betty George is not a charming, harmless granny."

"But we're supposed to be having rehearsals and decorating for Sunday," Loretta protested. "How will we do all that if you're hunting killers?"

Everyone dug into their food rather than answer that.

"All right, we'll only make one attempt early tomorrow morning." Evie's ADD mind played with a hundred scenarios as she spoke. "We get everyone, even Mackie, there. Maybe not Zoe. I need to talk privately with Betty's assistant. *We'll* be doing the camera/action though, not Mackie."

Evie smiled benevolently as even her mother and aunts raised their glasses—probably in despair.

All her life, she'd craved respect. Here was her opportunity. If she could pull this off, then she'd know she could be the wife Jax deserved.

Twenty-nine

"THIS IS A REALLY BAD IDEA, EVIE," JAX MURMURED FURIOUSLY AS HE WATCHED HER family hand scripts to all the film crew on Saturday morning.

The sheriff had read the script they had hastily penned last night. Troy lacked imagination and didn't see how it could hurt to re-enact the crime scene like some bad mystery movie. Jax could think of ten thousand ways people could die.

Wayne Wright was strutting around, directing the scene, theoretically. In reality, Evie had recruited every member of the family to keep an eye on the cast, and Reuben and Roark were rolling the film.

"Even Troy admits that questioning isn't working. They're all skilled actors and liars. This forces them to get their stories together in front of each other. It will be fun." Evie kissed his scruffy cheek.

They'd all been up late last night writing the script and up early this morning to organize the scene. Jax appreciated that they'd stopped the alcohol after the celebratory champagne. They didn't need to be doing this with hangovers.

For reasons unclear, Evie had assigned him to Roy O'Bryan, the aging cowboy actor and Betty's presumed lover. The older man was scowling as he leaned against the Buick he'd been told to drive over and watched the antics.

Setting up a food table on the porch, Pris and Dante guarded the front door.

"What the hell is this about?" Roy asked as Jax handed him a script.

"Sheriff is trying to piece together what happened the night Sandra died. I guess he thought a film crew would respond better to theater than interrogation."

Roy scoffed. "Wright couldn't direct his way out of a paper bag. He's Mackie's stooge and no more."

"Well, Mackie fired Brice, so we had to improvise." Jax leaned against the car to watch the actors scatter to their various positions.

"Brice never knew anything anyway. The only time he ever talked to us was on the set. Don't know why the hell he took the job. He hated Mackie."

"Guess that's why the sheriff didn't need him today." Although the sheriff had almost nothing to do with anything other than provide a cover for Evie's brainstorm. And the director was watching the whole proceeding from a video monitor in Iddy's office, ready to drive up as he said he had that night.

"Mackie wasn't there. Why's he here now?" Roy asked with a hint of suspicion.

"How do you know he wasn't here if you weren't?" Jax asked. As far as he was aware, Roy had never admitted to driving over that night. They only had Brice's word. Even Goody Two-Shoes Betty and Ray Anne hadn't mentioned Roy.

"Everyone said Mackie was at the hotel." Good actor that he was, Roy didn't hesitate in the half-lie. "He was holed up in his room with whiskey and his lawyer."

From the parking lot where they stood, they couldn't see any of the action inside the barn or house. Jax called up R&R's video feed on his phone. "Then I guess the sheriff wants to see Mackie's reaction to our little production." He showed the feed to Roy.

Mackie sat sullenly in the farmhouse front room with the sheriff, monitoring the action from all the cameras on a large-screen monitor. On his smaller screen, Jax had to switch links to see the various sets R&R were filming.

Watching the small phone screen, Roy appeared captivated as the crew who'd been staying in the house gathered in the kitchen. "They're *crew*. Ain't any of them actors by a long shot."

"Not expected to be. The script just reflects what they said happened that night. All they have to do is read."

Evie's sister Gracie had used her writing skills to form the sheriff's notes into dialogue. The rest of them had added a little extra drama, and Gracie had created logical connections. As theater, it was pretty bad. As real life—the crew was getting into it.

They watched as Ray Anne—playing Sandra in high heels and cowboy shirt—shouted about dirty dishes. The Steves flung towels at her. She whipped them with one.

Roy snorted. "That Ray Anne is something."

"Learned a lot from Betty, I assume."

"Yeah, Betty uses her to read the scripts. Guess that makes sense." Roy stared at the scene unfolding on the phone.

Steve Nancy, the camera operator, woodenly read his lines about Sandra being a useless bitch expecting everyone to do all the scut work. The second Steve—Nimrod, the set designer—agreed, saying even Parker was complaining that she had him doing all the heavy work of hauling feed.

Sandra had called Parker that day, ordering more feed for the animals. This morning, the long-haired film director was sitting in the back lot, twiddling thumbs with the rest of the crew that had been in Charleston. He didn't react to the scene being broadcast on a monitor.

Ray Anne/Sandra shouted that animals had to be fed, and they hadn't given her a truck. Everyone waited and turned to Wright, who was standing in a corner of the kitchen, trying to follow the script.

He finally found his place and shouted, "If you can't take the heat, you're fired! Get your bags and leave! I've got work to do." He looked a little startled and studied the script again. He growled when he read the stage direction. "If I leave now, I can't direct the action."

Beside Jax, Roy snorted. After a brief discussion, the group decided Wright could stay and play invisible. They all claimed he'd been in his room most of that evening.

They returned to the script with Ray Anne threatening that he couldn't fire her, or she'd tell Mackie what had happened to the film Nancy edited.

"What the hell does that mean?" Roy asked. "Parker does the editing. Nancy just operates the cameras."

Jax shrugged. "Came from the sheriff's notes. One of them must have said something in their interview."

Roy began to frown as the scripted argument escalated.

Darren, the blond sound tech and actor wannabe, was really getting into his part, Jax noted. As if this were an audition, he emoted his lines about Sandra sleeping with anything that moved, including balding old men. Ray Anne smacked him pretty hard. Darren objected. The squabble seemed to go off-script at that point.

Wayne Wright stepped in front of the camera to bring them to order.

Roy snorted. "If he thinks anyone will kowtow to him now he's director, he's about to lose his tech."

On the video, the group had returned to the script—although Gracie had added a twist not in the sheriff's notes. Jax watched with interest as Darren emoted his lines about Sandra being a lying blackmailer. After he read them, the blond sound tech looked puzzled and scanned the script instead of continuing.

"She wasn't a blackmailer exactly," Roy said while the scene paused. "People just paid her to keep her mouth shut."

"The difference being?" Jax asked. He hoped Betty was being as talkative to Evie as Ray was to him He kept half an eye on Pris. She was supposed to signal him if she picked up any mental surprises. He didn't exactly know how she operated, but she'd promised not to shut herself off as she usually did.

"Blackmailer sneaks around, finds evidence of dirty secrets, then promises to tell if the victim don't pay up. Sandra never sneaked. People asked her to do stuff, and she did, for a price. Once they knew she kept quiet, they kept using her, but her prices went up. Everyone knew it was the price of her silence."

"Huh. Did she ever snitch if someone couldn't pay?"

"Don't know. I didn't deal with her." Ray clammed up.

But if the initials in the little black book were indicative, *Betty* had. The price of Sandra's silence when she arranged her trysts? Booze runs?

Jax used a second phone to text Evie and R&R with what he was learning. He'd persuaded them that the team needed phones separate from their personal ones, and they'd jumped right on it. Evie hadn't been able to afford tech until this past year. Her grasshopper mind was all over it now. R&R, being tech nerds, had been juggling multiple info feeds all their lives.

In the backyard, Jax noted, Cade only had his one phone. He was patrolling restlessly, keeping an eye on the action. He still looked like a financier in button-down shirts, but pulling a T-shirt on with that shoulder probably didn't work.

In the kitchen, the Sandra blackmail argument grew. Out of curiosity, Jax switched to the image of Mackie. He didn't even appear to be listening. Old news?

He found the link for Evie's set in the barn. Although technically she should be in the trailer, Betty George was prowling the stalls, smoking a cigarette, and petting the remaining animals. Evie was studying her phone and leaning on. . . a shovel? She blew a kiss at the hidden camera as if she knew he was watching. R&R probably had a camera out here aimed at him, and she was watching it.

Jax could take care of himself, but he had insisted that the sheriff hide an officer in one of the barn stalls. A murder re-enactment as a wedding rehearsal was bad enough. He was taking no chances of getting married in a hospital.

Mavis and the aunts were scattered about, but amulets and reading tarot weren't of much use here. Jax figured they intended to swing brooms if any of their chicks were threatened.

Cade watched the farmhouse to handle any fireworks. Iddy, naturally, was hidden in the barn with the animals.

Roy had grown suspiciously silent. Jax switched back to the kitchen scene on the spare phone, scrolling back to where Sandra had been accused of blackmail. In Gracie's script, Sandra/Ray Anne charged the film crew with pandering to Mackie's pornography by filming his bedroom.

Giving up on pretending invisibility, Wright went off script, shouting that what a man did in his own bedroom was his own expletive-deleted business. R&R's hidden camera caught Steve Nancy looking twitchy, glancing from the script to the action.

As the argument escalated, Nancy finally tossed the script aside to shout at Wright, "*You* stole that film! I tried to find it, and it was gone. Mackie almost tore me a new one for losing it."

Everyone on the scene except the two combatants hastily scanned their scripts, looking for what wasn't there.

"*Parker* edits everything your lousy camera records." Wright shoved the papers back at the camera operator. "You wanta blame anyone, blame him. Stick with the script, moron."

Parker had been in Charleston that night. He was sitting in the back lot now, watching the monitor.

Jax glanced to see what Roy was watching. . . He'd turned to the link with Betty in the barn.

"Do they always fight like this?" Jax asked, just to hold Roy's attention.

"It's the reason I stay away from Mackie's crew," he said with a shrug. "I like to work as well as the next man, but Mackie is a dirtbag, and his crew are all scum. Makes for boring action where you hope they all pull out their guns and shoot each other."

Jax had to agree with that assessment—except Sandra had been the one to die.

Back in the kitchen, Ray Anne had found her place again. "I'm done here! I don't have to put up with this crap. Mackie is going down, and you're all going down with him!" She turned to Darren. "The least you can do is give me a ride to Charleston!"

Jax had added that line. Sandra's ghost had said Darren would help her, but Brice said he'd been the one with the truck. Until now, Darren had admitted nothing, but apparently recalling that night, he got into the emotion. "Anything to get rid of you. You're going to get us all fired!"

Well, if that had been Darren's actual reaction at the time, there was the reason Sandra hadn't relied on him. "Fired?" Jax asked idly. "Because Parker stole Mackie's porn? Does any of this make sense?"

Roy grimaced and looked uneasy. Even Pris shot a glance in their direction. The actor shook his head at Jax's question and didn't answer.

On screen, Ray Anne huffily stalked out the back door. The crew in the kitchen threw unscripted taunts and watched her go. Had they done that the night Sandra died?

"She didn't take suitcases," Jax commented when no further action ensued.

"She already had them packed," Roy responded, still frowning. "I don't know what the little schemer was planning by staging this scene, but she had already planned to leave."

Of course, if Roy was sneaking into Betty's trailer, he'd have seen the luggage —and hadn't said a word. The two actors were really experienced at cover-up.

Jax pretended he didn't know anything. "How did she move the suitcases without anyone noticing?"

Roy glanced at the barn. "Sandra always stayed here with the animals when everyone else went into town. Not difficult. Betty said she was in a snit about something. How do you switch this thing to see Mackie?" He handed the phone over.

Jax found the link to the front room camera. Mackie was sipping Perrier. The sheriff was on his phone "Why didn't you tell the sheriff that?"

"Betty only just told me." Which was quite likely a lie to cover up their trysts— provided Brice Kennedy wasn't the liar. "Can't see it makes any difference, but you're wasting time with this nonsense. One of the sleazeballs had to have followed her out, but they won't admit it. Mackie has them all by the balls. Where's she going?"

On the kitchen camera, Wright ordered the crew in the house to follow Ray Ann out back. No one claimed to have followed Sandra that night, but Evie had insisted they all be available for the barn scene. Darren and Steve Nimrod, the older set designer, did as ordered. Curious, the crew sitting in the backyard joined the parade. Why didn't Wright and Nancy follow?

"Sheriff figures Sandra went out to the barn to get her dog or check on the animals before she picked up her suitcases." Anxiously, Jax switched to the barn camera.

Apparently having watched the kitchen scene, Evie had left the shovel leaning against a hay bale and vanished. Betty was invisible as well, since no one had placed her on the scene. Iddy and Philomena, the sheriff's officer, were hiding in the empty-looking barn too.

Roy studied the phone screen uneasily as Ray Ann appeared in the barn door with an audience behind her. "Why am I here? Betty and I could have gone into a nice restaurant while you waste your time."

"The owner of the nice restaurant is laying out brunch on your porch." It was Jax's turn to shrug. "Since Betty was here that night, we're trying to keep it realistic."

The old boy still wasn't admitting he'd been here. Could Brice be lying?

"Horse and dog ain't here anymore," Roy pointed out. "So that's not realistic. Didn't she have a truck waiting too?"

On screen, a stall door opened and a collie raced out. Not Sandra's but one Iddy had borrowed. The dog raced up to Ray Anne/Sandra, probably at Iddy's direction.

"Depends," Jax said, strolling toward the barn. "If that whole scene in the kitchen was Sandra upsetting apple carts, then she might have called someone already."

On that note, he checked over his shoulder. Pris was saying something to Dante, who immediately jumped down from the porch to trail behind Jax and Roy.

Jax unfastened the holster under his jacket and switched his phone link back to Mackie.

Instead of joining the rest of the crew outside, Steve Nancy and Wright were in the front room, waving the script while Sheriff Troy looked on. Even as Jax watched, Mackie nearly turned purple and reached inside his coat pocket.

Thirty

As Ray Anne entered the barn, Evie almost regretted sending Sandra on to the next plane. But she couldn't play Goddess and imprison a spirit for her own convenience. Evie had a suspicion that would be evil.

All she could do was pretend she knew what Sandra had done, include it in the script, and see what happened.

Ray Anne's aura showed contentment—the poor woman was enjoying this acting opportunity, with all eyes on her. The hairdresser stooped down to greet the collie, glanced at her script, then pulled out her phone. Not knowing who may have been outside, they'd had to improvise this part.

"Brice, please, can you come get me? We just had a big blow-up, and I think Wright is suspicious. He fired me."

Stomping out her cigarette, Betty joined Evie in her hiding place behind the hay bales. "What did Wright have to be suspicious about?" she asked innocently, although her aura was its usual murky.

"Weren't you here when we found the microchip?" Talking distracted her from reading auras. Evie tried to stay focused on the people watching from the doorways. Jax and Roy were at the front. Almost everyone else seemed to be gathering in the back.

"What's a microchip?" Betty asked.

Her murkiness could mean she was lying, except all she was doing was asking questions. So maybe acting and lying brought out the same colors. That made sense.

In between the two doors, Ray Ann sat down to play with the dog. The sheriff had said the angle of the blow indicated Sandra had been crouching. He just didn't think it had happened in the barn since they'd found no trace of blood in the hard-packed dirt. But it was easier to control the action in here than by the bullpen.

"Sandra's microchip contained videos," Evie answered absently, switching her phone to the front room with Mackie.

The producer had pulled pills out of his pocket and was choking them down with his Perrier. She'd already noted he had serious health issues. She tried not to wish evil on anyone, but he was doing an excellent job of it all on his own.

Instead of calming down after taking the pills, Mackie screamed into his phone and lumbered for the door. Sheriff Troy followed, with Wright and the balding Steve on his heels, bringing the drama out here, she guessed.

Had they just figured out that Sandra had stolen the porn video? Poor babies.

"The sheriff has the chip now," Evie explained to the actress while watching her phone video. "Didn't you say Sandra had a camera?"

The angle on the porch showed Pris's table but no Pris. Mackie walked offscreen. The sheriff and his followers grabbed food from the buffet before following him. Evie switched back to the barn.

"Everyone has cameras," Betty said dismissively. "Do they come with microchips?"

"I only have a phone. I think they run on some kind of card, don't they? Look, they're letting Parker enter the barn. He wasn't there that night, was he?"

Betty frowned at the pony-tailed film director entering to stand over Ray Ann, reading lines from the script as if he were talking on the other end of the phone. "She called Parker?"

"At some point during the day, he called her," Evie said with a shrug. "But he's playing the part of the unlisted number on her phone, I think."

"What did you say to tick them off?" Parker read woodenly.

Ray Anne stood and started pacing. "Wright started shouting about missing film. They know it's gone. If they learn I have it. . . They'll kill me, I know they will." Not in the script but she was probably repeating what she'd heard.

Betty made an inelegant noise. "Not a one of those faggots would have lifted a hand to her if she'd stolen the clothes off their backs. Give me a real man any day."

"Like those two in the front?" Evie referred to Jax and Dante. The short old actor in between them didn't qualify in her books. His aura was murky with. . . guilt? Or maybe that was just anger and fear, and the daylight behind them interfered with clarity. No one ever said her gift was precise.

"Never discount older men, dear," Betty admonished. "Experience counts."

Parker leaned against the wall with an air of boredom as he pretended to speak into a phone. "Nah, Mackie might hire an assassin, but we'll all be out of jobs if you don't keep that thing hidden until the film is done. Once reporters get their hands on that. . ."

"But they all know!" Ray Anne/Sandra cried into her imaginary phone. "Even Roy and Betty! They hate me."

"We know what?" Betty asked with interest, but her aura flickered with fear.

Shoving Roy aside, Mackie barreled through the doorway. Dante stepped away to give him room. Evie winced as Jax's hand slid beneath his jacket.

Fortunately, Sheriff Troy sauntered along, munching a sandwich, and Jax relaxed his grip.

"Stop this farce!" Mackie roared. "Everyone go home. This show is done. You're all done. I'll make certain none of you ever work in this business again!"

Betty stiffened. "He can't do that, not after everything we've done to save his neck."

"If you weren't here the night Sandra died, Mackie," Roy called from the doorway, "then you have to step aside and watch like the rest of us. It's just an act."

Mackie shook a fist at him. "I'm not raising more funds to pay a bunch of backstabbers! This production is *over!*"

Betty said something very ungrandmotherly before stalking from behind the haybales looking as if she were carrying a jungle rifle and facing down a lion. "You can't do that, you old coot! We have contracts! You *owe* us. We'll ruin you if you quit now."

Interesting. Evie wiggled her fingers over the hay bales so Jax knew she was fine. On her phone, she saw him look exasperated and prepared to fling a bale so he could reach her. She loved that man dearly, but she didn't want to be revealed yet. She made a chopping motion that he grasped instantly. He leaned against a nearby stall, the one Iddy and Mena were hiding in.

Mackie swung around to shake his fist at Betty. "Finance your love nest on someone else's money. When I get through with you—"

Betty grabbed the shovel Evie had left leaning against the hay bale. "After all I've done for you, you're not throwing me out now, you massive coward!"

Done? As killed Sandra to prevent the microchip from going to reporters? Evie's eyes widened. She'd been gossiping with a killer?

"Cut!" Parker shouted in alarm.

Betty swung anyway. Jax leapt in and grabbed the handle, yanking it from her grip before the actress could connect. Mackie was taller. She would have only hit his shoulder. But she raged against Jax's hold.

Evie whistled to herself. "I did *not* see that coming." Then, noticing the red in Mackie's first chakra turn an ominous gray, she shouted a warning at Jax.

Before she could emerge from her hiding place, a man's voice shouted, "Betty, c'mon, I'll take you away from all this."

Roy? Evie peered around the haystack. The old actor was holding a big honkin' gun like a pro, aiming it at Iddy and Mena who'd emerged from hiding. In uniform and looking authoritative, Mena had her gun drawn. As did the sheriff. Shoving Betty and her shovel aside, Jax pulled his as well, damn the man.

Between all the guns, Mackie collapsed on the ground and lay still.

Evie couldn't even shout her triumph at evil going down, not when all she knew and loved was surrounded by guns.

Iddy whistled, catching the dog's ear.

Before the collie could attack, Betty kicked over a gas can, produced her modified gold lighter, and threw it on the leaking gas around Evie's bales. "Let's give them something better to do than follow us, babe."

The gas can exploded into flame as Betty ran to join Roy.

ONCE THE CREW IN BACK HAD ENTERED THE BARN, CADE HAD MADE HIS WAY AROUND front, keeping an eye on the action on his phone. He'd reached the front paddock when he saw the two aging actors fleeing for the Buick. What the. . . ? He turned to chase after them.

Iddy's screams electrocuted him. In horror he swung around to see flames leaping from the barn—

Roark jumping from his van jarred Cade's brain into gear. The Cajun was closer to the fleeing couple and the Buick. Grabbing a pitchfork off the fence, Cade flung it toward Roark, and heart in his throat, ran for the barn. He met Reuben dashing from the farmhouse, fire extinguisher in hand. They tore through the paddock together.

Smoke already filled the wooden interior. Flames licked at old stalls.

"The goats!" he heard Iddy cry through the haze.

She was alive and furious, not hurt. Cade tried not to breathe too deeply in relief. As Reuben sprayed the flames, he edged through the smoke in the direction of Iddy's voice.

Jax stalked past him carrying a still-smoldering Evie. She was screaming protests but looked decidedly scorched. Cade stayed out of that fracas and skirted around Mackie's entourage, surrounding the producer, flat on his back. Maybe the fire was the devil rising from hell to take the bastard's soul. He hoped someone was taking photos.

The sheriff and the skinny officer stomped on the flaming straw Reuben knocked away from the stalls. A line of flames licked across Cade's path. He grabbed the fallen shovel and dug up half the floor flinging dirt on the sparks as he made his way to Iddy.

"The goats!" she cried. "Get the goats before they asphyxiate."

With the sparks smothered, he opened the goat stall. The stupid creatures nibbled his jeans instead of moving. Using the shovel, he prodded them toward the opening, but they just milled.

"This won't work." Coughing, he stomped to the end of the barn where Iddy worked in the sheep stall.

She was nearly weeping while urging the equally recalcitrant sheep from their hay. Frightened by the noise and smoke, they resisted even her mental lures.

The raven flew in, screaming, adding to the confusion.

"Our mothers are out there, manning a hose brigade," Iddy warned him, although how she knew, he refused to ask.

"We'll all die of smoke inhalation if we don't get out now." Knowing the fool woman would drop dead before leaving the animals, he edged around the muddled sheep to the back of the stall and began poking them from behind. "Where are the porkers?"

"Owner picked them up last night, along with the chickens. It's just the sheep and goats." Coughing, she clucked and clicked her fingers to hold their attention on the open door.

Together, they urged the sheep out of the stall, where the collie could nip at their heels. The dog drove them out the back, away from the smoldering straw in front. Cade dived in with Iddy to work the goats next, until they were both hacking and nearly blind from the burning haze.

Nudging the final goat out the back, Cade wrapped his good arm around Iddy, and, choking on fresh air, followed the animals into the chaos past the bull pen. One of the Tres Madres handed them water, and he gulped it gratefully.

"Evie?" Iddy asked in between swallows.

"Needed a haircut anyway," the short woman in a caftan answered pragmatically.

"Everyone else?" Cade asked, counting heads.

"We think Fatso had a stroke. They're trying to find his heart to do CPR."

"Aunt Mavis," Iddy admonished gently. "Pris okay?"

"She's feeding the masses so they don't kill each other." The older woman nodded toward the farmhouse. "We'll look after her. We'll keep the dog with us for now. You two better beat it. There are a lot of angry, scared drama queens running around."

They'd all just been fired, even the innocent ones. Cade grasped that. "All right, that's my territory. Spread the word that I'm on it. Maybe keep Evie's team listening?"

Mavis nodded. "Drama queens ignore us. We'll keep our ears open."

Cade was pretty sure Iddy actually chuckled as he led her away. Not understanding, he halted. "Are the animals safe? Do you need to stay here?"

"They have an entire farm to roam." She wrapped a bare arm around his waist and urged him forward. "The animals are fine. Just don't tell Evie that our mothers think they're on her *team*. She'll insist Jax go to Vegas for their wedding."

Cade thought maybe he followed that thought. He'd like to follow it even further now that they seemed to be working in tandem. But his goal as of this minute had to be Brice Kennedy. He couldn't count on Iddy understanding that.

They passed a despondent Betty and Roy being read their rights by a triumphant Mean Mena.

The Buick's tires were nicely flat.

"What is their story?" Iddy whispered as he led her toward the Tahoe.

"I'm not the crime fighter here. I'm leaving that to the sheriff." He took the driver's seat and shifted gears before she had her seatbelt fastened. If he could, he might still save his uncle's business. "I'm out to save jobs and my uncle's investors."

She shot him a look he couldn't interpret and stayed silent.

At the vet clinic, Brice Kennedy was storming up and down the parking lot while Slate Cooper leaned against the paddock fence, arms crossed, stoically watching.

Cade helped Iddy out of the Tahoe out of habit. She certainly didn't need assistance. She pulled away and put distance between him and the others. He didn't know what she was expecting, but he was here for one reason. Once he'd accomplished it, he was gone.

Wasn't he?

Not to be distracted by personal concerns, Cade strode directly for Brice. "Did you know Sandra had that microchip?"

"I told you, no!" Brice shouted. "What in hell is going on out there? The cameras cut off."

"Answer my questions, then I'll answer yours. What was Sandra doing and how much did you know?"

Brice drove his hand through hair that was no longer there. "I knew she and Zoe had evidence on Mackie. She wanted to come out here to help her friend and unload her animals."

"I thought the two of you were an item?"

"Sandra was tired of Hollywood. I knew it was never a long-term affair. I'm an alcoholic married to my work. Sandra understood that. She just wanted to make a statement when she gave up her dreams."

"And bringing down Mackie was that statement? Who else knew?"

Brice shrugged his skinny shoulders. "I don't know who she told. A lot of people wanted him out of the way. She figured she'd go out, guns blazing, hero of her own story. She persuaded me to accept Mackie's blackmail and direct the film to help in their endeavor."

"And you hoped, after she brought down Mackie, the payoff would be the investors investing in you? So, all you did was sabotage the balloon and the Hummer?" Cade got that. A man did what he could to get ahead.

It just shouldn't cost lives.

"I didn't expect anyone to be hurt." Brice accepted a bottle of water Iddy handed him from her truck supply. "After Sandra died. . ." He gestured helplessly. "There was no point in going on. I had to stop the film. The stupid animals seemed to know she was gone. It was all out of control."

Cade thought he detected real grief and gave the man a moment to calm himself before asking, "What was Sandra's role in bringing down Mackie? Just carrying the microchip? But if no one knew about it, that didn't get her killed."

Brice closed his eyes, made fists, and confessed, "Sandra liked games. She decided she could wring a little cash out of Mackie and his thoroughly rotten crew."

"What kind of games?"

"I stayed out of it. I don't know how she got the film, but she didn't do it on her own. I have no idea what she was holding over anyone. For all I knew, she was scoring drugs. As long as it didn't interfere with the film, I didn't care. I was just there to watch her bring Mackie down and step in."

Cade had wanted to know what kind of man Brice was. Now he knew. He saw a little too much of himself in the single-minded focus on his career. Brice was giving the right answers for investor purposes, wrong ones on a personal level. A relationship meant caring enough to share—thoughts, burdens, futures. He thought. "So, you're saying you knew nothing until the night she died?"

"Exactly what I'm saying. We'd only been here a few days when she called me, said she was in trouble, asked me to come get her, just as I said. When I arrived, I received a text saying she changed her mind. I thought she'd found another way out. That's all I know."

There was a lot more to discover, but that was the sheriff's job. His was the production.

Cade glanced at Iddy's father. "You want to call my uncle and make the arrangements?"

Slate nodded curtly. "My farm?"

Cade turned back to Brice. "Can you film the rest without this town?"

Brice didn't look particularly happy but nodded. "We have enough in the can to edit in what we need. But Roy and Betty?"

"Have Ray Anne walk through Betty's part. She'll be cheap. Roy—" Cade gestured. "Think about it. The rest of the crew and the investors shouldn't pay for the mistakes of others."

He should know. He'd been paying for his father's mistakes for over half a lifetime.

Time to walk away.

Thirty-one

KNOWING EVIE'S HOUSE WOULD BE WEDDING CHAOS, AND THAT ASIA PLANNED TO take the rest of the weekend to visit family, Iddy led Cade into the clinic after Brice left. She set him in her office with the coffee machine, a telephone, and air conditioning. He wouldn't actually rest, she knew, but he might sit down while finishing his business transactions.

He would be gone tomorrow, or the next day at best. She had to remember that. Afterthought's moment of film glory had ended. Mayor Larraine would simply have to deal with it.

Planning on cleaning up, she left Asia to finish the morning's appointments. Outside, she found her father poking around the dog pen. She'd expected him to leave with Brice.

"You have a farm?" she asked as she filled the pen's water bottles. She still didn't know how she felt about his shooting a bull to protect her. He most likely didn't believe he'd hurt her at the same time. It was more denial than ignorance. She still wasn't happy with him.

"Yeah. Shooting range, training greenhorns to stay on a horse, office and classroom for sensitivity training. It's expensive out there. A man needs three jobs." He scratched the head of the three-legged German shepherd.

"It suits you?" she asked evenly.

He thought about it. "It does. I was a big frog in a small pond here. That's suffocating."

A small pond filled with irritating gnats who wanted him to turn into the charming prince he wasn't. Iddy understood. It had taken her a while to grow up and grasp that, but she'd learned her lesson well. It was only watching Evie and Pris and Gracie find good strong men who believed in them that had given her cause to question her cynicism.

Not all men were her father. She glanced at the window where Cade worked. He wasn't her father either, but here, he was a really big frog in a muddy pond.

Slate followed her glance. "Cade's a good man on a narrow path. He needs to wander in the underbrush more, camp under a full moon, hear the coyotes howl."

Iddy snorted at the image. "I believe that's his plan. Will you stay for Evie's wedding?"

"With the whole entire family there? Not on your life. I'm outta here. Sorry I'm not your dream dad. Will you still talk to me occasionally?" He straightened, already looking toward the road.

"I've always been here," she said in resignation. "You're the one who never shows."

For a brief moment, he looked regretful, then he tapped his hat and headed out.

After seeing her new partner off and closing the office at noon, Iddy watched with interest as the sheriff's car rolled into the lot. Cade had promised to finish up in time for lunch. She'd tried not to listen to his calls, but she was pretty sure one of them had been to the airline.

Instead of going inside, Iddy waited in the parking lot to greet the sheriff. While he talked on his phone, she sat on the fence and checked a string of family messages. She grinned at Evie's claiming to be held hostage in ER, and Pris telling her she'd save her some burritos. She quickly texted Loretta that the family was insane, and she should study hard and escape while she could. Loretta texted what appeared to be an elf rolling in laughter, so all was relatively well in her world.

Cade finally emerged to join her, and she shared the elf. "I'm learning a new language."

He took the phone and immediately found an image of a madly grinning bow-legged cowboy. He sent it before she could inquire into its meaning. Loretta hearted it, so Iddy had to assume she understood whatever he'd said.

By the time the sheriff got out of his car, Slate Cooper was well down the road.

"Just wanted to make sure y'all are okay," Troy said, dusting off his hat. "Philomena is cursing y'all up one side and down, but she brought in your pistol-packin' actors for questioning. They lawyered up pretty good. We're leaving them to the state police."

"Is anyone with the animals? Do I need to go back?" Iddy hadn't wanted to watch the aftermath. Unlike Evie, her thirst for justice was limited to the helpless. In her experience, humans usually deserved whatever they got. Animals didn't. She didn't ask after Mackie.

"I left them two PhD'd criminals cleaning up. Do 'em good dealing with real life. They'll probably tell you more than I know by dinner."

Iddy assumed that meant Reuben and Roark, although she thought only Reuben had actually completed his doctorate. Whatever. Two MIT grads cleaning up a barn made total sense.

"The owners should be out to fetch the animals today. I should probably corral them." Iddy wasn't in a hurry to play shepherd. She'd resigned, after all.

"I think your mothers are giving the critters the evil eye and using brooms to drive them out of the blackberry bushes. You're better off hiding from Larraine once she learns you threw the film crew out of town. Give my regards to your family, and I guess I'll see y'all at the wedding." He threw his hat in his car and departed.

"Weird." Iddy puzzled over the visit. "Did he just stop to tell us not to worry?"

"And that he appreciates Reuben and Roark for being the additional staff his budget can't afford. I've added a line item for police enforcement. Pays to keep a good man on our side." Cade glanced down at her. "Given your family's predilections," he added.

Iddy almost laughed, but if this was goodbye— "Are you and my dad meeting at the airport and flying home?"

"He did sneak out pretty quick when the sheriff showed up, didn't he? But nope, you're not rid of me so easily. Come inside, where we won't bake in the sun." He draped his good arm over her shoulder.

The familiarity woke the butterflies in her stomach. She didn't do casual flings, she reminded herself as she followed him inside. Everyone had left for the day. They'd have privacy. But. . . Maybe just once she could let herself go? It had been a harrowing morning. . . She'd like to know what comfort sex felt like.

Cade swung the door wide and stepped aside for her to enter. It took a second for her eyes to adjust to the dim light and another second to realize something was odd. Every object, even La Chusa's perch, had been decorated with her *I-need-a-good-home* ribbons. Wide-eyed in confusion, she turned to Cade, who was dangling one around his neck and tying another on his wrist.

She gaped, unable to process.

Putting a big hand at her spine, he nudged her back to her office. "Found them in your drawer when I was looking for a pen, and they just kinda jumped out and bit me."

"Ribbons? Ribbons bit you, and you decided my office needed redecorating?" She was being deliberately obtuse, she knew. She simply. . . didn't react well to surprises.

"I need redecorating. Maybe a mental realignment. I thought I knew what I wanted. . ." He sat her down in front of her computer. "But I knew you would never follow me to Thailand."

"Follow. . . ? I'd love to visit. . ." In bewilderment, she stared at the monitor he woke up. It took a moment before she recognized the photos rolling across the screen. "Fake," she warned him. "That old farmhouse is falling apart, and the fields are fallow these days. I didn't know the Shepherds were selling their farm. Who's showing you these lies?"

"I just went hunting for local real estate. It doesn't have to be this place, but I calculate it's only a mile down the road. I know farms, but I have no desire to be a farmer. I don't need land. I need a place to live. With my job, I can work anywhere."

Before she could tell him that the Shepherd farm was a terrible choice, Cade leaned over, caught her shoulders, and kissed her.

Farms and ribbons made a lot more sense when she was in his arms. They made even more sense when he lifted her to the desk and undid her shirt and bra.

Saturday afternoon, after rescuing Evie from the ER, Jax dropped her off at the hairdresser where Loretta waited. He assumed the fashionista mayor was inside, ready to personally direct hair cutting. Larraine had been too busy wedding planning to take off his head when he warned her that Mackie Productions was done. And he'd be on his honeymoon if she did decide to go nuclear later.

He kissed Evie's nose. "If you don't want me to have a stroke like Mackie, please spend the afternoon doing pretty wedding things."

She scowled, then pulled his head down so she could kiss him more thoroughly. Then she pushed him away. "I'll tell them to shave me bald."

Mournfully, he fingered the burnt side of her beautiful hair, carefully not brushing the red singed skin where he'd ripped off her smoldering shirt. "Even if they never nail Betty for murder, she's going down for arson and assault. I'll personally hire whatever the prosecutor's team needs."

"Just don't let our eager mayor bring in any more film crews unless you vet them first, or we'll turn into a Wild West show. Now go do whatever bachelors do on their last night of freedom." She nibbled his ear, patted his jaw, and strode into the salon as if she hadn't been giving him heart failure.

Jax wasn't too worried about his freedom. He'd had that. In his twenties, fast cars and fast women had made sense. In his thirties, he had a satisfying career taking down evil-doers. Gaining a family of his own and a woman like Evie to keep him on his toes fascinated him far more than cars.

To satisfy his need for justice, he'd texted Zoe David a photo of Mackie flat on his back, surrounded by flames. She'd returned a hysterical text involving tears and fireworks. It was impossible to repair the damage done by villains, but justice could start the healing process.

Knowing the women were decorating the house, Jax headed for the relative sanity of his office. He needed to tie up a lot of loose ends before he and Evie left for the Keys.

R&R were waiting for him when he arrived.

"I assume Cade paid you well for finding out who killed his ex? Does he need more?" Jax opened the compact refrigerator Evie had bought at a thrift store and handed them the cold drinks of their choice. He had a flask in his drawer but it was too early to hit the booze.

"The old lady ain't talking, but her bed buddy refuses to go down for murder." Reuben settled into the big Morris chair. Cleaned up and professionally dressed in business shirt and decent khakis, he fit into the stuffy, old-fashioned chair—except for the manbun with the stylus through it and the tribal scars

In his usual tank top and jeans, Roark paced off his energy. "Roy O'Bryan confirmed what the director told us. He rolled the Buick up quiet like just as Brice Kennedy's pickup left the night Sandra disappeared. He gave da Buick keys to Ray Anne, as usual, and she merrily tooted off to town. She confirmed dat, out of loyalty, she kept quiet about da lovers. She didn't think the police needed to know."

Jax sipped his water. "So, Evie was right, and Ray Anne is just an innocent dupe?"

"Looks like it. She was crying pretty hard during the interview, but she brightened up when Kennedy offered to take her into the city with the crew." Reuben studied his can of bubbly juice. "The old cowboy was the one who dug Sandra's grave after Betty whacked her by the bullpen. If it hadn't been muddy, he probably never could have done it. He made Betty help him roll her in the blanket out of respect before throwing mud in her face."

Jax grimaced at the grisly image. "If Roy testifies in court, that should be enough to convict Betty, even if he didn't witness the murder. Stupid move on his part to pull that gun, though. Now he's looking at more time." He called up the camera footage and shook his head. "Looks like a really bad western."

"Exactly. Dude isn't exactly a genius. He's an accessory just for flinging Sandra's phone out the car window when he returned to the city." Reuben relaxed and checked his phone. "We didn't give him a script at the barn, so he simply performed a scene from one of his old films. He claims he would have turned Betty in, but he was used to being the hero."

"Yeah, right," Roark said with a heavy dose of sarcasm.

"Since it has nothing to do with being paid, I don't suppose you tracked what happened with the pornographers and blackmailers and whatnot?" Jax asked. "I assume Betty was protecting her job and not Mackie so much when she bashed Sandra."

"That's all up to the attorneys in the sexual abuse lawsuits. Mackie's in pretty serious condition in ICU and can't defend himself at this point." Reuben sipped his juice and contemplated the ceiling. "We may have checked on a few bits and pieces. The whole crew used to work with Mackie way back when he was a porn producer. Wright scouted victims. Looks like Steve Nancy set up cameras in Mackie's bedrooms so he could watch his performance as often as he liked. Parker edited the film for quality. Sandra found out somehow. My guess would be the whole crew knew and one talked."

"She most likely seduced, bribed, and blackmailed one of them into giving her Zoe's tape," Roark said. "They stupidly didn't just copy it but gave her da original file, so one of dem knew it was missing. A falling out among thieves ensued when Sandra dropped the bomb that she had it."

"But what set *Betty* off? That's the point that makes no sense." Jax scrolled through the video until he reached the part with Betty telling the producer he couldn't fire her.

"Since she's not talking, we had to put pieces together." Reuben must have hit SHARE on his phone. The file popped up on Jax's screen. "She knew with her bad ticker that she wouldn't get more action parts. Her drinking has her on a lot of blacklists. Her husband is some snotty lawyer who likes having an actress to show off at the country club. She's not raking in big bucks these days, so she relies on his income to pay for the house and cars and face lifts."

"Ariel dug all that out, did she?" Jax knew his sister was a math whiz, but Roark had been teaching her bad habits.

"It's all out there pretty much," Roark said with a shrug. "Betty's agency is sitting on a contract for some big TV show, but they wanted proof she still has the right stuff, or they'd hand it to a more stable actress. The documentary was supposed to prove she can stay sober and look good and sound intelligent."

"Mackie was Betty's ticket to that lucrative, long-term TV contract that might allow her to retire to TV heaven with the old cowboy. She'd probably been drinking when Sandra stupidly bragged that she meant to bring down Mackie, thinking Betty was on her side." Jax had a lot of experience at piecing puzzles.

"And the old lady saw her future go up in smoke while smug Sandra cuddled the dog or fed the bull, whatever," Reuben finished for him. "We all saw Betty's temper."

"Chances are good Sandra was already blackmailing her over the trysts and drinking," Roark reminded them. "Sandra was costing Betty money she wasn't making."

"And Sandra was young and pretty and the crew paid more attention to her than Betty." Jax waved a weary hand at the old story. "The prosecutor will have fun. Turn everything legal that you have over to the sheriff. Cade will see you get paid."

Rising, they crushed their cans and tossed them at the recycle bucket.

"You really wearing a tux tomorrow in this heat?" Roark asked.

Jax shrugged. "You don't have to. Wear nice shirts and the green cummerbund to show solidarity. You'll look like pirates. Evie will love it. Somebody should warn Nick that Gracie will be a bridezilla."

"Knowing the Brit, he'll soak it up. They'll have to tie the knot in winter so we don't all roast in tweed and wool." Reuben headed for the door.

"Larraine's already suited Rube up in something fancy," Roark confided once his partner was out of earshot. "I've got cameras set up. We'll roast him into eternity."

"Have fun with that. I have plans for sun and sand and no family anywhere for a thousand miles." Jax hadn't revealed their honeymoon plans to anyone but Evie.

Roark laughed knowingly on the way out.

Thirty-Two

EVIE SWIRLED HER SEA-FOAM GREEN TAFFETA. SHE'D NEED LADDER HEELS TO KEEP IT from dragging the ground, but she didn't mind. It was green and swished and rustled and was everything a wedding dress should be—especially with the gorgeous bouquet of red roses and lavender and purple crape myrtle blossoms the Tres Madres had gathered for her.

"Loretta, you can't wear blue boots!" Gracie cried in another room. "Where are those pretty shoes we bought?"

Evie snickered and peered down the hall. Loretta and Gracie were nowhere to be seen, but Pris was sneaking up the stairs. Evie signaled her. Her cousin had dyed her gray streak green in honor of Evie's colors and blue to match her lovely sky-blue silk—not the pink Gracie had ordered.

"Well?" Evie asked eagerly.

Pris didn't do shy or blushing bride well, but she ducked her head and studied her toes. "We're doing it. He's over-the-top crazy and insisting we marry right now and wants me to stop working and eat ice cream all day or something. We have the license. Larraine said she'd say the words and sign it whenever."

Evie grinned in satisfaction. "Do it while I'm dancing Jax down the aisle. Processions are silly. I want music. And it's my day. And yours! What do you want? Do we throw rosebuds?"

Pris shook her head vigorously. "I want quiet and unnoticed. Dante doesn't care. We'll probably do something at his home for his family. This is your day."

Unexpectedly, she hugged Evie. "You've grown up, baby cuz. You'll be ruling the town like your mother one of these days."

Respect, from her multi-gifted, talented cousin, was the best wedding gift Evie could receive. She hugged back. "I want you to steer our English relatives this way."

"Will do. And maybe Cade and Iddy can drive the west coast family here to meet them." Pris leaned over and whispered, "She spent the night in his room."

Evie grinned. "So the ghosts told me. Now go, keep Dante calm, and send Loretta here before Gracie scalps her."

Loretta bounced in wearing a red satin shirt dress and blue boots, with her hair braided in red silk rose buds. She swirled around for Evie to admire "Will Aunt Gracie hate me forever?"

"Only if you wear that to her wedding. She's a teacher. She gets it. She just can't help scolding. Are Aster and the twins all appropriately outfitted in frills?"

"I think they're playing hide and seek and leaving your rose petals in trails. Dante is sorta distracted, and Nick is chatting up the guests, so no one is watching them. Will Nick be my uncle if he marries Aunt Gracie?"

"He will. Just don't try it on him yet. They're both a bit skittish. Maybe you'll be a matchmaker some day. You have a good eye."

Music blared from the back porch. Reuben had set up the dancing platform, but Evie had demanded classic rock, not country. She hoped he and Larraine had been practicing the Watusi. Somehow, she doubted it.

Mavis shoved open the door. "Come on, you two, before Jax eats his way through the shrubbery worrying that you've run off."

"Nah, he's just afraid someone will set fire to the bushes before we tie the knot. Let's rock our way to the altar." Evie grabbed her mother's arm and swung her around so her lovely midnight blue silk caftan adorned with constellations swirled like the heavens. "We are all goddesses!"

They met Gracie fretting in the kitchen. She wore the sedate pink gown she'd wanted all the bridesmaids to wear. She sighed in resignation as they gathered in their rainbow of choices. "Larraine needs to look for circuses instead of movie productions. They'd be far more successful."

Iddy emerged from Cade's bedroom looking a bit tousled but in a stunning golden sheath that set off her bronze coloring to perfection. She laughed at Gracie's despair. "We're a rainbow, a prism effect of color and light to tell the world that all is well."

"A prism effect," Gracie said thoughtfully. "That might work." Without explanation, she leaned out the screen door and signaled the band.

They broke out in "We Will Rock You."

Evie didn't care how they lined up the children and the bridesmaids and her mother to march outside to the podium stage where Larraine waited. She loved the colorful swirl of music and flowers and guests, but Jax waiting at the end of the line was her focus.

He wore a white tux coat, because of course he owned one. He'd politely worn the green cummerbund Gracie had provided, to make his new sister-in-law happy. His nicely fitted navy blue trousers hugged his narrow hips and could take whatever depredations the day would throw at him. And he wore a red rosebud in his lapel because she'd given it to him.

He hugged Loretta when she danced up. This day would make her their daughter. The glow on their Indigo Child's face would live in Evie's heart forever, right along with the peace and love in Jax's expression as he watched her approach.

She was loved. She had never thought herself lovable until Jax had opened her eyes. Glitter bombs of butterflies and stars exploded along her path—R&R at work. She might be dizzy with delight but not nervous enough to be seeing stars.

She squeezed Pris's hand in encouragement as they reached Larraine's podium. She stood on her toes and pecked Iddy's cheek because the serious vet had stars in her eyes—metaphorical ones and not glitter.

Evie took Loretta's hand, who took Jax's, then brought their hands together and stepped back. Jax's strong fingers clasped hers as they said their vows. She hadn't wanted more than the spoon ring he'd fashioned for her. His Ives cousins had sent him a signet with a family crest, and she slid that on his finger.

The instant the final words were said the crowd erupted in cheers, bubbles, and music.

"Distraction," she murmured to Jax, taking his arm and throwing out her other to encourage others to join in as she shimmied down the aisle. Jax caught on quickly, swinging her around and bending her backward, then neatly tangoing her toward the porch and the musicians. The audience followed, performing their own rocking maneuvers.

Behind them, Dante and Pris lingered at the podium, exchanging vows while holding the twins' hands, with aunts and cousins surrounding them in their wedding finery.

Amazingly, Jax's shy sister stood at the screen door, laughing as they danced. Roark abandoned the crowd to slip inside and spin her out of sight.

"I think I might cry of happiness for a week," Evie whispered as Jax swung her into a more sedate wedding waltz on the dance floor.

"I thought the world a bitter place until you surrounded me with love and happiness. I don't know how you do it, but wherever my hermit sister is accepted, I see life as it should be. You are magical, Evangeline Malcolm Ives-Jackson."

She snuggled into his broad shoulder. "It's all about acceptance and respect. I have learned that we can't judge others by ourselves. You were my turning point, lawyer man."

The band broke out in "Gypsy Woman," and they laughed as even the Tres Madres joined the dancing, crowding the floor with Judge Satterwhite and the sheriff and half the older generation.

Upstairs that night, Jax and Evie hastily shed their wedding finery and slipped into travel clothes. The suitcases were already in the Subaru, hidden in the locked garage. Iddy had left her raven guarding the doors and had reported no one had entered to wreak mischief.

They stopped to kiss all the way down the stairs. Revelry continued in the backyard and cellar. The kitchen looked like it had been bombed. Evie didn't attempt to determine who was here and who had slipped away for Beltane high jinks. She simply knew the spirits were restless and ready. So was she.

Once they hit the highway out of town, she gestured at Witch Hill. "We need to stop there and speak to the ancestors."

Unquestioning, he pulled off on the property her family had owned since settling here in the 1600s. A nearly full moon lit their way as Evie led him down a well-worn path to the cemetery.

He raised his eyebrows at the bower of evergreens and linen she'd created.

He did not question at all when she opened his shirt and tugged him down on their bridal bed.

"Spirits speak to me," she reminded him as they stripped each other in the moonlight. "Does this bother you?"

"Does it look like it bothers me?" Naked, he leaned over her.

She smiled up at his chiseled face, which looked stern even in repose. "Tonight, they'll enter me. Are you ready to be a father?"

His answer to that was in affirmative action.

Characters

MALCOLM FAMILY AND FRIENDS

Evangeline (Evie) Serena Malcolm Carstairs—sends spirits to light, reads auras
Mavis Malcolm Carstairs—Evie's mother; reads crystal ball
Grania Malcolm Carstairs Jenkins (Gracie) —Mavis's elder telekinetic daughter
Aster—age 6, Gracie's daughter
Idonea (Iddy) Malcolm—Evie's cousin, veterinarian who talks to animals
Priscilla Broadhurst—Evie's cousin; telepathic
Loretta Aurora Post—eleven-year-old heiress; sees souls
Aunt Felicia—Mavis's sister; Iddy's mother
Aunt Ellen— Mavis's sister; Pris's mother
Great Aunt Evangeline Valerie Malcolm Brindle—Aunt Val, Civil War re-enactor
Damon Ives Jackson (Jax)—fraud and family lawyer; Evie's significant other
Ariel Ives Jackson—Jax's sister
Roark LeBlanc—hacker friend, former military intelligence
Reuben Thompson, PhD—Roark's engineer partner
Dante Alfonso Ives Rossi—archeologist; distant Italian cousin of Jax
Nicolas Gladwell—British marketing expert
Philomena Marquette (Mena)—police officer; went to school with Evie
Mayor Larraine Ward—fashion designer and business owner
Sheriff Troy—beleaguered, bewildered law enforcement

BOOK SIX:

Caden Ives Garcia—investor, temporary line producer
Slate Cooper—Iddy's father; Cherokee sensitivity teacher in Hollywood
Sandra Harris—animal trainer
Sean Mackie—film producer
Betty George—film star, plays a wildlife expert
Roy O'Bryan— aging cowboy actor
Ray Anne—wardrobe and makeup, hairdresser
Wayne Wright—production assistant, Mackie's right-hand man
Parker—film director; looks like hoodlum
Darren—sound tech; surfer blond, actor wannabe
Steve Nimrod—set designer
Steve Nancy—film tech, camera operator
Brice Kennedy—director
Enrique Garcia—owner of Garcia and Sons Insurance
Asia Brown—deaf veterinarian
Zoe David—owns horse training center

The Prism Effect
Patricia Rice

Copyright © 2021 Patricia Rice
Cover design © 2021 Killion Group
First digital edition Book View Café March 2021
ebook 978-1-63632-086-1
Print 978-1-63632-087-8

Published by Rice Enterprises, Dana Point, CA, an affiliate of Book View Café Publishing Cooperative.

Book View Café
304 S. Jones Blvd. Suite #2906
Las Vegas NV 89107

BOOK VIEW CAFE

About the Author

With several million books in print and *New York Times* and *USA Today's* bestseller lists under her belt, former CPA Patricia Rice is one of romance's hottest authors. Her emotionally-charged contemporary and historical romances have won numerous awards, including the *RT Book Reviews* Reviewers Choice and Career Achievement Awards. Her books have been honored as Romance Writers of America RITA® finalists in the historical, regency and contemporary categories.

A firm believer in happily-ever-after, Patricia Rice is married to her high school sweetheart and has two children. A native of Kentucky and New York, a past resident of North Carolina and Missouri, she currently resides in Southern California, and now does accounting only for herself.

Also by Patricia Rice

The World of Magic:

The Unexpected Magic Series

MAGIC IN THE STARS

WHISPER OF MAGIC

THEORY OF MAGIC

AURA OF MAGIC

CHEMISTRY OF MAGIC

NO PERFECT MAGIC

The Magical Malcolms Series

MERELY MAGIC

MUST BE MAGIC

THE TROUBLE WITH MAGIC

THIS MAGIC MOMENT

MUCH ADO ABOUT MAGIC

MAGIC MAN

The California Malcolms Series

THE LURE OF SONG AND MAGIC

TROUBLE WITH AIR AND MAGIC

THE RISK OF LOVE AND MAGIC

Crystal Magic

SAPPHIRE NIGHTS

TOPAZ DREAMS

CRYSTAL VISION

WEDDING GEMS

AZURE SECRETS

AMBER AFFAIRS

MOONSTONE SHADOWS

THE WEDDING GIFT

The Wedding Question

The Wedding Surprise

School of Magic

Lessons in Enchantment

A Bewitching Governess

An Illusion of Love

The Librarian's Spell

Entrancing the Earl

Captivating the Countess

Psychic Solutions

The Indigo Solution

The Golden Plan

The Crystal Key

The Rainbow Recipe

The Aura Answer

The Prism Effect

Historical Romance:

American Dream Series

Moon Dreams

Rebel Dreams

The Rebellious Sons

Wicked Wyckerly

Devilish Montague

Notorious Atherton

Formidable Lord Quentin

The Regency Nobles Series

The Genuine Article

The Marquess

English Heiress

Irish Duchess

Regency Love and Laughter Series

Crossed in Love

Mad Maria's Daughter

Artful Deceptions

All a Woman Wants

Rogues & Desperadoes Series

Lord Rogue

Moonlight and Memories

Shelter from the Storm

Wayward Angel

Denim and Lace

Cheyennes Lady

Dark Lords and Dangerous Ladies Series

Love Forever After

Silver Enchantress

Devil's Lady

Dash of Enchantment

Indigo Moon

Too Hard to Handle

Texas Lily

Texas Rose

Texas Tiger

Texas Moon

Mystic Isle Series

Mystic Isle

Mystic Guardian

Mystic Rider

Mystic Warrior

Mysteries:

Family Genius Series

Evil Genius

Undercover Genius

Cyber Genius

Twin Genius

About Book View Café

Book View Café Publishing Cooperative (BVC) is an author-owned cooperative of professional writers, publishing in a variety of genres including fantasy, romance, mystery, and science fiction — with 90% of the proceeds going to the authors. Since its debut in 2008, BVC has gained a reputation for producing high-quality ebooks. BVC's ebooks are DRM-free and are distributed around the world. The cooperative is now bringing that same quality to its print editions.

BVC authors include New York Times and USA Today bestsellers as well as winners and nominees of many prestigious awards.